Sugar and Spice

LEDA SWANN

red

AVON

An Imprint of HarperCollinsPublishers

This book was originally published in trade paperback by Avon Red in October 2006.

AVON RED
An Imprint of HarperCollins*Publishers*
10 East 53rd Street
New York, New York 10022-5299

"Obsessed," "Enslaved," "Exposed" copyright © 2006 by Leda Swann
ISBN: 978-0-06-136339-9
ISBN-10: 0-06-136339-1
www.avonred.com

First Avon Red mass market printing: July 2007
First Avon Red trade paperback printing: October 2006

Avon Trademark Reg. U.S. Pat. Off. and in Other Countries, Marca Registrada, Hecho en U.S.A.
HarperCollins® is a registered trademark of HarperCollins Publishers.

Printed in the U.S.A.

10 9 8 7 6 5 4 3 2 1

Contents

Obsessed

One

"Please." To her horror, Gwendolyn Farrell felt tears well up in her eyes. She blinked them back, not wanting Adam to see just how desperate she was. He could not refuse her. His refusal would toll the death knell of their marriage, a marriage that she was not willing to give up on. Not yet. Not until she had done everything humanly possible to win him back, to make him love her even just a tiny fraction as much as she loved him.

She gazed at the man in front of her, at the hard planes of his face and the even harder look in his eyes. Being married to him was supposed to be her dream come true. Instead, it had turned into a waking nightmare.

She swallowed convulsively. The very worst of it was that he was in no way to blame. Their estrangement, the utter desolation of their marriage, was all her fault.

"You want me to come away with you to a house in the country?" His lip curled into a sneer. "It sounds like hell."

"Would you not like to take a week's holiday out of the London fog and the miasma of the City?" Almost imperceptibly she inched closer to him, hoping to persuade him with her closeness if she could not persuade him with her words. "To walk in the fields and along the rocky beaches, and breathe the clean sea air?"

"The country I could handle. But the company?"

"It would just be me." Despair, thick and black, boiled up in her soul. He had to come with her. Her happiness, her very life depended on it. "There would be no one else there you know."

He lifted one eyebrow. "Exactly."

"You have to come." She could not hide the pleading tone in her voice.

"And if I do not? What then, princess? Will you bribe the footmen to waylay me, truss me up like a goose ready for the oven, and deliver me to you?"

Her eyes dropped to the floor as she fought back the telltale blushes. How had he guessed her plan? She had not so much as spoken to the footmen about it yet, though she did have a secret stash of gold sovereigns tucked away in her reticule for just such an eventuality. It was a mark of her desperation that she would entertain such a wild idea even for a moment, let alone plan to bring it about.

He cursed under his breath. "You *were* planning to abduct me, weren't you?"

For the briefest moment she thought she saw a flash of amusement in his eyes, but it was gone so quickly she must have been mistaken. "Only if you refused to come with me."

"What a pearl of a woman I have married," he said, his voice full of mocking self-contempt. "I knew you would lie and steal to get your own way, but I had not thought you would stoop to outright violence."

His words dripped burning acid into her soul. She dropped to her knees in pain and threw her arms around his knees. "Please, I am begging you. If you ever held any affection for me at all, do this for me. I will never ask anything else of you ever again."

"You do not have the right to ask anything of me. I thought we had already agreed that. A twelve-month ago, on our wedding night," he added cruelly.

The blood rushed from her head so fast she almost fainted, and she had to clutch his knees tightly to stop herself from toppling over onto the floor. That awful night was engraved forever on her memory. It would never leave her. "I know I have no right to ask you. That is why I am begging."

"It means so much to you?"

"It means the world to me."

His chest rose and fell in a sigh of irritation. "Then I suppose, just this once, I can suffer a week in the country with you. Particularly if it will save me from your importuning in the future."

She raised her eyes to his face, but it was as hard and closed as ever. His eyes gave away none of his secrets. "You will come with me?" Was he going to allow her this one last chance to save them both? To save their marriage from becoming a wasteland of spoiled hopes and despair. She hardly dared hope that he would come with her willingly.

He shrugged. "I suppose I will make the effort. If I have nothing better to do."

Adam disengaged himself from his wife with a grimace of distaste. There was no need for her dramatics or her falling on the floor in front of him and clutching at his knees as if he were an ogre. He had treated Gwendolyn well enough during their year of marriage. Better, certainly, than she deserved.

She, more than anyone, had reason to know that he was an honorable man. If he had not been so damned honorable, he might never have married her. For all the dark temptation of her lush body and the way her naked skin smelled so tantalizingly of warm, ripe peaches, he had married her out of honor and nothing more. She knew that as well as he did.

Despite his noncommittal words, however, he was intensely curious as to why his dear Gwendolyn was so set on taking him to a health spa in the wilds of Cornwall of all places. When she had first asked him to accompany her, he'd been concerned she might be secretly ill, but she had insisted she was perfectly well, and he did not think she was lying. Not this time.

Still, she had some scheme or other planned. He could feel it in his bones, and, despite himself, he was eager to discover exactly what it was. Just exactly what was his sneaky little wife up to now?

Two

Gwendolyn looked beseechingly over the tea table at the older woman seated opposite her. Though she was exhausted from the long train ride from London and wanted only to stretch out on her bed until dinner, she could get no rest until she had spoken with her hostess and solicited her aid. "Please. I need your help." If Mrs. Bertram could not help her, Gwendolyn was doomed.

"I gathered you didn't come all the way to Cornwall just for a little rest and relaxation." Mrs. Bertram picked up the teapot and filled Gwendolyn's bone china teacup nearly to the brim, then added a dash of cream and a spoonful of sugar to the brew. "Does your husband know why you have brought him here?"

Gwendolyn shook her head, setting her corkscrew curls shaking around her shoulders. "I didn't tell him anything. I was afraid he would not come with me."

Mrs. Bertram raised her eyebrows. "Even if he knew?"

Leda Swann

"Especially if he knew."

"Most men, I have found, while at first nervous or apprehensive when first introduced to the notion that their wives are interested in such matters of the flesh, are delighted at the eventual outcome. Maybe your husband will be one of those."

"He is not . . ." Gwendolyn's face grew hot, and her words trailed off into an embarrassed silence. There was no easy way to say what she needed to say.

"Not what?" Mrs. Bertram prompted.

"He is not . . . not uninterested in me as . . . as a woman." In the dark of the night he would reach out for her with desire and make love to her until she was senseless with pleasure.

"But?"

But when the morning came and his lusts were sated, he would not look at her. "But he does not love me." She did not even care that she was wailing like a baby.

"And you want him to love you?"

"I want him to love me like I love him." Her tears were dripping into her tea, and she swiped them away with the back of her hand. "But he doesn't and it is all my fault and now it is too late and he will never even like me ever again."

Mrs. Bertram took a sip of her tea. "That sounds serious."

"I fell in love with him the first time I met him." She hiccuped through her tears. "He was so handsome, so kind, so easy to talk to. How could I not love him? I had never met anyone half as wonderful as he was."

"Did he return your feelings?"

"I thought he was falling in love with me, just as I had fallen in love with him. But then he stopped coming to our house quite so often, and when he did come he was preoccupied, withdrawn. I was losing him, I knew, and I couldn't bear that." Her heart had been breaking when she realized that he did not love her as she loved him. She had wanted him so badly, more than she had ever wanted anything in her life, and she had not been able to let him go. Not without a fight. And when she fought, she played dirty.

"So?"

"So I paid one of my servants to bribe one of his to purloin his seal and a scrap of paper with his handwriting on it, and I forged a note from him to my father." She picked up her teacup for a comforting swallow of tea, but her hands were shaking so badly she had to put it down again untouched. "The note asked for my hand in marriage."

A smile spread over Mrs. Bertram's face. "And it worked?"

"My father was delighted at the match, and Adam, as a gentleman, could hardly proclaim his innocence and lay the blame on me for writing the letter. He was forced to pretend that he was equally delighted at the prospect of marrying me."

Mrs. Bertram gave a bark of laughter and set down her tea. "A very effective plot. Sneaky, but effective."

"He is a good man. I knew he would not disappoint me."

Mrs. Bertram reached out and took one of Gwendolyn's hands in hers. "But he has disappointed you," she said gently. "Or you would not be here."

"When we are in company he plays the part of the devoted husband to perfection. He is too proud to admit to the cracks in our marriage by shaming me. But when we are alone together every word he speaks is cold and cruel. He will not even look at me, let alone touch me, if he does not have to."

"And in the bedroom?"

"It is the same there. He will approach me with desire, but with loathing, too, as if he could not help touching me though he hated himself for his weakness."

"I see." The older woman's words were soft and thoughtful. "He has not forgiven you yet for the trick you played on him."

"He never will forgive me. It is too late. I have destroyed any affection he ever felt for me, and now he despises me." Gwendolyn held her head in her hands, tears rolling down her face. "He will always despise me."

"And yet he married you. That says a good deal about him."

Nothing could soothe her anguish. "What choice did he have?" she cried. "I left him no choice."

"Nonsense. A man always has a choice in such matters. He might have accused you. He might have blamed your father for sending the letter himself and refused to have anything more to do with your whole family. He could even have blamed one of his own household for playing a cruel trick on you and wriggled out of it that way. But he chose to go along with it and marry you."

She knew the reason why. "He wanted to make me pay for my sins."

Mrs. Bertram shook her head, a faint smile curving her mouth.

"Believe me, Gwendolyn Farrell, a man does not wed a woman just for revenge. He marries her for her wealth, or for her connections, or because he wants her for himself."

Gwendolyn looked up, confused. "Adam could not want me for my wealth or my connections. My family is solidly respectable but nothing more than that, and I only brought him a modest dowry."

"So he must have desired you for yourself. That is a good start. The trick will be to make him acknowledge it instead of fighting it."

Mrs. Bertram's voice was so calm and matter-of-fact that, despite herself, Gwendolyn found herself starting to hope that her situation was not as desperate as she had feared. Was it possible that Adam really did care for her, deep down inside? Was that the real reason he had married her? She had to hope so, or she would go mad. "How should I do that?"

Mrs. Bertram tapped her fingernails on the top of the table for a few moments, her face creased in thought. "I do believe I have an idea." She stood up from the tea table and held out her hand to Gwendolyn. Her eyes were brimming with mischief. "Come with me. Let's make a plan."

Adam ate well of the excellent five-course dinner served up that evening. The long train ride to Cornwall in Gwendolyn's company had been a trial to his patience. The whole way she had sat opposite him in the carriage, looking so sweetly innocent and yet so forlorn that he had longed to take her into his arms and cover her with kisses just to put a smile back into her eyes and the lilt of happiness back into her voice. Only the sure knowledge that her innocence was nothing but a sham could have stopped him.

Still, he was looking forward to a week in Cornwall with his wife. He was hoping the time they spent together would have a good effect on her character. It might even be possible for him to teach her a better respect for honesty and integrity.

She was not inherently vicious, just misguided. As her husband, it was now his place to see her on the right path.

In the meantime, he would enjoy the dinner and the company. Two other married couples, a Mr. and Mrs. Rutherford and a Mr. and Mrs. Hughes made up the rest of their group. Mr. Rutherford he knew slightly by sight—they worked together in the City. Mr. Hughes he knew only by his reputation as a self-made man who had built a fortune through taking well-calculated risks that had paid off handsomely. Though neither of their wives could compare with his Gwendolyn in looks, they were both pretty enough and perfectly pleasant to converse with.

All in all, the company did not displease him and might even be useful when he returned to the bank in a week's time. His wife had good taste and had chosen well. Thank Heaven he would not have to spend the week dining on cold mutton in the company of fools and charlatans.

Gwendolyn, however, did not seem to be enjoying herself. Though the dinner was nearly over, she looked positively bilious and had eaten next to nothing. He frowned as he looked at her. Now that he thought about it, she had not been eating well for some time. Since their wedding last March she had lost much of her pleasing plumpness and was almost verging on the scrawny.

She must start looking after herself properly—he would have words with her on that subject later. Maybe tonight it was simply that the train ride had disagreed with her. He hoped there was nothing more seriously wrong.

Despite his nagging worry about Gwendolyn's health, he was feeling remarkably mellow. Gwendolyn had been right—he *had* needed a holiday.

He sat back at his ease as their hostess, a well-endowed lady of a certain age, tapped her knife gently against her glass to command the attention of the table. "I bid you all a warm welcome to Mrs. Bertram's Sugar and Spice Health Spa for Married Couples. From time to time we are all in need of a little sugar and spice and all things nice in our lives—and that is exactly what we strive to provide for you here. I am Mrs. Bertram, your hostess for the week. I trust you have found everything to your liking so far."

Adam felt distinctly uneasy at the polite murmur of agreement went around the table. *Sugar and spice?*

"Good, good. If there should be anything you need, pray don't be afraid to ask for it. My staff will be pleased to attend to *all* your needs." A gleeful smile spread over her face, as if she were keeping a delicious secret all to herself. "And I do mean all. For what man, or what woman either, can be said to be truly healthy if that sensual part of him or of her is left unsatisfied. And at Mrs. Bertram's Sugar and Spice Health Spa we want you all to be truly healthy."

Adam choked on his wine, his mood considerably less mellow all of a sudden. Gwendolyn was staring at him, her face flushed and anxious, her fingers clenched around her napkin so tightly that her knuckles were white. It was only too clear that Mrs. Bertram's words had come as no surprise to her.

"During the day we have a number of healthful exercises for you to indulge in. Any of us will be happy to show you around the choices available to you at a convenient moment. In the evenings, after dinner, we will have group exercises, or indulge in some entertainment that I have no doubt you will enjoy. Tonight is no exception."

With a gracious nod to all at the table, she stood up, shaking her skirts out as she did so. "Ladies, will you follow me. Gentlemen, please, feel free to linger over your port. Once I have settled the ladies, I will be back to see to you. Now, if you will excuse us."

Adam eyed Gwendolyn with anger in his heart as she followed Mrs. Bertram out of the room. Though she had clearly known what kind of house this was, she had chosen not to warn him but instead to bring him here under false pretenses. Yet one more sin of manipulation and deceit to lay to her account.

His blood was boiling at this new evidence of his wife's dishonesty as he poured himself a tumbler of port and drank it down in one gulp. He would not stay here for the week. As soon as it was light next morning, he would leave and take his errant wife back to London with him. Sooner or later she would have to learn that he would not tolerate her attempts to manipulate him. She was his wife, and she would learn to obey him in this.

By the time Mrs. Bertram returned, he had worked himself into a fine temper. When she asked them to accompany her, he stalked out of the dining room after her feeling like a steam engine about to explode. His tolerance had definite limits, and he was very close to reaching them.

Mrs. Bertram led them into a luxurious sitting room decked out in rich colors and draperies, with long, low sofas and piles of huge cushions on the patterned rugs. The total effect was as if he had just stepped into a sultan's harem. The impression was strengthened by the presence of three young ladies in the room lounging on the sofas dressed in the costumes of harem slaves. Baggy silk pants of a fabric so sheer it was almost as if they were naked, a bodice that bared their shoulders and arms, glittering bangles around their wrists and ankles, and a headdress of gold from which hung a veil that obscured their faces.

"Welcome to our Turkish room. Gentlemen, meet your companions for tonight, Sofia, Lela, Helena. Girls, make our guests welcome."

There was a tinkling of bangles as the three of them stood up and stretched like languid cats interrupted in the middle of a nap.

One of the girls made her way over to him. "Tonight we will

be doing a Turkish massage," she said in a lilting and heavily accented voice. "Come with me, and I shall make you ready."

She reached for his jacket to pull it off his shoulders, and he backed away. Make him ready? His blood was still boiling, but no longer with unadulterated rage. What had Gwendolyn gotten him into now?

"To do Turkish massage you need to have bare skin," she explained, correctly interpreting his reluctance. "You must take off silly English clothes that stop you from breathing and put on a proper Turkish robe." A silky robe of dark blue was thrust into his hand, and before he knew what was happening, he was throwing it on over his naked body.

"Lie down on the sofa and let me give you massage," she said as she pushed him onto one of the low sofas.

The idea of a Turkish massage intrigued him. Had Gwendolyn known exactly what was on offer here? He did not think so, or surely she would never have brought him here to be serviced by a seminaked young woman. Still, that was Gwendolyn's lookout, not his. She had brought him here and now must suffer the consequences.

He stretched out on his stomach on the long, low sofa, his stiffening cock pressed up hard against his stomach. For the short time he remained here, he might as well sample the new experiences available.

A few drops of oil dripped onto his back, making him gasp with the sudden cold. The woman's hands on his back were warm and soothing as they dug into his muscles, rubbing the warming oil into his shoulder blades and up and down his spine, finding sore spots that he did not know existed and massaging them into submission. Pain mingled with pleasure as her hands worked their magic first on his back and shoulders, and then down his thighs and calves.

With his eyes closed he could almost imagine it was Gwendolyn's hands on his back, her hands caressing his legs, her breath panting in his ears as she stroked him.

"Turn over."

Drugged with the feeling of her hands on his body, he did as she instructed, discarding his Turkish robe completely. His cock was standing up stiff and proud, but he did not care. His Turkish masseuse was so comfortable with his nakedness that he could not feel embarrassed.

"Mmmm, you have a nice body," she murmured in her softly accented voice, recoating her hands in oil and rubbing her hands across his chest. Her gaze was firmly fixed on his cock, which swelled still further under her eyes.

His balls grew tight and hard with desire as the girl stroked over his shoulder and down his chest and stomach. Just as she reached the lower part of his stomach and he was anticipating the delicious feeling of her oil-slicked hands on his cock, she raised her hands and placed them on his thighs instead.

He groaned with disappointment as she began instead to massage his legs, running her hands over his thighs and calves, to his feet and toes.

"You are relaxed now?" He could hear the mischief in her voice.

Her hands were busy giving each of his toes individual attention. Nice as it felt, he wasn't in the mood for nice anymore. "You know damn well I'm not."

"You want more Turkish massage?"

In one fluid movement he sat up and grabbed her hands. "I do." He placed her hands firmly on his cock. "Massage me here."

She encircled his cock with her oily hands, sliding them up and down. "Would your wife mind if she were to catch me?"

He shook his head, his breath catching in his throat. A hand job from another woman was of no significance. As far as he was concerned, it did not even count as infidelity. "I doubt she would care. After all, she brought me here. She cannot blame me for enjoying the entertainment on offer."

There was a small silence as she continued to stroke up and down his throbbing cock with her eager hands. "Ah, I see." Her voice held a world of knowing laughter. "She wanted the same for herself."

Her words doused the fire in his loins more effectively than a bucket of cold water would have. He rose up on one elbow and stared at her veiled face in horror as the implications of her words burst in on his lust-drugged mind. "What did you say?"

His Turkish girl gave a slight shrug as she continued to stroke his cock with one slick hand, reaching down to stroke his balls with the other. "Lie back and let me give you pleasure. Your wife wants you to be entertained and out of her way. She will not come to bother us."

Her hands had lost all their appeal. He sat up and pushed her aside more roughly than he had intended. "Excuse me, I must go and find my wife." The thought that Gwendolyn might be lying in another room in the house with some scoundrel in the garb of a Turkish slave pawing at her naked body, touching her breasts, stroking her mound, even putting his fingers inside her wet pussy, made him fume. God damn it, she was his wife, not some cheap harlot. No man had the right to touch her but him.

"Do not bother her. She will be busy and will not want to be disturbed." She gestured around the room. "See, the other husbands are not so fussy as you are."

He looked around the room, noticing the others for the first time since his Turkish girl had approached him, and then wished he hadn't.

On one sofa, Mr. Hughes was lying back as his Turkish girl, her long dark hair streaming down her naked back, rode him hard and fast. On another, Mr. Rutherford was thrusting into the willing pussy of the last Turkish girl as she bent over for him, her ass up in the air.

Everyone was fucking except for him. His erection had wilted to nothing. He leaned over and put his head in his hands to shut out the sight and sounds of the other men fucking. He could not touch the girl. Not when he thought of Gwendolyn.

His Turkish girl was leaning closer to him, her breasts close to his mouth. Surprisingly, she smelled of peaches, warm, ripe peaches. A very familiar scent. "Stay for a while longer and let me sit on your cock. Let me take you into me and ride you up and down until you come inside me."

How had he missed the signs before? They were right in front of his nose. He had been so blinded by anger and by lust he had not been thinking straight.

With a quick flick of his wrist he pulled her veil aside, ignoring her gasp of shock. "Gwendolyn."

"I am not Gwendolyn." Her eyes were large with trepidation. "Tonight I am Lela, your Turkish slave girl."

He pulled her to her feet and gestured around him. "This is not the sort of place I would have expected to find you," he hissed in her ear.

Intensely relieved as he was that she was not in one of the other rooms letting some stranger paw her body, he was furious with her for exposing herself to such sights as this. She was his wife, dammit, not a harlot to be fucked in company.

Her bottom lip quivered at his harsh tone. "I only wanted to please you, Master."

"It would please me better if you were not to expose yourself in such a manner. You look like a whore."

"Tonight I *am* a whore. I am *your* whore to do with as you like." She drew closer to him, writhing her scantily clothed body against his naked one. His cock was instantly hard again. "I can be very obedient when I choose to be. Tonight I will do whatever pleases you."

He thrust his arms into his Turkish robe and wrapped it hastily around his body. Then taking her by the hand, he dragged her to the door. "It pleases me to get you out of here. These are games that my wife ought not see, far less partake in. Indeed, any well-bred young lady ought to run away from here as far and as fast as she can. And since you lack the good sense to leave of your own accord, I will take you away myself. Tomorrow morning we will return to London."

A pout of disappointment settled on her face, but she followed him through the hallways willingly enough. Maybe obedience came as part and parcel of the harem-girl costume. If so, he'd buy twenty of them and make her wear them every day.

He did not loose his hold on her until they were back in the bedroom they shared. "What on earth possessed you to behave like that?" he asked, towering over her in the dim gaslight. Dammit, but she had made him feel worse than he ever had before. The thought of his wife in the hands of another man had infuriated him beyond belief. Though she was innocent of infidelity, he was still mad with rage that she had taunted him with the prospect. "To dress up in a harlot's costume and to proposition me like that? What would you have done if I had not realized it was you? Would you have sat on me and let me fuck you on the sofa until I came? Would you have fucked me in the company of other men, of men that you might have to meet one day in respectable company? What would they think of you?"

She shrugged, her breasts heaving up and down in her transparent top. "I thought you would like it."

He could not put the real source of his anger into words— the thought she had been with another man while he was playing

21

with a harlot in the Turkish room. It would reveal too much of him. "You thought I would like the sight of my own wife playing the harlot?" he asked, seizing on a peripheral matter.

"I wanted you to see me in a new light, in a new way," she said, her voice small. "I wanted you to see me as Lela, your Turkish slave girl, not as Gwendolyn, the wife you hate so much."

He crossed his arms over his chest to ward off the uncomfortable feeling that assaulted him at her accusation. "Do not be foolish. I do not hate you." Since their marriage he had treated her with nothing but respect. Coldness sometimes, he admitted as much, but always with respect.

"I wanted you to make love to me," she sniffled, sitting on the side of their bed, looking disconsolate. "To turn to me with affection in your eyes, not disdain."

Was there any understanding women? "You went to all that trouble to get me to make love to you? Dammit, Gwendolyn, you need only have asked."

She blotted her eyes with a corner of her bodice. "Would you have come to me if I *had* asked?"

What kind of a question was that? "My cock spends half its existence burning to fuck you," he said crudely. "Of course I would have."

His words sparked a light in her eyes. "You want to make love to me? Now? Even after . . . ?"

Her voice tailed away as he untied the cord around his robe and allowed the edges to fall apart, exposing his cock standing up stiff and proud again. "What do you think? Does this look like a man who is indifferent to his wife?"

She stepped closer to him, flicked the veil over her face, and took his cock into her hands. "I think you are a very finely built man, Master," she said in her Turkish slave accent as she stroked him up and down. "What would you like me to do to you?"

She still wanted to play Turkish slaves and submit to his every whim? Now they were alone together, the idea of his wife being his love slave was too good to pass up. Besides, he would enjoy seeing just how far she would take her obedience. In the mood he was in, he hoped she was prepared to take it very far indeed. "Very well, then, I want to see your breasts."

Her fingers dropped obediently to her bodice. The ribbons were soon untied, and her bodice gaped open to expose her breasts.

Reaching out, he pushed her bodice right off her shoulders. Clad only in a headdress and a pair of diaphanous trousers, with her breasts swinging free, she looked like any sultan's wet dream.

"Touch your breasts for me."

She looked at him, startled. "But—"

"Are you arguing with me, slave?" he asked in a voice silky with menace.

"No, Master." Her voice shook a little.

"Then do as I say. Touch your breasts. Rub your nipples until they are hard as pebbles. I want to watch you touching yourself."

Her face flaming, she placed a tentative hand on each breast, more to cover her nakedness than to titillate herself.

"Good. I see you can be obedient when you choose. That isn't so bad now, is it?"

Her fingers were spread wide over her breasts so that one pink nipple just peeked through. "No, Master."

He could stand there all day and look at her, but her obedient demeanor was too good not to make use of. What man alive could resist a woman like Gwendolyn? "Your hands are far too passive and still. I want you to touch yourself as a lover would touch you. As I would touch you. I want you to pant and moan at the feel of your hands on your breasts. I want to see your pussy start to drip with excitement and to know that you made it so yourself."

Her head shot up in protest. "Adam—"

"Did I give you leave to address me in such a familiar manner, slave?" His voice was coldly authoritarian.

"But—"

"You are my slave, and I am your master. You will call me master when you speak to me, and you will not speak unless I first give you permission. Is that clear, Lela?"

Her eyes were wide as she looked at him, their pupils so dark they were almost black. "Yes, Master."

His foot tapped out an impatient rhythm on the floor. "I'm waiting, Lela."

"Waiting, Master?" Her voice was the merest whisper of sound in the silence.

"For you to start touching yourself."

Her eyes grew wider still, and he thought he saw the glint of unshed tears in her eyes, but tentatively she moved her hands over her breasts, stroking herself as he had ordered her to do.

His hand moved down of its own volition to cup his balls. God, watching his wife was more erotic than he would ever have guessed. He stroked his balls and the base of his cock. "Does that feel good, slave girl?"

"Yes, Master." Obedient, even a little breathless, but not yet excited enough for his taste.

Throbbing with need himself, he wanted her hot and ready to be fucked, so ready that she came for him as soon as he entered her. "Touch yourself between your legs."

She froze and stared up at him, her eyes begging him mutely to have mercy, but he was adamant. "Touch yourself between your legs," he repeated. "Put your hand inside your trousers and stroke your pussy. Feel how wet you are and make yourself even wetter for me. Fuck yourself with one of your fingers. Push your finger right inside your pussy to make you wet all the way up right to your womb. I want to see your cunt juices staining your pretty silk trousers."

"Adam," she said tentatively, making no move to comply with his orders. "I do not think I want to be your slave any longer."

He was not going to let her give in quite so easily, his cock was too damn excited at the sight of her touching her breasts. He badly wanted, no, he needed, to watch her go even further, further than he would ever have dreamed of asking her before.

"You should have thought of that before you put on the costume, Lela. Now do as I have ordered you, or I shall have to punish you as disobedient slaves are punished."

A prickle of interest lit her eyes at this new threat. "How are they punished?"

"They are spanked." His groin tightened further at the thought. Christ, he hoped she would disobey him. He would enjoy spanking those soft, white buttocks of hers until they were hot and red under his hands. And afterward he would make her touch herself anyway.

"I cannot t . . . touch myself. Really, I cannot."

Excellent. Just as he had hoped. "Then come here, slave. I will have to find another use for you."

Her legs shaking, she rose from the bed and approached him. "What do you want with me, Adam?"

He chucked her under the chin. "I told you to address me respectfully as master. Your disobedience really does need to be punished, doesn't it?"

She shook her head bravely. "No, Master."

"Are you being insolent, slave?"

Her voice dropped to the merest whisper. "No, Master."

"I think you were. You will have to be punished for that, too. Now take off your trousers, slave. I want to see you naked."

Her hands fumbled with the ties that held her trousers around her waist and her face lost its color. "Please, Adam . . . I mean, Master, do not beat me."

"Do not dawdle, slave. You are trying my patience."

Obsessed

The trousers fell to her ankles, and she stepped out of them. "No, Master. But—"

Striding past her, he flung himself down on the bed, lolling on it supported by his elbow like any sultan in his harem. "No buts. Turn around. I want to look at your ass."

She turned her back to him. Her body was shaking like a leaf.

Her ass was everything a woman's ass should be and more. Well rounded but not overlarge. Pert and bouncy. Ah, how he would enjoy spanking her soft flesh. He reached out and stroked down her smooth hip. She gave a start at his touch but relaxed again as he continued to stroke her gently.

With a sudden twist, he grabbed her by the waist and upended her across his lap, pinning her there with the weight of his arms.

She let out a muffled yelp and fought to get free. "Let me go."

With one hand he stroked the smooth, white skin of her buttocks. God, she had a nice ass, cool and firm against his palm. It was almost a shame to smack it, to turn that cool white firmness into swollen red heat. Almost. "Not until you have been punished as you deserve." He drew his hand up and gave her a stinging slap right on one of her buttocks.

If she had not been firmly anchored to his lap, she would have fallen right off in surprise. As it was, she gave strangled gasp. "Owww, that hurt," she wailed.

He smacked her sharply on the other buttock. "It was meant to."

"You are beating me." Her voice held a world of incredulity.

He smacked her again, once on each side, so hard that it made his palms sting. "I'm glad you noticed, princess. It would lose the effect if you didn't."

She was squirming in earnest now, trying to get away, but he had no mercy. Smack after smack rained down on her ass until the white flesh turned hot and red, and his palm ached with the effort. Yelping with each slap, and wriggling on his knee, she fought him every inch of the way, but he did not let her go until she hung across his lap, limp and exhausted.

When she finally gave in and lay quietly, he raised her and laid her on the bed on her side so as not to aggravate the pain she would be feeling in her red and swollen ass. "Now then, slave," he ordered her. "Touch yourself between your legs."

Her lips were swollen from biting them, and her hair was in disarray over her face. "No," she said baldly, staring him straight in the eyes with what looked very much like hatred.

He grinned at her. "Do you want to be punished again?"

That gave her pause. "No," she admitted, her eyes dropping.

"Then touch yourself between your legs for me."

Sulkily, she put one hand between her legs and let it lie there.

He shook his head. "Not good enough. Roll over onto your back and put your knees in the air."

With a grimace, she did as she was ordered, wincing as her ass came into contact with the bed.

Reaching out, he spread her legs apart, leaning in to touch her pussy gently with his fingertips. Her cunt lips were as red and swollen as her ass was. For all her protests, she had evidently enjoyed the spanking as much as he had. Or more.

As he watched her, a trickle of liquid seeped out of her pussy and ran down onto the counterpane beneath her.

He took hold of her hand and ran it over her pussy, first ruffling the hairs that grew over her mound, then making her fingers stroke the delicate skin underneath.

Letting go of her hand, he encouraged her to take over where he had left off. "You do not need my help. I want to watch you."

And watch her he did as she slowly began to stroke herself. Gently as first, and then harder and a little faster and more intently. Her eyes drifted shut, and her breath came in short pants.

He wanted her attention on him, not just on the demands of her own body. "Open your eyes."

Her eyes snapped open again, and her hand stopped its rhythmic stroking for a moment.

"I want you to watch me. I want you to look at me as you are touching yourself." He took his cock in one hand and began to stroke it up and down in long, lazy strokes. "I want you to look at my cock, slave, and imagine what it would feel like to have it thrusting in and out of your wet little pussy."

She began to play with her pussy again. "Yes, Master." Her eyes slowly glazed over with lust again as she stroked herself.

"Put your finger inside yourself."

She hesitated.

"Slave," he said in a warning tone.

She shivered and put the tip of her finger inside her pussy.

"Deeper."

She inserted it a little deeper.

He swallowed convulsively. Christ, he was ready to spurt on her breasts watching her do that to herself. "Good. Now move it in and out. Tease yourself."

At his command, she began to fuck herself with her finger, dipping it slowly into her cunt and taking it out again, glistening with juice.

"Are you imagining what my cock feels like inside your cunt, slave?" He rubbed the head of his cock, imagining in his turn how it would feel when he thrust into her dripping pussy. "It's bigger than your finger, isn't it? Bigger and more satisfying."

"Yes, Master." Her breaths were so short she could barely get the words out.

"Does it feel good?"

"Yes, Master, it feels very good."

"Would it feel better to have my cock inside you, where your finger is now?"

"Yes, Master, it would feel even better than my finger." She looked at him, her eyes wide with entreaty. "Please will you put your cock inside me?"

Not yet. Not until she had reached the brink where he was already standing. "Keep stroking yourself, slave, until you are ready to come. I want you to tell me when you are ready to come, slave."

"I'm ready now, Master," she said, her finger moving in and out of her pussy furiously. "I'm so ready now that I'm about to come just with thinking about having you inside me. Please, Master."

That was the way she ought always to be—so wet and ready for him she was begging him to fuck her. "Get on your knees, slave. You have pleased me well. I will fuck you now."

Obediently, she took her finger out of her cunt, turned over onto her stomach, and got up onto her hands and knees.

He parted her legs, and then drove his cock home, hard and fast deep into her cunt.

At the first thrust he felt her pussy start to convulse around him. "Hold it in, slave," he commanded her. "I do not want you to come too soon. You must wait until I give you permission."

"Oh, Master, I am coming," she panted. "I do not think I can hold it back any longer."

"Hold it back, slave," he ordered, fucking her fast and shallow, refusing to give her the satisfaction that she craved just yet. "Hold it in until I say you may come."

His own need was spiraling out of control. He thrust into her again and again, until he was teetering on the very brink. "Now, slave," he gasped, as he thrust into her deeply one last time. "Now."

As he thrust, his seed spurted out of him in a burst of ecstasy that robbed him of breath and of thought.

At the instant his seed spurted into her, her pussy convulsed around him, milking him of every last drop of semen as she writhed beneath him, lost in her own pleasure.

She collapsed on the bed, her breath loud in the silence of the room. Boneless with satisfaction, he lay on top of her, careful not to rest all his weight on her.

His cock, satiated for the moment, slipped out of her wet pussy, and he rolled to the side and gathered her into his arms. He patted her ass affectionately, enjoying the sensation of lingering heat from her spanking. "You make a damned good slave girl. That was the best fuck I've ever had." Any better, and he'd go up in flames. His balls were aching from the power with which he'd shot out his seed.

She snuggled close in to him. "Does that mean that you're staying here for the week with me?" she murmured.

He raised his eyes to her face. Her voice was sleepy enough, but her eyes, her damned blue eyes, were bright and calculating.

The bottom fell out of his stomach. Had Gwendolyn's erotic obedience been nothing more than yet another attempt to manipulate him? His temper began to rise anew. "Is that what this has all been about?" he asked, his voice cold. "Fuck me senseless so you get this damned holiday in a bawdy house that you want so much?"

Her eyes, wounded with his harshness, met his. "No, it wasn't about that."

She was lying. He could tell she was lying through her teeth.

He rose from the bed and pulled on a pair of trousers, suddenly disgusted both with himself and with Gwendolyn.

God, when would Gwendolyn ever learn to be honest with him? And when would he stop falling for the innocent look in her big blue eyes? "I said before we would leave on the morrow, and I meant every word. I see no reason to change my mind. That fuck," and he imbued the word with as much disgust as he felt for his own damnable gullibility, "changes nothing. We will be returning to London in the morning."

Three

The next morning brought no respite to his ill temper. He had slept badly, the wounded look in Gwendolyn's eyes haunting him even in his sleep. What else could she expect? That he would lie down and allow her to walk all over him? The prickles of guilt he felt for not treating her kindly were simply a sign of weakness and to be resisted with all his strength. She was a mere woman, not a damned princess, and needed to learn her place.

His temper did not improve when Mrs. Bertram regretfully informed him there was no train back to the City until the afternoon. Adam glowered more darkly than ever at the news. Gwendolyn had won. Again.

Still, while he was here, he might as well find out what the Sugar and Spice Health Spa had to offer. Who knows, he may just want to come back one day—without his wife in tow.

At least, that was what he growled inwardly as he followed

Obsessed

Mrs. Bertram around the establishment. "You have already seen our massage room," she said, as she passed by the door to the room they had been in last night. "But there are many others I am sure you will enjoy at least as much, if not more. The sunroom, for instance," she said, as she opened the next door along.

The room was empty save for a carpet on the floor, a wardrobe in one corner, and a number of long, low settees. He looked around it, wondering as to its purpose.

"The windows face due south," Mrs. Bertram explained, indicating the floor-to-ceiling windows across one wall. "The room is filled with sun for most of the day. It is very healthful to have the sun on your body for some part of every day. On your naked body."

Adam looked around him with renewed interest. Even this early in the morning the sun was peeking through the windows, bathing everything is a soft warm light. A whole room simply to be naked in and let the sun warm your body. The whole idea was decadent in the extreme and more than a little attractive. Especially since his dratted wife was here to share it with him. Maybe he would bring Gwendolyn here this afternoon to soak up the sunshine on her naked body with him, and take the train back to London the following day.

Next, Mrs. Bertram led him out of the house proper into an annex in the courtyard. "We find water to be very healthful here. I do not mean just the ocean, though certainly sea bathing is to be recommended. Many people around the world use water in different ways to promote health and well-being. We have learned from them and brought you the best the world has to offer.

"Take a look in here." And she pushed open the door to a small room, windowless save for a few skylights set high up on the walls and containing nothing but a heavy iron stove in one corner and a slatted wooden bench that ran the length of it. "This is a sauna. The Finns have been using them for centuries. When you are ready to use it, have one of the maids build you a fire in the stove. When the stove is hot and the room so warm you can hardly bear it, sit in here and sweat out all your impurities. Then come next door and plunge into the cold pool. I guarantee you will feel the better for it."

A sweating room and then a cold pool. He had heard of the health benefits of such things but had never had the chance to experience them before. Sugar and Spice certainly took the well-being of their guests seriously.

"And to top it all off, a hot pool to relax in when you are done with the rest."

A hot pool? He felt his muscles glow in anticipation of sinking down into the warmth of the water, being surrounded and cushioned by liquid heat, floating in luxurious comfort on a bed of moving, swirling water.

He squared his shoulders. The hot pool had settled it. Gwendolyn could be taught her much-needed lessons another time, in another place. His pronouncement the previous evening had been made in the heat of his temper—it was not a fixed decision. Now that he thought coolly and rationally on the matter, he adjudged it best to stay. Particularly when there was a fair prospect of getting Gwendolyn to be his Turkish slave in a hot pool.

He followed Mrs. Bertram around as she showed him the rest of the house and the gardens, storing every detail for future reference. It didn't matter anymore that Gwendolyn had tried to manipulate him into staying. She had been right—he would like it here. There was no point in cutting off his nose to spite his face and leaving before he had experienced a half of what this house had to offer him, particularly as he had already paid for it. Why should he throw his money away and get nothing in return?

Besides, she wanted so badly for him to stay, and it was little enough trouble for him to humor her just this once.

The tour once finished, Mrs. Bertram stole a look at his face. "So, shall I order you the carriage to take you and your wife to the station? Or can I tempt you with a walk along the beach? The views from the top of the cliff are remarkably fine, and the water is unusually warm for this time of year."

He squared his shoulders. "Thank you, but no, we shall not be needing the carriage. We shall be staying the full week, as arranged."

She gave him a regal nod that didn't quite manage to hide her satisfaction. "I am glad to hear it."

Hands in his waistcoat pocket, he took his leave of Mrs. Bertram and headed off over the fields toward the cliffs that led down to the beach. It was petty of him not to let Gwendolyn know right away that he had changed his mind about staying, but he was still not feeling in a generous mood toward his beautiful young wife. He had decided to humor her and stay the week, and that in itself would have to be enough for her.

Gwendolyn. That one woman had caused him more heartache and trouble than any woman ever had before.

He needed some time to himself for quiet reflection, not to mention some exercise after being cooped up in the train all yesterday. A quiet walk along the beach would fulfill both his requirements.

The grass was springy under his feet as he strode along in the sunshine, surprising himself with how eager he was to see the sea again. He had not been to the shore since he was a boy and his father had taken them to Ramsgate every summer for a couple of days of playing in the sand with buckets and spades and running barefoot in and out of the salt waves.

The house in which they were staying stood in a small, sheltered hollow a little way back from the coast. Just a few minutes walk away huge, foaming waves crashed into the cliffs at the entrance of the small bay, funneling a channel of less turbulent water onto a rocky beach.

This beach was very different from the one he had known as a boy. That beach had been tamed, domesticated. The shores in Cornwall were wilder and more strange, threatening even.

A steep path led down the cliff to the shore. Careless of the state of his trousers, he slipped and slid down the rutted path to the bottom.

The white-sand beach was worth the scramble down the cliff face to get to it. He strode purposefully across the sand and over the rocks, working off his ill temper.

His dear wife, Gwendolyn, could not force him to do anything he did not want to do. That was not the issue.

Though he had not particularly wanted to come, now that he was here and knew exactly what was available, he was excited and more than a little intrigued to see exactly what else she would do. Certainly her performance last night had had him randier than he had ever been before. She was more erotic and more wanton than even the best-trained courtesan could hope to be.

What irritated him more than anything about her, though, were her deceit and brazen attempts to manipulate him. It galled him to the depths of his soul that she believed she could make him dance to her tune.

Even in marrying her he had consulted his own inclination. Dammit, but he had been in love with the wench and had thought her the most perfect creature in all England—until she had tried to force his hand. He had considered turning his back on her and letting her stew in the mess of her own making, but he had not had the heart to treat her with such cruelty. He loved her.

Whatever he felt about her, though, he did not dance to anyone's tune but his own. Maybe this week *would* be a good time for him to teach her that, once and for all. There was no business to take his attention. All his time could be spent on teaching his young wife how to behave.

A faint rustle of clothing was all that alerted him that he was not alone on the beach. Instantly on guard, he swung around to face whoever was following him, but it was too late. In an instant, his arms were pinioned behind him, and a couple of burly men in outlandish pirate garb complete with black patches over one eye and curved swords at their sides were dragging him up toward the entrance to a small cave in the rocky cliff face.

Just inside the entrance, a solid iron ring was hammered into the wall. The pirates clasped iron bands around his wrists and fixed them to the iron ring with a length of chain. He was firmly anchored, but not uncomfortably so. Judging by the dryness of the walls and the sand beneath his feet, he was well out of the reach of the high tide. Whatever they intended to do with him, he doubted very much his life was in danger. His dignity was in far greater peril. Nevertheless, he fired off a heartfelt volley of curses at his captors as they disappeared out of the cave.

"Dear me, my prisoner ees een a temper."

He had been so busy cursing out his captors that he hadn't noticed the figure approaching him from the back of the cave.

He heaved a sigh. Though she had tried once more to disguise her voice, this time with a French accent instead of a Turkish one, he knew instantly that it was Gwendolyn. "Untie me."

She moved closer to him until she was standing right in front of him, nearly touching him. Her breasts were spilling out of her striped pirate gown, a red scarf held back her luxurious brown hair, and her calves and feet were bare. No real pirate, he was quite sure, had ever looked half so tempting as she did. Reaching up, she stroked his face. "Are ze bonds hurting you?"

His body could not help but react to her closeness. "Just untie me and stop playing these silly games."

"Zis is not a game. I am a pirate captain, and you are my captive." Her fingers trailed down the side of his face and onto his shoulders. "And what a handsome captive my men have caught me, for sure. I am so glad that we are alone together in this cave, you and I. So very very glad."

"Gwendolyn."

Gwendolyn shot him a mock glare. "My name ees not Gwendolyn. It is Long Meg ze pirate. Captain Long Meg," she corrected herself absentmindedly, as she ran her hands over his shirtfront. "And I intend to have my wicked way with my handsome captive."

"Gwendolyn." He wasn't sure whether his exclamation was an exhortation for her to stop or to continue touching him like that.

Her smile was evil personified. "You can weep and cry and beg for mercy all you like, but I won't let you go." Her hands moved to the fastenings of his trousers. "At least not until I've had my wicked way with you."

There was no way he could hide his reaction to her when finally she freed his buttons and his cock sprang out stiff and hungry.

"Mmmm, nice," she breathed, taking it in her hands and stroking it with long, languid movements that only stoked the fire in his loins. "My pirate comrades chose an excellently well-endowed captive for me to sport with today. I will have to reward them well when I get back to my boat."

Still he fought the temptation that she offered him. They were in a cave, for God's sake, not closeted in their bedroom as they had been last night. Someone might walk by at any moment. "You can't be serious."

She fell to her knees in front of him. "Why ever not?" Her breath was hot. "You are mine, and I can do whatever I want to do with you. And I want to do this." With those words, she bobbed her head closer to him and took the very tip of his cock in her mouth.

The feel of her soft mouth on him was more than he could resist. She had never done such a thing to him before—it was not a subject he'd felt he could easily broach with her. Proper gentlemen did not ask their wives to suck their cocks over the tea table, or at any other time, either. It came as a surprise to him that she knew such things took place between a man and a woman. His hips bucked involuntarily toward her, pushing his cock deeper into her mouth. "Oh, God, Gwendolyn." The words were dragged out of his very soul.

She drew her head back from him, leaving him bereft as her lips and tongue broke contact with his cock. "My name is Captain Long Meg, the pirate queen," she said sternly. "Say it, captive, if you want me to pleasure you."

He'd call her Queen bloody Victoria if it would get his cock back in her mouth again. "Whatever you command, Long Meg, the pirate queen," he said, bucking his hips at her and not even trying to disguise his impatience.

"*Captain* Long Meg."

"Captain Long Meg." He stressed the word *captain*, eager to feel her mouth over his cock again.

"Thank you. That wasn't so hard now, was it?" Opening her mouth wide, she welcomed his thrusting member again. Her lips closed around him, sucking on him greedily, as if she longed to taste every part of him.

A sigh of contentment escaped him as she began to suck on him. Under her ministrations, his cock swelled tighter and harder than it ever had before. The warm wetness of her mouth surrounding him, the tantalizing motion of her tongue on his sensitive tip, and the suction of her lips, added to the knowledge that it was his Gwendolyn, his wife, who was pleasuring him in this way.

Or rather, Long Meg, the pirate queen. Captain Long Meg. He was damned if he'd call her anything else as long as she had his cock in her mouth and was pleasuring him with her tongue.

She broke the massage for a moment to look up into his eyes. "You taste soooo good."

One of her hands cupped his balls, squeezing them gently until he thought he would expire with pleasure on the spot. With the other hand she stroked the base of his cock while she moved her mouth up and down over the head and down the shaft.

It was too much—he could not take it any longer. Furiously, he rattled the chains that held him bound, but he could not move. He could only stand there as she tortured him with her mouth and her hands.

The first spasms of an orgasm started to tremble through him. "God, Gwendolyn, I'm going to spend in your mouth if you do not stop now."

Her only answer was an appreciative murmur in the back of her throat and a renewed vigor in her sucking.

He took that as permission to do just that. Indeed, he had no choice—he could not stop himself. His hips bucked, his whole body jerked, and, with a burst, he spent his seed into her mouth.

She milked him with her lips and tongue, sucking every last drop of cum from his cock like a cat licking up cream from a saucer. Held captive by more than physical chains, he could say nothing, do nothing. Even panting for breath took too much effort. He was like clay in her hands, and she had molded him like a master potter.

When all his seed was spent, she finally had mercy on him and let his cock slide from her mouth again. "Did you like that, captive?" she asked, fondling his balls with one hand.

His breath slowly returned until he could speak again. "If I'd liked it any more, I'd be dead at your feet."

With a crow of triumph, she got to her feet, wiping a few

errant drops of cum from her chin with the back of her hand. "You have performed well, captive, and I will show you unaccustomed mercy. My pirate crew will be along to release you shortly."

He looked down at himself, his trousers around his ankles and his now-limp cock dangling wetly in the breeze. "You are surely not going to leave me like this." He did not want to expose himself to such ruffians at the best of times, and particularly not now, when he was tied up, vulnerable, and had clearly just been taken advantage of. The prospect was humiliating in the extreme.

She shot him a sideways look. "Ask me nicely, and I may not."

"Please." The word did not come easily to him.

"Please what?"

"You know exactly what."

"Maybe I do." There was a glint of mischief in her eyes. "But maybe I also want you to spell it out for me."

He glared at her.

She crossed her arms in that silly pirate costume of hers and leaned against the cave wall. After a few moment's silence, she pushed herself off the wall. "Well, if you have nothing further to say to me, I think I'll be off. Maybe we'll meet again some time on the high seas."

"Please," he muttered.

"Excuse me, I didn't quite hear you."

"Please pull my trousers up over my hips again and fasten them," he forced out between gritted teeth. "With my cock inside."

"With pleasure, captive." She knelt back down at his feet and drew his trousers back up over his hips. With a sigh of appreciation, she gathered his cock and balls in her hand and tucked them gently back into his trousers and fastened the buttons. Then she smoothed down his shirt and straightened his jacket.

"There," she said, stepping back to admire her handiwork. "No one would ever know now that Long Meg the pirate captain had held you captive and had her way with you."

"Release me, Gwendolyn."

"I'm afraid I cannot do that."

"Why not?"

"Because I do not have the key. But never fear, I have promised you your freedom, and Long Meg never breaks her word." She leaned in to him and placed a kiss on his cheek. "*Au revoir, Monsieur.*"

And just like that she was gone.

Fuming again, he stood calmly in his bonds until the ruffians who had first captured him returned. Without a word, they reached up and loosened his shackles. As soon as he was loose, he strode out of the cave, not deigning to favor them with a word or a glance. It would not be fair to take his annoyance out on them—they were nothing more than his wife's hired helpers. No, it was his dear wife who was to blame in this, as in everything else.

The sunshine hurt his eyes after the darkness of the cave. He looked around, blinking, but Gwendolyn had long since disappeared. His temper still ruffled, despite the ache of satisfaction in his loins, he strode up the beach and back to the path that led to the house.

Gwendolyn, the little witch, would pay for her latest trick. A smile curved his lips. Oh yes, she would pay.

On shaking feet, Gwendolyn hurried back to the house through the old smugglers' tunnels. She had achieved her aim of delaying Adam so he could not take the train back to London today, but would her act convince him to stay the week? She wanted him to stay so very badly.

Her steps slowed as she drew closer to the cellar where her day clothes lay hidden. Surely their marriage deserved a second chance. She had so much to give him, if only he would accept it from her. And once he had gotten over his annoyance with being captured and tied up, he had enjoyed her attentions.

She'd enjoyed sucking him like that. Having him in her mouth in such intimacy had made her hot all over. Even as she'd sucked him and licked him, she'd felt her pussy grow wet and start to drip. His cock had been so hard and proud that she'd wanted to impale herself on it and ride him until she came, but she hadn't wanted to stop sucking on him either. In the end the need to pleasure him with her mouth had won out over her own desires.

But her own desires were insistent now. She hoped he would soon recover from the aftereffects of his captivity.

A determined smile crossed her lips. Nothing would stop her now. If he showed any signs of being a laggard in this arena, thanks to Mrs. Bertram she had a few more tricks up her sleeve to reengage his interest.

By the time Adam returned to the house, Gwendolyn was sitting calmly in their private sitting room, a piece of delicate sewing on her lap. He approached her and bowed low over her hand.

She felt herself color at the memory of how they had been engaged just a half hour ago. When Mrs. Bertram had explained to her how to suck on her husband's cock, she had thought the idea far-fetched and rather off-putting, but the reality had proven to be quite different.

"I apologize for being delayed," he said smoothly, "but I went for stroll on the beach and was abducted by pirates."

"Pirates? How extraordinary."

"Indeed." His voice was wry. "Given the history of this part of the coast, I might have believed smugglers, but pirates? They were most unexpected."

"I hope you were not seriously inconvenienced by the experience."

"Ah, but I was. I greatly fear that I was delayed far beyond what I had expected. We will not be able to take the train back to London today as I had planned."

Did he want her to pretend she was sorry? "How disappointing for you."

"But not for you, I suspect."

She bowed her head briefly in agreement. "You know I wanted to stay."

"Then you have cause to be grateful to the pirates. And to the most interesting experience I had at their hands."

"I *do* have cause."

"Still, I am not sure I would care for my interesting experience to be repeated. Pirates are, on the whole, rapscallions of the lowest order, and I would not want to make a habit of associating with them."

She could not stop a slight smile from fleeting across her face. "I would not be afraid of such an event happening again. Such interesting and unexpected experiences rarely repeat themselves."

Why should they, indeed, when Mrs. Bertram had given her a thousand and one ways in which she could get his attention. She was determined to show him that there was more to her than a spoiled young woman intent on getting her own way, no matter what the cost.

"Now, if you will excuse me, my dear wife, I believe I have just enough time to try out Mrs. Bertram's hot pools before it is time to dress for dinner."

Adam lay back in the steaming water of the hot pool with a groan of appreciation. The half hour he had spent by himself, just quietly and peacefully enjoying the warmth of the water, had not been enough. He could spend hours in here, just basking in the warmth of the hot pool. He knew he should get out and dress for dinner or he would risk being late, but somehow he lacked the willpower. What did he care for dinner anyway?

Miracle of miracles, but the house had hot water piped straight from the huge kitchen range that kept the hot pool warm all day and night, all year round. Hot running water would have been a treat in itself, but this! He'd never been in a private house that offered such a luxury before. This week would no doubt cost him a small fortune, but he would not begrudge paying for it.

It was hard to admit, but Gwendolyn had been right to bring them here. In these unfamiliar surroundings, he could almost forget for a short while the way she had deliberately and cold-bloodedly manipulated him into marrying her. Almost.

It would be easier if she didn't continue to manipulate him into making love to her.

Easier to forget her sins, maybe, but not half so fun. He had surprised himself by finding it so exciting to make love to her as a slave girl, and even to be tied up to a wall in a cave and ravished by a pirate queen.

A soft knock on the door interrupted his thoughts. Ah, the maid with the clean towels he had been promised by Mrs. Bertram. With any luck, she would be at least passably good-looking. "Come in."

It was not a maid, however, but Gwendolyn who walked through the door, a bundle of fresh white towels in her arms.

She shot him a saucy look from out of the corner of her eye and dipped into a demure curtsy. "Your towels, sir."

She was even dressed for the part in a maid's simple dress, though cut far too short, with a white apron and mobcap. Even though she'd just sucked him off a few hours before, he felt a renewed stir of interest. "What are you playing at now?"

Hips swaying, she made her way over to the side of the bath and put down the load she was carrying. "I was just bringing you the towels you wanted, sir." There was definitely a naughty glint in her eye as she peeked into the hot pool and unashamedly gave him the once-over. "Coo, sir, you're all man and no mistake."

Four

Adam lay back in the hot pool, just staring at her. Now the towels were no longer covering her, he could see the full glory of her maid's outfit. Certainly no maid in a respectable establishment would ever wear such a bodice. The shift was cut so low that her breasts were covered only by the flimsy apron, whose white fabric could not hide the dusky pink of her nipples. Her skirts were cut so short that not only her shapely little ankle, but also her calves, knees, and even a good few inches of stockinged thigh were exposed.

The temperature of the hot pool suddenly seemed to climb several degrees, and his cock could not help but respond both to the view and to her appreciative scrutiny of his own naked body.

"Would you like me to wash you down, sir?"

To his surprise, he did want her to. Very much. "Please." He liked this saucy new Gwendolyn, in her outrageous costume, ready and willing to do his bidding.

With a flirtatious smile, she rolled up her white apron sleeves and knelt beside the bath. "Allow me to assist you out of the water," she instructed, leaning over him so that her breasts were brushing against his cheeks.

Without hesitation, he took her hand and stood up. There was little point in trying to hide his erection, and in any case, he wanted her to see his cock fully hard despite the relaxing effects of the hot water.

His body steamed in the cooler air as he clambered out of the tub. Just what had Gwendolyn planned this time?

She placed a small wooden stool on a patch of tiles next to the pool that sloped in to a small drain at the bottom. "Sit here and let me wash you."

Sitting on the stool, he leaned forward so she could reach his back.

The soap foamed up into a thick lather on the washcloth. Deftly, she rubbed the soapy was cloth over his shoulder blades, across the top of his neck, and down his spine. Her hands were firm but gentle as they scrubbed away at his skin. He did not want her to stop.

With his back rubbed pink with the lather, she took a bucket of hot water from the tub and rinsed him off.

"Wash my hair," he suggested, more for the sake of keeping her hands on him for a few more minutes than for any other reason.

"Yes, sir," she replied obediently, but the glint in her eye let him know that his suggestion tallied perfectly with her own desires.

She dribbled the last of the hot water over his head and neck, then rubbed his hair into a lather with the cake of soap. Once his hair was thoroughly soapy, her fingers massaged his head, the gentle pressure all over his scalp having a curiously relaxing effect. His eyes closed of their own accord as he wallowed in the luxury of her attentions.

"Now I can wash the rest of you," she said, rinsing off his hair.

She moved to lather up the washcloth again, but he shook his head. "Leave the cloth alone. Wash me with your hands." Being sucked off in the cave had only been an entree, and already he was looking forward to his main course.

She laid the cloth aside and, her hands covered in soap, she reached out for his shoulders.

Her touch was surprisingly tentative as her hands explored his chest. Her fingers brushed lightly over his nipples, making him groan aloud. Dammit, he'd never known that Gwendolyn, his scheming little wife, had such a streak of fun-loving mischief in her. Before they had come away on holiday together, he had only seen the selfish side of her, the side of her that took everything and gave nothing back, the side of her that showed a fierce determination to get her own way, whatever the cost to others. This Gwendolyn was different.

Her questing hands had reached his belly. They were taking too long to get to the main course, and he was more than ready for dessert again. Grabbing her wrists, he tugged her hands lower on his body and placed them firmly on his cock. "Wash me there."

"Yes, sir." Her voice shook a little and her chest was heaving enticingly as she breathed. At the flush of her cheeks, he revised his earlier opinion of her unselfishness. Her little game was for her just as much as it was for him—she was enjoying it quite as much as he was. More, probably, as he'd already orgasmed at her hands today, which was more than she had. She had probably been hot for him ever since she'd captured him and tied him to the wall of a cave in order to make him miss the train back to London.

Not that it mattered. Nothing mattered now but the fact that her hands were slick with soap as she squatted in front of him and stroked along his cock. He spread his legs as he sat on the low stool to provide her better access to his balls, which he loved being massaged. Taking the hint she obliged, gently fondling his sac while her other hand stroked the base of his cock in teasingly short motions. Her nipples were standing to attention under the flimsy fabric of her apron, and not from the cold. The tiled pool room was steamy hot and getting hotter by the second. The knowledge that she was as turned on as he was by her little game excited him even further.

He did not trust the wench for a minute, but this was not about trust. This was about sex, pure and simple. Right now he wanted to fuck his wife more than he had ever wanted to before.

She had been having that effect on him a lot lately. Every time he turned around she had a new trick for him, a new way of enticing him into making love to her.

It was just as well that their holiday at Sugar and Spice was only to last a week. Any longer than that, and the pace would surely kill him.

Right now, however, the pace seemed pretty damn perfect to him. Her hands were stroking up and down his cock with just the right amount of pressure to make him randy as hell. Much more of this, and he'd shoot his seed straight across the room and into the hot pool. Which would be a waste given that she had a hot wet pussy to spend into instead.

Her indecently short skirt had ridden up farther as she squatted before him, exposing the best part of her thighs to his sight. This maid's costume had already proven to be almost as much fun as her obedient-slave outfit. He liked her to dress up in these outfits.

Naked, she was only Gwendolyn, his wife, whom he had a right to fuck whenever he wanted to. Dressed up as she was, she was as tempting as forbidden fruit. He could fulfill one of his fantasies of fucking a servant girl in her maid's uniform, not that he'd ever fuck one of his servants like this in real life, but a man could dream . . .

Gwendolyn stopped her ministrations and once again rinsed him off with a bucket of hot water.

He stood, allowing the water to drain off his body. The cool air of the room after the heat of the hot water whispered over his skin like a caress. The chill of the tiles seeped through the mat and into the soles of his feet, but the rest of his body stayed hot as hell. How could it not, when Gwendolyn the maid was avidly watching his every move.

He tossed her a towel from the pile she had brought in with her. "Dry me."

She caught the towel in midair and bobbed a curtsy. "Yes, sir."

Reaching up so that her breasts strained against her flimsy bodice, she tousled the water out of his hair, then patted dry his shoulders, his back, his buttocks, his thighs.

His cock was hurting with need again, standing up as straight and as stiff as a flagpole. Unwilling to wait any longer, he snatched the towel out of her hands and tossed it on the floor. "That will do for now." Grabbing her by the hand, he strode over to the armchair that stood in the window and sat down. "Come and sit on my lap."

Her skirts were so short that when she sat on his lap only the thin material of her bloomers lay between him and her naked skin.

He pulled her close to his chest, his cock pressing into her back, and put his hands between her legs. In short order he had found the slit in her bloomers, tugged it wide open, and put his hands on her pussy. His fingers found her clit and gave it a little tease, flicking it gently and rubbing it between his forefinger and thumb until she groaned under the torment.

His cock grew harder at the knowledge that she wanted him again. One of the things he liked best about her was that she was always ready for him, never complaining of a headache or some other trifling feminine ailment to evade his attentions. She liked being fucked as much as he liked fucking her.

He lifted her up a little and set her down again, carefully positioning her so that his cock slid home right into her cunt. His fingers still teasing her clit, he urged her on. "Ride me. Ride me up and down like you would ride on a horse."

At his urging, she moved up and down on him, sliding her cunt over his cock.

His fingers teased her without mercy, while with his other hand he stroked her legs, still in their stockings. God, it was erotic to be naked and to be fucking a woman with all her clothes on still. The slide of the silk under his skin, the restrictions on her bloomers, the layers of material separating them— all of it added to the delicious naughtiness he felt in taking her like this.

The knowledge that someone else might want to use the pool-room at any moment and interrupt them in their fornicating just heightened the feeling of excitement. He was fucking a servant with all her clothes on, and he had to come in her quickly before they were caught.

On and on he urged her with his caresses until he could take no more. He was going to come in his servant's cunt. With a guttural moan, he thrust her down hard on his cock and held her there, immobile, as he spurted his seed into her with great force.

Dammit, and the maid hadn't even come yet. He redoubled

his caresses of her clit, rubbing her intently, until he felt her
pussy muscles tighten around his wilting cock and explode into
little tremors. She held herself rigid in his arms, then, with a
sigh of delight, she relaxed back onto his lap with a satisfied
wriggle.

Christ, that had felt good. "You can be a good girl when you
want to be," he said, giving her a quick pat on the bottom.
"Now be off with you and rustle up something in the kitchens
for us to have for dinner. You have made me too late to dine with
the rest of the company."

Gwendolyn slunk back to the bedroom she was sharing for the
week with her husband. Though she had insisted at the time
that one bedroom would do for the both of them, all she wanted
right now was a dark place to hide and solitude in which to lick
her wounds.

Their lovemaking had been wonderful—that was not what
was making her want to cry. Adam had been tender and passion-
ate and everything that she had ever dreamed of him being.

She pulled off the maid's dress, wadded it into a ball, and
threw it into the corner in a burst of ill temper. What hurt her
was the manner in which he had dismissed her the instant the
deed was done. He had taken her and sent her on her way again
without a second thought. Though she was dressed as a servant,
he had no cause to treat her like one, as if she was nothing more
than a convenient vessel for him to spill his seed in. She was his

wife, God damn it, not some floozy he had chanced to run into in the servants' quarters. Surely he owed her more respect than to treat her like that?

Respect. That was the key. Why was she fooling herself? Shaking, she sat down on the edge of the bed, her ill temper suddenly replaced with shame and guilt. Adam's respect was the last thing she deserved. He owed her nothing, less than nothing. On the contrary, she owed him more than she could ever repay.

Mrs. Bertram had warned her that winning Adam's heart would not be easy. There was no cause to despair just because her first few attempts had led to nothing more than a good, hard, but ultimately soulless, fuck. She would not give up until every weapon in her arsenal was discharged and she had nothing left.

A proper marriage to him was all she had ever wanted. No man, not even Adam, would be able to resist all the plans she had made for their week together.

The thought of all the plans she had set in motion made her feel strong again. Drying her eyes, she reached for the first of the scandalous new gowns she had had made in London just for this occasion. Bright red and cut to reveal rather than conceal every curve of her body, it made her feel like an expensive mistress rather than like a neglected wife. It was exactly the armor she needed to be able to face the rest of the evening alone with her husband with a measure of confidence.

Adam waited until the pool-room door had closed behind his

wife before he dared to move. His legs shaking, he managed the few steps to grab his dressing gown from the hook on the wall, wrap it around himself, and collapse back into the armchair by the window. Making love with his wife this evening had once again shaken him to his core.

For the first time since their unfortunate marriage, he had been able to forget about her betrayal instead of letting it taint her every touch. Her costumes had done that much for her—and for him. The taste of her, the rose-petal scent of her hair, the feel of her satiny skin under his hands, had been, for the first time in over a year, unmixed with anything bitter or unpleasant.

Thankfully, the persona in which she had chosen to accost him this time had allowed him to send her away so easily once their lovemaking was over. He could not afford for her to guess at the power she could wield over him. He did not trust her—and rightly so. Only a fool allowed himself to be kicked in the teeth twice over. If ever she realized the extent of her influence over him, he would never know a moment's peace. However sexy and desirable she was, she was also a liar and a thief, and it would be well for him that he did not forget it.

He would forgive her for manipulating him into marriage— truth to tell, he had already forgiven her long ago—but if he were wise, he would not forget.

The next morning was fine and fair. After his early night, Adam rose early, breakfasted lightly on tea and toast, and wandered back down to the seashore. There would be no pirates around to kidnap him at that time of the morning, especially given that their queen was still fast asleep, curled up in her bed. A perfect time for him to escape out on his own for a few hours.

He loved the sea. Or more correctly he loved being by the sea, for whenever he had had the misfortune to find himself on a boat of any kind, he suffered horrifically from seasickness. Nonetheless he loved to walk along the water's edge, to breathe the clean, windy air, invigorated by its passage over the water. How different it was from the stale, smoky air and unhealthy miasma of London.

He needed a walk along the wild shoreline to clear his head. For a sensible banker, not given to flights of fancy, he was starting to feel perilously obsessed with his wife. Even her little attempts to manipulate him were starting to strike him as charmingly sweet and naive.

A steep path down the crumbling cliff face came into view, a different path from the one he had taken when he was kidnapped by pirates. He laughed out loud as he scrambled down the path, clinging to tree roots to keep him from tumbling head over heels to the bottom. Pirates, indeed. Her Majesty's Royal Navy had stamped out those vermin years ago.

At the bottom of the cliff he crunched along the stony shore, watching ravenous seabirds wheel and dive into the water for their fishy breakfast. Ahead, a seal lazed on a rocky outcropping, and he stopped to watch as it idly scratched with an unwieldy flipper.

Its deep brown eyes looked back at him with almost human

intelligence. No wonder the folks in the Orkney Isles had considered seals to be their cousins and made up tales of selkies, creatures that were half-human and half-seal and could change their shape between the two at will.

Judging by the bawdiness of the stories, selkies were as well-known for their wanton ways as they were for their shape-shifting abilities.

Selkies. He snorted and kicked a loose rock into the waves with the toe of his boot. They were even more preposterous than pirates. An excuse for a bit of fun in the sand with someone other than your own spouse, he would like to bet. How typical it was of those people of the north to dream up such an improper legend to explain away their lack of moral backbone. True Englishmen would never stoop to such a sham.

Gwendolyn sat up quietly as the bedroom door closed softly. She could hear Adam's booted feet walk along the hallway, then descend the staircase. As soon as she was sure he was not coming back, she rose from her bed and padded over to the wardrobe in the corner on her bare feet.

A glimmer of bright green peeked out at her from the dark recesses of the wardrobe. Ah, there it was. She reached in and brought out the unusual garment, glittering as green as fish scales in the morning light.

Adam had gone, and she was sure she knew where he would be heading, if not immediately, then eventually. There was no rush—she would wait for him there all day if need be.

She threw on a morning gown, slid her feet into some slippers, and tucked the glittering green garment under one arm. There, she was as ready as she could get here. If she left right away, she would be sure to find Adam before the day got much older.

Continuing past the outcrop with its resident seal, Adam reached a small headland. He paused for a moment, his ear catching the incongruous noise of singing.

Yes, he was certain he could hear singing—a woman's voice, high and clear—but he could not tell the direction with the rocks and cliffs bouncing the faint sound around.

He scrambled over some rocks to be confronted by a perfect beach of fine white sand that stretched in an arc to another headland perhaps a mile ahead. It was hard to judge distance in the shimmering light.

With the faint singing still perplexing him, he walked along the fine sand in his usual brisk, straight-backed manner, his footprints joining those made by crabs and birds marring the otherwise smooth sand.

Striding closer to the headland, Adam thought he could make out a figure sitting on the sand before the rocks. His eyes staring intently into the bright summer light, his first thought was it looked like a mermaid.

Preposterous, of course. First selkies, and now a mermaid singing her siren song. What had gotten into his head lately? His mind did not usually stray along such a fanciful path.

And yet the closer he approached, the more the lone figure appeared to be a mermaid. Although her back was to him, Adam was certain he could make out a naked torso over which streamed a quantity of long, brown hair, and a fishlike tail that gleamed jade green in the sunlight. And yes, she was singing, crooning a wordless tune to herself as she dragged a comb through her hair.

Though he made no effort to hide the noise of his approach, she took no notice. Mermaids were evidently not as shy as they were reputed to be.

As he strode closer, he could clearly see it was no mermaid but a woman sitting on a blanket, naked from the waist up and wearing a tight skirt with a texture and color that gave the impression, at least from a distance, of being the skin of a bright green fish.

It could only be one woman. The same woman whom he had just left fast asleep in their bed. That same woman who had first surprised him on the beach as a pirate queen.

And now she was a mermaid. A half-naked mermaid singing to herself on a deserted beach.

Just at that moment she laid her comb down on the blanket beside her and turned to face him. Gwendolyn.

Her long hair was flowing free over her naked shoulders leaving her breasts and belly as naked as sin.

He swallowed uncomfortably. "You should cover yourself, or you will catch cold." Even to his own ears, his voice lacked conviction. He did not really want her to cover herself. Her breasts were too damn fine to be smothered in a corset when he could be gazing at them like he was now.

She gave him an enigmatic smile as she continued her wordless crooning, and reached to cover her breasts that were so proudly displayed in the warm sun. Instead of making herself more decent, she made matters worse by teasing her nipples to attention between her thumb and forefinger.

He watched, mesmerized, as she massaged her nipples until they became tight and hard, little pebbles of rock under her fingers.

As her nipples hardened and became erect, so did his cock, until it was standing to attention in his trousers.

"Gwendolyn, where are your clothes?" He did not expect an answer. He knew her well enough by now to know that she would play her fantasy out to the full.

She held out her arms to him. "Is your cock hard, sailor boy? Are you interested in making love to a lonely mermaid on this deserted beach?"

He looked around him, scanning the horizon in all directions, but he could see no one. The beach truly was deserted. He swung his gaze back to her, his tongue snaking out involuntarily to lick his lips. Dammit, but he was actually considering fucking his wife out in the open on a sandy beach.

"I can see by your trousers that your cock must be standing to attention. Do you know, my pussy is quite wet. And not from seawater, oh no. Does my wet pussy interest you? Or does it at least interest that lovely hard cock of yours?"

"But Gwendolyn . . . outside . . . people . . . not proper." His jumbled and disjointed thoughts escaped from his mouth as the remnants of his resistance crumbled. When she was sitting in front of him like this, all but naked and practically begging him to take her, what else could he do but acquiesce to her request.

Gwendolyn could sense the moment that he surrendered to his desires—and to her.

His mouth opened and shut without a word coming out, and he stood immobile, just looking at her naked breasts, making no further protests and no move to turn away.

She was sure of him now.

With fluid fingers she unwrapped the mermaidlike material that covered her from the waist down and tossed it aside with the last of her modesty.

Now completely naked, she lay back on the rug and spread her legs wide. "Do you like what you see?" she asked coyly, as he stared at her.

It was not often in her life that she had been able to catch him unawares and make him speechless. He always took control of the situation and of her so masterfully, as if she had never caught him by surprise in the first place.

Not that she had a problem with that. She liked him to take charge. A man who could not control her, a husband who arranged everything for her pleasure and never for his own, would be a namby-pamby thing of milk and water and not for her. She couldn't abide weakness in a man.

Leda Swann

But she also liked to have the upper hand herself once in a while, without having to resort to tying him in chains. And now, it seemed, she had it.

His fingers were fumbling at his buttons. As she watched, his trousers slipped down to his ankles and his cock sprang free. She gazed at it hungrily. Adam might not love her, but he certainly desired her. The naked and decidedly large truth was impossible to hide.

She reached down to her cunt and with one finger stroked her clit with soft short touches. As she did so she arched her back, affording Adam the best sight of her parts she could give him. She knew he liked to look at her there.

She glanced down at herself, her pussy so lewdly exposed, her juices glistening in the sunlight as they ran down past her asshole, soaking the blanket. If he was as excited as she was rapidly becoming, he would not be able to resist her for long.

"Come on, sailor boy," she urged him as she continued to stroke herself, admiring the glistening pink of her pussy and the way her clit swelled under her hand. "You look foolish standing there with your trousers around your ankles and your cock in your hand. Wouldn't you rather lie here on the sand with me? Wouldn't you like to feel the sun on your bare skin? Wouldn't you like to sink that big sailor's cock of yours into my wet little mermaid pussy with one thrust?"

She sneaked a glance at him out of the corner of her eyes. "I want you to, you know. I'm ready. Look."

With that she slid one finger, then two, into her pussy as far as

68

they would go, withdrew them, and sucked her own juice off finger by finger. She had never tasted herself before—would never have thought of doing so if Mrs. Bertram had not suggested it.

Her juice tasted strange, but not unpleasant, and the look of utter lust that settled on Adam's face at the sight was reward enough for her boldness.

His body jerked as if he had suddenly been released from a spell, and her husband, her oh-so-proper husband, began to stumble out of his clothes as fast as he could rip them off his back, barely pausing to grumble at the sand getting into his socks.

As soon as he was naked, he stood astride her, his cock erect in the ocean breeze.

"Come to me, sailor," she entreated, holding out her arms.

He lowered himself to his knees, his cock tantalizingly close to her face. She lifted her head to taste him, but he pulled away, teasingly. "You made me watch you. Now it is your turn to watch me."

She was not ready to cede control to him just yet. Wriggling under him a bit further until his tight balls were directly over her mouth, she reached out with her tongue and flicked his sensitive sac.

The moan of delight that escaped him encouraged her to be even more daring. Grabbing his muscular buttocks, she pulled him closer, where she could gently suck one of his testicles, then the other. As she licked, she reached up and applied a feather touch to the end of his cock, inches above her.

All too soon he took charge again. He jumped up, spun around, and once more knelt astride her. Bending down low over her, his mouth so close to her pussy she could feel the heat of his breath, he gently teased her with his tongue.

His touch was magic. Pure magic. She almost forgot to keep stroking and sucking him in her turn as she lay back and reveled in the new sensation. Her lusty sailor boy was licking her pussy, and she couldn't get enough of it.

What else had Mrs. Bertram said? Ah, yes, she remembered it now. With one exploratory finger, she applied a light questing pressure to his asshole.

He moaned deep in his throat, and his licking intensified.

Thus encouraged, she gently entered him, her finger lubricated with her own juices, while with her other hand she pumped the base of his cock. She wanted him to feel the same pleasure she was feeling, the same desperate need.

She had not had nearly enough of both giving and receiving pleasure when his mouth left her pussy. Reluctantly, she released her intimate hold on him as he slowly straightened up and once again spun around to kneel between her widespread thighs.

Taking his cock in his hand, he rubbed it up and down her pussy, smearing her juices over the purple head. "Are you ready for me?"

She wriggled her body deeper into the sand beneath her, steadying herself for him. Yes, she was more than ready.

Taking her silence as assent, he leaned forward and plunged fully into her.

She gasped as he penetrated her deeply, stretching her to accommodate his width. Nothing, not even the touch of his tongue on her most sensitive parts, was better than the feeling of his cock buried to the hilt inside her.

Still kneeling, he thrust in and out of her, while his thumb teased her exposed clit, sending shivers of pleasure tingling all through her body. She was going to reach her pleasure far too soon if he did not stop, but she did not want him to stop. She never wanted him to stop.

As if he could read her mind, he leaned forward and lay down full length on top of her, his body pressing hers into the sand. He kissed her passionately as his cock made short, sharp, thrusting movements that teased her while they did not satisfy.

She was on the brink of dying with frustration when he withdrew almost completely, until just the head of his engorged cock probed the entrance to her pussy.

Then with deliberate slowness he eased fully inside her and started to fuck her with long, slow strokes. In the background, the waves were lapping softly with a rhythm of their own onto the sand.

The sun on her face and his weight on her body caused her orgasm to build quickly.

The pace of his thrusting quickened, and she saw that he was not far from his own peak. She reached up and squeezed his nipples hard. As she hoped it would, the pain only heightened his pleasure. His strong arms pulling her close to him, he pushed his cock deeply into her pussy and held it there. The first warm spurts of his cum burst into her, triggering the waves of pleasure that rolled over and over her until she thought she would drown in them.

Later, exhausted, he lay on top of her, limp in more ways than one.

She held him to her in a warm embrace, not wanting the moment to end. If only she could capture such a feeling forever, she would be a happy woman.

All too soon, he rolled off her and sat up on the blanket. He ran his hands through his thoroughly mussed hair. "That was madness. I cannot believe I just fucked you on a beach."

She simply lay back on the sand, admiring his nakedness still. His crude language was a sign of how much she had affected him—it did not bother her. "That is generally what happens when a lusty sailor boy happens upon a mermaid on a deserted beach."

He was shaking out his clothes, the clothes he had discarded in such a hurry when she had first started playing with herself, and grumbling to himself. "Damn mermaids."

She raised one inquiring eyebrow to see what had unsettled him so much.

He glowered back at her. "There's sand in my socks," he complained, sounding like a small boy in a pet. "I hate sand in my socks."

Obsessed

His sudden display of grumpiness could not upset her. Not when her whole body was still humming with the aftereffects of her orgasm. Reaching out with one leg, she hooked the glittering green gown with one toe and kicked it over the bottom half of her, arranging it carefully to keep the sun off her delicate skin. "That," she said demurely, "is what naughty young sailor boys get from playing with mermaids."

Five

After-dinner entertainment was in the music room that evening. By now Adam had learned to expect the unexpected. The week away from London was proving to be an education in more ways than one.

Gwendolyn, in particular, had not ceased to surprise him. There were so many different aspects to her that he had never seen before: obedient love slave, demanding pirate queen, saucy servant girl, and entrancing siren. How many other Gwendolyns were there hidden inside the small person of his wife? And how long would it take him to search them all out? For he was determined to find them all, to explore every aspect of his enchanting wife's character.

No secrets would be left between them. Then, and only then, could he begin to trust her once again.

Mrs. Bertram took first seat at the piano. She ran her fingers softly over the keys, flexed her fingers once or twice, and turned to the others in the room. "I will, as always, start off the musical evening with a traditional song, the song for which our house is named."

A short introduction and she began to sing in a surprisingly excellent mezzo-soprano voice.

> *What are little girls made of*
> *What are little girls made of*
> *Sugar and spice*
> *And all that's nice*
> *That's what little girls are made of*

> *What are little boys made of*
> *What are little boys made of*
> *Muscle and bone*
> *And cocks hard as stone*
> *That's what little boys are made of.*

The women giggled behind their hands, and Mr. Hughes let out a great belly laugh. Even Adam could not help but chuckle at the new words she had put to the traditional tune. Really, the woman had no shame. He had not enjoyed himself so much for a long time.

Mrs. Bertram rose from the piano stool and gave a short bow to the enthusiastic applause that greeted her. "I know there is some real talent among the ladies gathered here," she said, gesturing at her guests. "But before I open the floor, may I please present Mrs. Sally Stevens, one of the most entertaining singers of my acquaintance."

A stout woman of a certain age with a heavily rouged face stepped up to the piano. "I am going to sing a pretty song of my own composition called 'The Adventures of Ernestina.' This is an action song—the words tell a story and you, my dear audience, must play along with the words." She waggled one fat finger at them. "I am expecting you all to be good sports and play along with me, or I shall be very angry with you."

With that, she sat at the piano and struck up a merry tune. "Gentleman, take your partners for a waltz."

Adam offered his arm to Gwendolyn. "Madam, will you dance?"

She took his arm with a blush. "You have not danced with me since we were married," she murmured to him in a whisper.

"I have not?" She must be right. Now that he thought about it, he couldn't remember the last time he had danced with her. "How remiss of me. I will have to make amends."

Her touch was light on his shoulder as he steered her around the floor to the strains of the piano. Her dancing was too proficient to give him any excuse to hold her closer to him.

He was so wrapped up in the feel of Gwendolyn's body tantalizingly close to him as they waltzed slowly around the floor that he barely noticed when Mrs. Stevens began to sing.

Gwendolyn squeezed her hand on his shoulder. "The words," she murmured at him. "We are supposed to follow along with her."

He tuned his ear to the words being sung. The Ernestina of the song had attracted the attention of a libertine, who had evil designs on her innocence. The libertine had asked her to dance with him, and was whirling her around the room in a waltz, holding her just a little too close.

He drew Gwendolyn closer to him so the tips of her breasts just grazed his chest. "Just following the song," he said, and winked at her.

The libertine of the song was soon not satisfied with such a minor indiscretion. Before poor Ernestina could protest, he was leaning over her and whispering naughty suggestions into her ear and making her blush.

As the song did not specify exactly what the naughty suggestions were, Adam felt at liberty to improvise. Judging by the scarlet that rushed into Gwendolyn's face at his words, he was quite successful.

The libertine in the song didn't stop at whispering naughty words, either. Like a vampire, he fastened on Ernestina's bare neck and shoulders, kissing every inch of them until Ernestine was ready to faint with pleasure.

Adam was only too happy to follow suit, kissing every patch of Gwendolyn's bare skin that he could reach. He liked this song.

Soon enough the libertine in the song had Ernestina up against a wall, having abandoned any pretense of dancing.

Adam found a patch of wall that lay in the shadows and maneuvered Gwendolyn up against it. He had a definite hunch that he would prefer the darkness for what was about to come next.

He was right. In short order the libertine had his hands up Ernestina's skirts and was fondling her most private places, while Ernestina was squirming with delight at his touch.

Gwendolyn put up her hands to ward him off and tried to sidle away. "You can't do that," she hissed at him. "Not here."

He advanced on her, intent on her capture. "Hmmm—I can't, you say?" He pinned her up against the wall, using his weight to stop her from retreating any farther. A pirate queen can molest me in a cave, a saucy maid can accost me in a hot pool, and a siren can make love to me in full view on the beach beside the waves, but I cannot fondle my own wife among friends?"

"Tonight I am Gwendolyn. I have to be proper."

"I know you are Gwendolyn. Pirate queen or Turkish slave, you have always been Gwendolyn. And I like you best when you are improper." He put his hands under her skirts and grabbed her ass, pulling her toward him until all her curves were plastered nicely against him. "The more improper the better."

His cock was already standing in his pants at the feel of her body against his, and he was randy as a schoolboy again. He couldn't get the feel of her, the taste of her, out of his mind. It seemed the more he fucked his delectable little wife, the more he wanted to fuck her.

She gave a shiver as he pressed her to him. "You have changed. You did not use to be so . . ."

His eyebrows raised in a query. Just how did Gwendolyn think he had changed? "So?" he prompted her.

Obsessed

She squirmed against him, rubbing her body against the hardness of his cock. "So predatory."

"You are my wife. You belong to me. I have to look after what is mine."

"I have been your wife for almost half a year and you have never behaved this way until now."

"True." One of his hands slid through her legs from behind and found the slit in her drawers. "But until now we have never been in a music room at a house of entertainment for married couples, with a woman singing bawdy songs at the piano and encouraging me to seduce my wife on the dance floor."

His fingers found their way through the slit in her drawers to the damp flesh beneath. For she was wet. Adam could not resist a grin of satisfaction. Gwendolyn was always wet for him. Wet and ready.

Slowly he teased her, touching her gently, running the tip of his fingers lightly across her hair and only occasionally dipping in to touch her skin.

She was shivering in his arms, but not from the cold. Her chest, where it was pressed against him, was fiery hot. "You can't do this to me. Not now. Not here."

He looked around. It was dark enough, they were in a secluded corner, and everyone else was too busy in their own dalliances to pay any attention to them. "Why not? It seems like the perfect place to me."

"Because you were dancing with me."

"Mmm, so I was. Until the idea of putting my hands under your skirts instead occurred to me." He rubbed one of his fingers along her pussy, moistening it with her juice, and then thrust it deep into her cunt. "I like feeling your wet little pussy more than I like to waltz."

"You can put your hands under my skirts anytime you like, but you never dance with me." She looked up at him, her eyes wide and pleading. "Won't you keep dancing with me? Talking to me? As if we weren't married anymore and you were still courting me?" Even as she spoke, she moved herself up and down on his finger, thrusting it deeper into her.

Was this another one of her games? If so, he wasn't sure he knew what she wanted to play. "I don't want to court you. I'd rather fuck you."

"I know you would." She did not sound happy about it. "That is all you ever want me for."

"You can hardly pretend you don't like it." Her pussy muscles were clenching around his finger, and her juice was dripping down onto his fist. "You've been panting for it all week. You're panting for it now."

"I *do* desire you. You know I do. But there is more to a marriage than two people who want to make love to each other all day and night. A marriage should be where two people talk to each other, care for each other, respect each other. A marriage should be where two people love each other. That is the kind of marriage I want to have with you. Not this . . . this empty coupling."

Mrs. Stevens was singing now about Ernestina's skirts up around her hips and the libertine nailing her up against the wall. That was what he should be doing to Gwendolyn now, not having some damn fool conversation about what made a good marriage.

"Damn our marriage," he growled, lifting her skirts up and fumbling with his buttons to free his cock from his trousers. "Right now I just want to fuck you." All the blood in his body had left his brain and gone straight to his prick. Once he'd nailed her up against the wall he'd be able to concentrate better on talking. But until then, he could only feel.

"Damn fucking you," she shot back at him, pushing him away so that he lost his intimate grip on her and stumbled backward. "Right now I want to talk about our marriage."

"We don't have a marriage," he growled at her. "Or at least not that kind of damn fool marriage that you think you want. You tricked me into a situation where I had to wed you, and wed you I did. What more do you want from me? What more can you reasonably expect from me?"

Her face was flaming with embarrassment or with shame, but she did not back down. "I want your respect. I want you to talk to me as if I were your partner in life instead of having you talk down to me as if I were a naughty child who needed to be chastised."

"You have done nothing to earn my respect, and I sure as hell don't want to talk to you at all right now."

She backed up against the wall. "You never will want to talk to me, will you?"

Hell, she sure had managed to choose a great time to pick a fight with him. No doubt she'd thought he'd be more vulnerable if she caught him with his cock up and his pants down. "Probably not," he said brutally, just wanting to shut her up so he could deal with his disappointed lust. Judging by the look on her face, Gwendolyn wasn't about to let him get under her skirts again tonight. "Not when there's anything else on offer."

"That's all I am to you, isn't it? A warm body to spill your seed into. You want nothing more of me than that." She shook her head as a fat tear rolled down her face. "That isn't enough for me, Adam. It never has been enough for me."

There was no understanding women. None at all. "What more do you want?"

"Nothing that you can give me. That is the pity of it." Patting her skirts down, she stepped away from the wall and walked with dignity past the other couples embracing in their dark corners, past Mrs. Stevens on the piano, toward the door. In the doorway she turned and gazed at him for a long moment, then shook her head. "Nothing at all." And she was gone.

Gwendolyn tossed her gowns into her traveling valise without a thought for packing them properly so they would survive the journey unwrinkled. It was no use. She might as well give up trying. Whatever she did, however hard she tried to win him over, Adam would never love her.

This whole holiday had been a mistake from beginning to end. She should never have brought him here, or tried so hard to make him stay when it was clear that he did not want to remain. Her selfishness and her foolish arrogance were to blame. She had thought she could make him care for her, trick him into loving her as she had tricked him into wedding her. More fool her.

Not only the holiday but her whole marriage, too, had been a mistake. It was time that, too, was brought to an end.

She had no grounds for divorcing her husband. He had not been physically cruel to her, and as far as she knew, he had not even been unfaithful. No court in the land would grant her a divorce for no reason other than that her husband did not love her.

Though divorce was out of the question, she could still set him free. If she were to return to her father's house, her papa might storm and shout at her to return to her husband, but in the end he would not turn her away. Once he realized she was adamant, he would accept her decision even though he did not agree with it. She could live with her father and keep house for him. Then Adam, though no longer able to marry where his heart led him, would at least be free of her.

That was the only way to redress at least a part of the great wrong she had done to him.

The wardrobe was empty now but for her thick gray traveling cloak. She swung it over her shoulders, picked up her valise, and started for the door.

At the last moment she hesitated, then stripped off one of her gloves and picked up a pen. She supposed she must leave Adam a note informing him of her intentions.

A few scrawled lines later, she had replaced her glove, picked up her valise once more, and was away.

Adam stalked back through the hallways to the room he shared with his wife. After Gwendolyn had left, the evening had lost all its spark. There was no fun in watching other couples share the closeness that he longed to share with her.

His cock was still half-stiff, too, despite her sudden change of heart. His lust was not a water tap that he could turn on and off at will. He considered wandering outside and taking care of it himself in the bushes, but the prospect held little appeal. It was not so much the sexual relief he craved, it was Gwendolyn herself.

That was the truly frightening thing about it. He did not want to take her to his bed because she was his wife, or because to fornicate with another woman would be an act of immorality and debauchery and would carry with it the risk of catching some nasty disease. He wanted her because she was his Gwendolyn, and she enchanted him.

Maybe if he reined in his lust for long enough to talk with her and find out what was making her so unhappy, then he would be able to coax her into a more compliant mood once their talking was done. And if Mrs. Bertram could help by rustling up another slave costume for Gwendolyn to wear, his satisfaction would be assured.

Their room, when he finally reached it, was quiet and empty. Far too empty. Gwendolyn's lacy nightgown was no longer hung over the end of the bed, the feminine clutter on the nightstand had disappeared, and not a single dainty slipper lay discarded in a heap on the floor.

The bed was undisturbed, and Gwendolyn was nowhere to be seen.

He stood in the middle of the room, stunned. His wife had packed up and left without a word to him, without even so much as a good-bye. She had really gone.

His gaze fell on the sheet of paper lying on the writing desk. He picked it up and scanned the contents, his temper mounting with every word he read.

When he had done, he tucked the note into his waistcoat pocket. So, Gwendolyn thought she could give up on their marriage, did she? She thought he would stand by and allow her to return to her father's house, abandoning him, deserting him, without putting up a fight?

He had allowed his disappointment to get the better of him a few moments ago, and he had spoken to her harshly. Far too harshly. He had not meant to drive her to despair.

Gwendolyn was his wife. She had made a vow to stand by his side for better or for worse, and by God, she would stick by the vow she had made. He would not let her run from him in the middle of the night. It was time his spoiled little princess realized life did not always go the way she wanted it to. Sooner or later she would have to learn that some decisions were irrevocable—and that her marriage to him was one of them.

Dammit, she could not want her freedom so badly that she had to leave him this instant. It was dark out, and cold, and a long, lonely carriage ride to the nearest train station. Was he that vile a husband to live with that she had to run from him at such an unseasonable hour?

Surely his sexual appetite had not been to blame, or could his newfound ardor really have been enough to frighten her off? Had she not enjoyed his attentions, even sought them out on more than one occasion? But what else bar a sudden fright could explain her hasty departure?

She had loved him once—enough to trick him into marriage—and she could do so again. He wanted to see the adoration in her big blue eyes as she gazed at him and feel her body tremble when he came close to her. He wanted her to love him as desperately and as passionately as she always had.

Dammit, he didn't care if she thought she had fallen out of love with him and was tired of his demands on her body. She was wrong. He would prove her wrong by making her want him again.

His fists clenched at his side, he strode back down the hallway to find Mrs. Bertram. A plan, or at least the glimmerings of a plan, was starting to form in his brain. All he needed was some small assistance to put it into execution.

If he was going to recapture his errant wife tonight—and there was no doubt that that was what he was going to do—then he would need Mrs. Bertram's help.

"Stand and deliver!"

The coach came to an unexpected stop, rocking on its soft springs. The shouting of the man, the surprised whinny of the horses, and the sudden stillness woke Gwendolyn from her uneasy slumber. She drew the curtain back from the window and peered out into the gloom.

There blocking the road stood a large, black horse and a rider in very strange attire, dressed as he was in old-fashioned clothes complete with coattails, eye mask, and tricornered hat.

She eyed him skeptically. "A highwayman?" she sputtered. Surely this was all a bad dream. "There haven't been any highwaymen in all of England since my grandmama was a little girl!"

"Best remain calm, love," advised the coachman, leaning over from his box toward her. "Highwayman or no, he looks like he means business."

The masked figure in his outlandish clothes guided his horse over to the coach door. "Easy, Bess," he said as he reined the horse to a standstill.

"Stand and deliver!" he repeated, as he waved a mean-looking sword over his head. "I am the ghost of Dick Turpin, come back from the grave to take care of unfinished business here on Earth. I need to right a wrong, to fix a mistake I have made."

Leaning down from his mount, he peered in the coach window. "Well, well, a strumpet. There's nothing I like better than an armful of willin' woman. More fun than a handful of pennies any day." He gestured at her with his sword. "Out of the coach with you!"

Gwendolyn stared back at the highwayman. "Don't be ridiculous," she scolded him. "This is modern England, not some fairy-tale history. Now please remove yourself and your knacker's yard horse from the roadway so I may continue my journey." With that she rapped on the coach panel in front of her and called in an imperious voice, "Carry on, driver!"

The coachman lifted his reins, but before he could stir the horses into motion, the masked man leapt off his horse and wrenched open the door of the coach.

To her immense surprise, Gwendolyn found herself being dragged out and onto the ground.

A heavy dew had fallen earlier in the evening, and the roadway was slick with mud. One of her slippers made a squelching noise as it came into contact with something decidedly unsavory.

Her husband did not love her, her marriage was falling apart, and now her favorite pair of slippers was ruined. That was more than any woman should have to bear in one evening.

She stomped her slippered feet on the ground and stuck her hands on her hips. The highwayman had chosen the wrong coach to hold up this evening. She was a respectable married woman and would not suffer such treament at the hands of any man, robber or no. "Now look, whoever you are, stop this nonsense . . ."

"Quiet!" With this command the highwayman brandished his sword under Gwendolyn's nose, and rather inexpertly, too, she thought. But a sword is a sword, so for once she held her tongue. Now that she was standing out on the road without the protection of the coach, she was starting to feel horribly uneasy.

She turned to the coachman hoping for assistance, but to her horror he flicked his whip and urged his horses to a gallop. In just a moment, the coach rounded a corner on the wooded road and was out of sight.

Gwendolyn started to feel real fear when her assailant produced a length of rope.

"So, my little pretty," he said with a leer. "You have the look of a wench who enjoys a bit of sport. How would you be liking a taste of my sword then?" He thrust his hips back and forth, giving her clear meaning to his words, as he sheathed his rapier.

"Don't be crude," she scolded, squelching her fear in a show of bravado. "You would not dare touch me."

"I wouldn't?" Roughly grabbing her, he forced her arms behind her back.

She struggled free and took several steps of flight, but he caught her and threw her to the ground.

She ended up on her back, the damp soil of the forest floor adding to the chill she felt in her heart. Still, she would not make it easy for him. With his weight pinning her down and her arms trapped by her sides, she looked up into his masked eyes. "You'll not get away with this," she spit. "My husband will avenge any insult you offer me. I suggest you let me go this instant if you value your worthless hide."

"Ahh, yes, your husband. Do you love him?"

Gwendolyn stared at him, too surprised by the question to struggle for a moment. "Of course I do," she retorted. "I never would have married him else."

"And your husband? Does he love you back again?"

Love? Adam would not know the meaning of the word. "He will protect me from you," she temporized. "That is all you need worry about."

"Are you so sure about that?" Still trapped with his weight, she watched with a mixture of fear and curiosity as her captor raised his arms and removed his mask.

"Adam!" For the merest moment she went limp with relief at the realization that her attacker was none other than her husband, and then she renewed her struggle with vigor.

Freeing one of her arms, she tried to beat him around the head. "You despicable man! You're a fool and a scoundrel, and you frightened me half to death with your silly games. Now let me up this instant."

"No, I will not let you up. Today, Gwendolyn, my princess, you are to play *my* game." With that he once again trapped her arm, rendering her helpless. Replacing the mask over his eyes, he bent down close to her and whispered to her, his breath hot in her ear. "So, princess, will you play with me tonight?"

He had come after her. She was not sure why, but he had come after her. Even so little as that was enough to make her heart leap with joy. Maybe, just maybe, their marriage still had a chance.

If he really wanted to be free of her, he could have stood back and simply watched her go. He must want her to remain with him. He must.

"You'll not have your wicked way with me, Mr. Highway-man," she said, entering into his game. Her fear was quite gone now—replaced by quite a different emotion. Adam would never hurt her. "I bet you aren't the swordsman you claim to be." She gave a malicious laugh, egging him on to be even more outrageous. "Indeed, I'd wager your sword is more dirk than rapier."

He sat back on his heels and glared at her. "No one insults the ghost of Dick Turpin, wench."

Distracted as he was by her insult, she managed once again to release an arm, but he held it and used it to flip her over so that her face was pressed into the moist vegetation on the forest floor.

Grabbing her other arm, he tied her wrists together behind her back and stood her up. "Soon, princess, you will discover the talent of my rapier. You'll be sorry you ever entered these woods. But for now I'm tired of your ranting."

He placed a gag over her mouth, roughly tying it in place, and led her, still struggling, off the road to a tree several hundred yards in the forest.

Looped over a branch of the tree was a large rope. He briefly released her hands only so that he could tie them up again, this time in front of her. Once they were securely fastened, he tied her wrists with the large rope and pulled her arms above her head, stretching her so that she had to support her weight on tiptoe.

She writhed around, trying to find a way out, but she could not. Her bonds were tied too firmly. She was tied up and at the mercy of a handsome highwayman, unable to stop him from taking his pleasure with her, whichever way he chose to. She could not even cry out to voice a complaint or beg for mercy. He would make her his plaything, and she could do nothing to stop him. Her pussy was tingling at the thought.

Her highwayman stood in front of her and pulled out a small dagger. "You were right about one thing, wench. I do indeed have a dirk. And this is what I use it for."

Spellbound by the blade, she could only watch as he started cutting away her clothes piece by piece.

Slowly her naked torso was revealed to the chill night air.

And as each item of clothing fell away, she felt his lustful eyes take in her captive nakedness.

Then his tongue followed his gaze, teasing, causing goose-flesh to rise.

She could only make muffled sounds around her gag as the highwayman turned his attention to her nipples. He flicked them into painful hardness, one at a time, taking his time on each point of pleasure.

Leaving her breasts, he resumed removing her clothes until finally she was naked.

She could feel her calves starting to cramp with the discomfort of her position. Her arms ached, and the rope bit into her wrists. But all this was nothing to the fire in her pussy, the fire that he was deliberately stoking. She wanted him to fuck her, to take her now, on the wet leaves of the forest floor.

"Mmmm—nice." With one last wicked leer, he walked behind her, and out of sight.

It went quiet, and all she could hear was the sounds of the

forest. Then behind her she heard the sound of a twig breaking, followed by a swishing sound that ended in a sharp pain across her buttocks.

She arched her back trying to escape the sting, her cry muffled by the gag across her mouth.

Her highwayman came into view in front of her brandishing a switch of flexible birch. "Now, princess, we shall see who likes to play games and who likes to be dominant. Or will you give in to me now, and confess yourself beaten?" As he spoke he waggled the switch in front of her wide-open eyes.

She shook her head, refusing to give in. A little whipping never hurt anyone. She would take it all, and more, to hold out on him as long as she could. He did not deserve her capitulation. Not yet.

He moved to stand behind her again, swishing the birch menacingly through the air.

She braced her ass for the next blow, but it was a while coming. She had just relaxed when the switch stung again.

He chuckled at the squeak of surprise that she could not help making. "Give in?"

Once again she signaled her refusal.

This time the birch hit and didn't stop. Each time the switch landed her body gave a little start, with a whimper gagged by the cloth over her mouth.

As the flogging continued, she felt her pussy getting hot and excruciatingly sensitive. Her upper thighs were dribbled with juice, and her ass felt like it was on fire as the light blows rained on her buttocks. The pain was almost pleasurable, especially when she rubbed her legs together in an attempt to alleviate the sensations that were building.

Suddenly the whoosh of the switch stopped, leaving her squirming on the end of the rope.

Behind her she felt her highwayman spread her ass apart, his breath cooling on the stinging redness. "I can see the wetness of your cunt, princess. I can smell how aroused you are. Do not pretend you are not attracted to the ghost of Dick Turpin."

In reply she arched her back as much as her bindings allowed, affording him better access to her cunt and ass. Her whole body was on fire for him. So lost in lust was she that she had no hope of hiding it.

Without warning she felt his tongue dip into her very wet pussy where it lingered for a while before teasing her sensitive asshole.

With his tongue teasing her tight hole, the highwayman slipped two fingers into her soaking cunt.

Her eyes closed and her breathing drew ragged as her climax approached, when unexpectedly he stopped, leaving her gasping on the brink.

Reluctantly, she opened her eyes to see her highwayman now standing before her. He still wore his mask, but was otherwise naked. Very naked.

Her gaze was drawn immediately to his cock. In the back of her mind she knew this was her Adam, but the mask hid his face, and his cock jutted out, not from the usual mat of hair, but from invitingly smooth skin. Around its base was tightly wrapped a narrow leather thong, causing the head of his cock to become engorged seemingly twice as big as usual.

His balls, also trapped by the thong, looked very sensitive, swollen as they were by the tourniquet effect of the leather cock ring.

"You like that, princess?" He ran his hand up and down his cock. "I'm very hard, and very sensitive. It would take but a few strokes for me to splatter over your whipped ass. Or maybe I should release you so you can taste me."

He loosened the knot, allowing her to sink to her knees before once more tying the rope. "I'm going to remove your gag, but don't call out, or it will the switch again. Only much harder!"

She coughed as her gag was removed, and ran her tongue over her dry lips, but remained silent as she had been bid.

"So, you want a taste, do you?"

She opened her mouth as her highwayman brought his cock closer, and she sucked on the large head, running the tip of her tongue round the rim and underneath over his sensitive glans. There was enough slack in the rope to allow her hands to run over his hairless torso, down to his cock and over his captive balls. The feeling of smoothness was exquisite, the leather thong causing his balls to stand proud of his body.

She could stand no more of this sensual torment. She wanted him, and she wanted him now. "Adam, I can't take any more. I give in."

"Be quiet, wench. I am not Adam, I am the ghost of Dick Turpin. And I say whether or not you have had enough."

He maneuvered Gwendolyn's body around, then brought her arms up over her head, tying them to the base of the tree. Next he tied a soft rope to each leg near her knee. The loose end of these ropes he also tied to the tree, causing her legs to be brought back close to her shoulders, exposing her cunt and ass to the soft breeze and dappled sunlight of the forest.

She lay still, completely unable to escape. Never had she been as aroused as she was now. She could feel his gaze on her wet pussy, so open and throbbing with need.

He stroked her cunt a bit before sliding a finger inside, immediately followed by two more.

Then withdrawing his well lubricated fingers he gently eased one into her ass. He paused for a bit, allowing her to get used to the feeling before adding a second finger and slowly moving them in and out, sending exquisite sensations through her body.

With his other hand he slid two more fingers into her cunt.

It was too much for her. In a matter of moments she came, her limbs straining against her bonds as the climax seared through her body. She cried out, not caring who heard, so intense was her pleasure.

Unable to hold off any longer, Adam guided his cock to the entrance of her cunt and, without hesitation, plunged into her as far as he could. Gripping her legs tightly he pushed his cock repeatedly into her pussy, seeking as much depth as possible.

His own climax imminent, he pulled his cock, slick with her juices, from her cunt. After only a few strokes of his own hand, a stream of white cum jetted out over her belly and breasts. His face contorted as the jets continued until finally he was spent, and he collapsed by her side.

Adam lay on the wet ground, Gwendolyn, free of her restraints now, cradled in his arms. "I have treated you badly, Gwendolyn. I hope you will forgive me."

"The spanking?" He felt rather than saw her shake her head. "You must not apologize for that, indeed, or I shall feel guilty for enjoying it so much."

"Not the spanking. But I have allowed you to think that you could manipulate me into doing what I would not otherwise have done. And then I have been angry at you for thinking so. For thinking that I was weak."

"But I did manipulate you." Gwendolyn's voice, muffled against his chest, was so sad and sorry it almost broke his heart. "You know I did. I made you marry me."

"No. You made me do nothing that I did not want to do."

"But—"

"If I had not wanted to wed you, I would never have done so."

She raised her head from his chest. "You mean you wanted to marry me all along? You loved me? Even though I was selfish and deceitful?"

"I was furious with you. After all, you tried to trick me with a silly stratagem that a child could have seen through, and it hurt my pride that you thought I would fall for it. I wanted to punish you—I thought you deserved to be punished. And the more I let my hurt pride fester, the harder it became to forgive you, and the more I needed forgiveness in my turn. But yes, even when my pride was smarting most of all, I always loved you."

Her eyes were flashing fire. "You made my life a misery. For months. You made me sorry I ever married you."

"I am a blackguard, I know it. I wanted you to be sorry." He put his hand on her ass, still warm from her whipping, and held her tightly against him. "But don't forget, I'm also the black-guard who just made you come so hard that you screamed."

She slapped him on his naked torso, an open-handed slap that showed her fury. "*You* deserve to be punished."

"I have been already," he said, as he grabbed her hands and held them prisoner so she could not attack him again. "When you ran away from me, and I thought I had left it too late, that I would never win you back again."

"So that was what all this was about? The horses? The costume? The playacting? It was all about winning me back again?"

"Yes, of course it was. I could not let you get away from me. Did it work?"

She closed her eyes in thought for a moment. "It's too early to say," she finally said, though the twinkle in her eyes belied her words. "Though I suspect that if you try very hard, and are very attentive and inventive, by the end of our week here in Cornwall, I might have an answer for you."

"Then I shall have to wait until the end of the week, shan't I?"

She reached over and stroked the smooth skin above his cock. "How did you do this?"

"Carefully!" he replied, laughing.

"Perhaps," she said, wriggling closer to him, "you could do the same to me?"

He took her in his arms. "Only if you dance with me."

Her heart soared as she kissed him. It seemed things were going to work out very fine indeed.

Enslaved

One

Lillian Rutherford stared into the mirror, her unblinking reflection staring straight back at her. Her fists were clenched out of sight in her lap, her knuckles white with tension. Her rapscallion husband would not make a fool of her. He absolutely would not.

Felix, the rapscallion husband in question, lounged at his ease against the doorjamb, looking at her with a mocking grin.

How she wanted to jump up from the seat at her dressing table and smash that grin right off his face with one angry blow of her fists. That would take him by surprise, wouldn't it, if his placid, obedient, nonentity of a wife were to turn on him with murder in her heart.

How she wanted to scream and yell at him, to rail and curse at him like a fishwife for breaking his vows to her. Again. And again. And again.

But she was nothing if not a lady, and ladies did not scream or yell, curse or fight. Ladies always kept their voices low and their expressions calm. Ladies did not harbor anger so deep it corroded their soul, or hurt so painful it robbed them of breath.

So she merely inclined her head a fraction. "You will be gone all week?" Her voice was as calm and as expressionless as always, despite the inner turmoil threatening to rip her apart. Her mother would be proud of her.

"All week. Or longer, if the sea air agrees with me."

She knew what that really meant. He would stay for as long as it took him to get bored with his new lover, and no longer.

His lovers, numerous as they were, did not hold his attention for long. Two months was the longest she'd ever known him to remain faithful to one.

It was longer than he'd ever remained faithful to her. Less than a month after they had married, she had found him in one of the attic bedrooms with Suzy, the underhousemaid, who had a reputation for sleeping with anything that moved. To her certain knowledge, the girl had already made her way through the butler and both footmen in their household, as well as the butcher's delivery boy and several ostlers from the nearby hiring stables.

It was the noise that had drawn her to the attic bedroom—a rhythmic thumping punctuated by groans that sounded as if an animal was in pain. Opening the door, she had found instead her husband lying on his back on the small truckle bed while Suzy, her short blond hair bobbing around her head, rode him with every sign of enthusiasm. The thumping she had heard was the sound of the head of the bed knocking against the wall, while the groans were not of pain but of a pleasure she could neither understand nor share.

She had shut the door again right away before either of them had noticed her, but the sight was still seared on her memory. "And the address where you shall be?"

He looked at her with one raised eyebrow. "You intend to write me a letter? A kind thought, but really quite unnecessary."

"I would prefer if you would leave me a direction where I could reach you if I need to."

His grin twisted. "And I would prefer if you would deal with whatever comes up in my absence."

It had not been Suzy's fault. Turning her out of the house would serve no purpose except to alert her husband that he had been caught out in one of his amours. Her pride would not allow her to admit to anyone, least of all to him, she had found him with one of her maids. It did not reflect well on her that she was unable to keep him happy, that he sought other pleasures even so early in their marriage. So she had swallowed her hurt, and Suzy had stayed. "And if I cannot?"

"Then it can wait until I return."

She inclined her head briefly. "As you wish."

"Enjoy your week of solitude." He moved toward her and chucked her under the chin, an empty gesture of casual, even contemptuous, familiarity.

Her reflection did not waver by even so much as the blink of an eye. He had no power to deepen the hurt she felt.

His mocking laugh rang in her ears long after he had left. "If you know how to enjoy yourself, dear wife. If you know how."

She was still sitting staring sightlessly at the looking glass when her lady's maid knocked at the bedroom door. "If you please, ma'am, there is a Mr. Hughes in the parlor."

"Mr. Rutherford has already left."

"He did not ask for Mr. Rutherford, ma'am. He asked specifically for you."

A Mr. Hughes? Her memory came up blank. "Do I know him?"

"I'm sure I can't say, ma'am," the maid answered doubtfully. "I haven't seen him call at the house before."

She rose from her seat, smoothing her skirts down with the palms of her hand. "Tell Mr. Hughes that I will be down to see him shortly, then order a pot of tea and a plate of biscuits from the kitchen." It was her duty to entertain morning callers, be they ever so uninvited and unwelcome.

Mr. Hughes proved to be a tall man with coal black hair in a suit of excellent cut, though sadly rumpled, and a complete stranger to her.

Dipping into a curtsy, she hid her concern under a polite smile. Complete strangers did not usually call on her in the middle of the day just to pass the time of day. "Mr. Hughes?"

He tipped his tall black hat to her, his gaze focused intently on her face. "Mrs. Rutherford."

"I must apologize for my husband's absence," she said smoothly, as she moved over to the window. She did not sit down, and neither did she offer him a seat. "I presume you wanted to talk business with him, but I fear he has left this morning for a short holiday."

"And do you know where he has gone?"

The question startled her, but no one looking at her would have known so much. She was an expert at hiding her feelings. Years of practice had honed her techniques to near perfection. "I'm afraid I do not have his direction to hand. If you call back in a week, I'm sure you will find him at home."

"You don't know where he's gone, do you?"

The obvious pity in his voice grated on her. She was Lillian Rutherford, respectable young matron and leading light in the Bloomsbury Benevolent Society. No one dared to pity her, at least not in her hearing. "That, sir, is none of your concern," she said in her coldest voice, reaching toward the bell to call the butler and have the stranger escorted from her house. "Now, if you will excuse me, I have business to attend to this morning."

"I did not want to talk to your husband. I wanted to talk to you."

"I do not know what you can possibly have to say to me." Whatever it was, she was sure she did not want to hear it.

"It concerns your husband."

The vise around her heart tightened another notch. This did not sound like good news. She glided to a sofa and sat down. One seldom fainted when one was sitting down. "Please, take a seat."

Either he did not hear or he ignored the invitation. With one distracted hand rumpling his hair, he strode up and down in front of the unlit fireplace, his elbows missing her precious ferns by the merest whisker.

"Felix Rutherford, your husband, is having an affair with my wife. They have gone away together. To Cornwall."

She had always wanted to visit Cornwall, to see for herself the land where King Arthur and the Knights of the Round Table had lived and loved. A foolish fancy, she knew, and one she had not admitted to anyone for a very long time.

"You are smiling?" Mr. Hughes's voice could have raised the rafters. "I tell you that your husband has gone away with my wife, and you smile in my face? What is wrong with you, woman?"

"Would you rather I cried?"

That stopped his ranting. He opened his mouth and shut it again. He looked, she thought with an incipient giggle, remarkably like a goldfish. "It would at least be a more natural reaction," he replied at last, the volume of his voice thankfully rather more muted.

"I cannot cry." She gave a helpless shrug. "There have been too many lovers for me to cry over all of them. I have no more tears left."

His gaze caught hers and held it for a few moments. She could not look away, even though it seemed as though he was looking into her very soul. "You knew already, then."

"I knew." She bowed her head, defeated. "I knew he was leaving me for a week with a new lover. I did not know it was your wife."

"And would you have come to tell me if you *had* known?"

She felt her face grow pink at his unspoken accusation. "My husband has never been faithful to me. I have long since ceased to expect it, or even to wish for it."

Just then the maid arrived with a tea tray. She placed it on the low table in front of Lillian and, with a small bob, backed away again.

"You have forgiven his behavior?" he asked in a low tone as the maid scurried out of the room again.

"No, I have not forgiven him." Her voice was calm despite the rage she felt in her soul. The hand with which she poured him a cup of tea did not even shake. "I will never forgive him. He does not deserve forgiveness. May I offer you a cup of tea? A macaroon?"

Mr. Hughes ignored the tea she had poured for him and shook his head at the offer of biscuits. "But you remain in his house. You do not accuse him publicly of infidelity."

"What would be the point?" She sipped at her own cup, grateful for the time it gave her to cement her composure in place. "People are not kind to a woman in my situation. He would still do as he pleases, and I would be shamed."

"The shame would be all his."

She looked at him steadily, her grip on the china teacup almost enough to break it. He did not understand her world, the world of women, with its petty jealousies and the pointed barbs they stabbed into each other's hearts under the guise of friendship. "No, the fault would be his. The shame would still be mine."

He walked about the room, his booted feet thudding heavily on the carpeted floor. "I love my wife."

She could only feel his pain rather than do anything to alleviate it. "Then I am sorry for you."

"She is a woman of fire, white-hot heat and golden passion," he continued, as if he hadn't heard her. "And right now she is angry with me. Very angry."

So Mr. Hughes was another one cut from the same cloth as Felix—inconstant to the core, despite the love he professed for his wife. "What did you do to her to upset her so?"

He gave a grimace. "I married her. She has not yet forgiven me for that. I do not know if she ever will."

"I see," she replied, although she did not see at all. She had been so sure that Mrs. Hughes had caught her husband with another woman and was angry with him on that account. Why would a woman be angered by an offer of marriage? Especially one she had accepted?

"She does not love your husband. If she did, she would keep their affair a secret. Instead, she threw his name in my face and boasted of all she would do with him, daring me to try to stop her. He means nothing to her except as an instrument for her revenge."

If only she had the same courage as Mr. Hughes's wife possessed, to treat men as meaningless playthings. "I am glad to hear it. She would be a fool if she counted on his constancy." She took a large mouthful of tea, deliberately scalding her mouth with its heat. She deserved the pain. Trusting a man as she had once trusted Felix was a fool's game. That way led to heartbreak.

"She is using him for her own purposes. She wants only to hurt me. To hurt me so badly that I would reject her as she has rejected me. But I will not do that. I will not allow her to poison our marriage before it has even begun."

She shrugged, helpless in the face of his pain. "I am sorry, but Felix will not leave your wife alone even if I were to ask it of him. He cares nothing for me. I cannot help you."

"Ah, but you can, Mrs. Rutherford." He stopped his pacing and fixed her with a steady gaze. "You can help me if you would deign to do so."

She took a macaroon and nibbled one corner carefully. "What would you have me do?"

"Your husband, my wife. They have gone away together to a house in Cornwall, a house for the entertainment of married couples. I hardly need to spell out to you exactly what the house has on offer."

She had no idea what he meant, but neither did she want to appear a fool, so she merely nodded. "Indeed."

"Come there with me."

He had finally managed to shock her. She took a sharp breath of surprise, and choked on a crumb of macaroon. "I beg your pardon?" she asked, when she had finished coughing and finally regained her voice.

"Come to Cornwall with me. Help me to win back my wife."

She cared nothing for his marriage. Nothing at all. Why

should she care about him when it was too late for her to save her own marriage? Her pain threatened to rise up and overwhelm her. She set her teacup back down on the tray. "I cannot."

"My wife has run away with your husband," he reminded her starkly, not giving an inch. He was all steel and flint. "You owe it to me."

She was as much a victim as he. More so, as she had been in pain for longer. She would match his steel with her own, finely tempered with years of suffering, and they would see who would prove stronger in the end. "I owe you nothing," she said fiercely. "Nothing."

"Then do it for yourself. Win back your husband, and I will help you."

Felix. The inconstant Felix. Right now she would rather murder him than welcome him into her bed. "You are assuming I want to win him back."

The rush of his indrawn breath told her he had not considered such a possibility. He started pacing again, tracking up and down across the room until she wanted to scream at him to stop his incessant movement and sit down. Finally, he came to a stop right in front of her. "You would not like the scandal, would you," he said, his eyes on hers to gauge her reaction to his words, "if I were to divorce my wife and cite your husband as her seducer?"

Her eyes closed involuntarily at the dreadful thought. To have her inadequacies as a wife paraded through the courts, for her name to become a byword through all of England for frigid wives, a jest for every drunken wharf rat to snigger over. To be pitied, yes, pitied, by the other ladies of the Bloomsbury Benevolent Society. No, she could not bear that. Anything but that. "You would not." Her voice was faint.

"I would," he said baldly, pushing his advantage now that he had discovered her one weakness. "My dear wife can push me so far, but no further. If she takes your husband as her lover, so help me God, I will divorce her, and your husband will share in her disgrace."

The blackness in front of her eyes was a safety net, a refuge from the horror of the world. She wished she never had to open them again. "And if I come with you to Cornwall and you do not win her over?" she asked, her voice faint. "What then? Will you still divorce her and drag my good name through the mud?"

"Divorce her? Yes, if I cannot win her love, then I will divorce her. I have no wish to be tied for life to a woman who refuses to accept the affection I can offer her. But your good name will be safe."

Her fingernails were digging into her palms. "How so, if my husband is named in your suit?"

"Once she has started on this road, she will no doubt eventually tire of your husband and take another lover in his place. When that happens, I will name her new lover in my suit and leave your husband be."

Some threats were more than a mortal woman could bear. Having her husband publicly named as an adulterer was more than she could stomach. Braving Felix's wrath in Cornwall was nothing in comparison. She was beaten, and she knew that Mr. Hughes knew it. "When do we leave?"

"We can catch the afternoon train and be there by this evening. I will have my carriage brought around in an hour if you can be ready by then." His voice was matter-of-fact and businesslike without a trace of the satisfaction he must be feeling. At least he was gentleman enough not to gloat at her defeat.

What choice did she really have if she wanted to save her reputation? It was, after all, the only thing she had left. "I will be ready."

Felix handed Cora Hughes down from the carriage and offered his arm to lead her into the house. He was more than a little curious about the place. A health spa for the enjoyment and entertainment of married couples? The idea intrigued him. He was eager to discover exactly what would be available.

When Cora had first suggested they escape the city together for a week's affair, he had agreed mostly because of the novelty she had promised him rather than for any particular fondness he had for Cora herself. Not that she was unattractive—far from it. With her long auburn hair and her lush figure, she really was quite a tempting armful. Well worth spending a week in her company getting to know in every way they could invent and a few more besides.

Looked at dispassionately, she was not as classically beautiful as his wife, but then few women were. Cora, however, had other virtues—an apparent enthusiasm for fucking not the least of them. Not, unfortunately, a virtue that his dear wife Lillian shared.

If Lillian had suggested they spend a week in the country together to conduct an affair, he would drop dead with surprise. All his wife's beauty could not make up for the coldness that lay beneath that glittering exterior. She did not feel as other women felt. How could she, when she had a stone where her heart ought to be?

They had been married for half a dozen years now, but he had found nothing that could shake her out of her coolness, her calm self-control. Though he had baited her unmercifully, deliberately indulging in actions that would send any other woman into a fit of hysterics, she had remained unmoved. She had simply looked at him with that cool stare of hers, not even deigning to despise him.

That was what hurt most of all—that she did not care enough about him even to despise him. The very worst of his antics could not elicit even that much emotion from her.

In time, his efforts to get her attention, any attention at all, had become a habit. Now he played around not to bait his wife but to console himself for the lack of her affection. Even if she would not welcome him to her bed, there were plenty of other women who would. For as long as he remained drowned in their smiles, his wife's indifference hurt him less.

He drew the lush body of his new mistress-to-be, the quite delectable Cora, close to his side, causing her breasts to brush against his arm and enjoying the shiver of anticipation that ran through her body at the touch. Cora, at least, did not find him lacking. She would not turn from the sight of his nakedness with disgust, or shake with fear when he approached her. Yes, playing around definitely had its own advantages.

The afternoon train steamed and puffed its way toward the coast of Cornwall as Lillian sat opposite Mr. Hughes in the dark-paneled carriage, both of them too lost in their own thoughts to speak to the other. Though they had agreed to join forces to re-claim their respective spouses, she owed him no particular cour-tesy on that account. She was not in the mood for politeness, particularly not politeness to the man who had more or less blackmailed her into this trip.

What would Mr. Hughes's wife say to his interrupting her liaison with her lover? Would she be pleased that he cared enough for her to come after her? Or would she be coldly furious and turn away from him forever?

More to the point, what would Felix think of her? Would he be jealous that she had arrived in the company of another man? Angry that his liaison was interrupted by the wife he cared for so little? Or would he simply turn away from her, not seeing her, not caring to see her, as he had done all through their marriage?

Sometimes she still wished they could mend what had gone so wrong between the two of them, but it was a futile wish. The rift between them ran too deep and too wide to be bridged, even if Felix were to want to meet her halfway.

The train clanked and rattled along the tracks, every so often letting out a great hiss of steam. They left the outskirts of London, traveling through the outer suburbs and into the sprawl of the countryside. Every turn of the wheels bringing her closer to Cornwall, closer to the husband who despised her.

Cornwall—that place of magic and myth and legend she had dreamed about since she was a child. She had spent hours looking at her schoolroom window daydreaming about knights and fair maidens and fierce battles for a lady's favor when she should have been attending to her books.

A wistful smile crossed her face at the memory. How her mother had reprimanded her for her foolish fancies when she had once summoned up the courage to ask to be taken to Cornwall, to the land of King Arthur. Her mother held no truck with foolish fancies. She had been scolded for a month and more after her ill-considered request.

It was odd how quickly her long-buried childhood yearnings toward King Arthur and Queen Guinevere and the Lady of the Lake were revived now that she was actually on her way there.

Despite her apprehension, she could barely contain her excitement. The very air of Cornwall, she was sure, would feel different from the air of London. London was all prosaic business and mercantile interests and rates of return on capital invested. Cornwall was magic and mystery, gallant knights and lasting loves. If any place could soothe her wounded spirit, Cornwall would surely be that place.

Whatever happened at this house of ill repute she was forced to visit, she hardly cared. For once in her life she would be selfish and attend to her own wants, her own desires. She had not wanted to come, but now that she was on her way, she would experience all that Cornwall had to offer and her husband could be damned.

The afternoon was darkening into evening by the time they arrived at the manor house. In the evening light, the stone walls took on an almost ethereal glow. Lillian could well imagine the sinister Green Knight of the legend living in just such a place as this.

The manor house itself was grander and more imposing than Lillian had expected, well-made and clearly prosperous, with extensive grounds.

Nothing about it indicated that it was a tawdry place where married men came to break their wedding vows. Even the servants were as attentive and polite as her own staff in London.

The patroness of the house itself, a Mrs. Bertram, came out to greet them as they alighted. "I am very pleased to welcome to you my house, though I confess we were not expecting more guests tonight." She led the way through to a pretty sitting room on the ground floor. "If you will make yourselves comfortable here, I will have another room made up for you at once, Mr. and Mrs. . . . ." Her voice tailed off into an inquiring silence.

Lillian gritted her teeth. How she hated to have her shameful secrets exposed in this way. "Lillian Rutherford. My husband Mr. Felix Rutherford arrived earlier today. Mr. Hughes was polite enough to accompany me."

"Gareth Hughes, at your service. My wife, Cora, also arrived earlier today."

Mrs. Bertram's eyes glinted with understanding. "I see. If you will excuse me, I will show you to your rooms and inform Mr. Rutherford and Mrs. Hughes of your arrival as soon as may be."

She led them up the stairs and down the hallway. "Your room, Mr. Hughes," she murmured, pushing open a door and gesturing him inside.

Dismissing Mr. Hughes's offer of attendance with a cool shake of her head, Lillian followed Mrs. Bertram to another room down the hall. Hesitating at the doorway she stared mutely at Felix's traveling valise lying untidily in one corner. Once inside, she stood by the window and looked out over the shrubbery, both relishing her solitude and wishing that it would end. The sooner that Felix heard of her arrival, the sooner she could leave here again.

Now that she was in Cornwall, she would take a cottage to herself for a week or two and enjoy all the sights before she returned to London. Truth to tell, she did not know why she had never come on holiday by herself before. Self-abnegation had become such a habit to her that she no longer even questioned the impulse.

It was high time she looked critically at her habits. Why should she be more careful of Felix's wants and desires than he was of hers? She had every right to be as happy as she could make herself. He would not go out of his way to please her, so why should she go out of hers to please him, either?

The door to the bedroom crashed open. She did not need to turn around to know that it was him. She knew by heart the tread of his feet, the smell of the sandalwood soap he preferred. "Good evening, Felix."

"Lillian. Mrs. Bertram told me you had arrived, but I didn't believe her. What the devil are you doing here?"

His reaction was exactly as she had expected. Irritation that she was spoiling his plans—nothing deeper. She squelched the feelings inside of her that had foolishly hoped he would be glad to see her, or even that he would fly into a towering rage. Anything but this cold, cruel indifference. "I have always wanted to come to Cornwall. I decided that since you were away for the week, I would go on holiday, too. How interesting that we both chose the same place."

"You came by yourself?"

"Oh, no. Mr. Hughes was coming this way, and he was kind enough to accompany me," she said rather vaguely. Never before had she given him the slightest cause to suspect her fidelity. She hoped the suspicion would cut him like a knife.

"Mr. Hughes?" The shock in his voice was most gratifying.

"He is a very gentlemanly man. I like him very much." A lie, but no matter. There were worse sins than lying.

"You came here, to this house, with Mr. Hughes?"

"What could be the harm in it? It must be a perfectly respectable place with plenty of genteel amusements on offer. Did you not come here with Mrs. Hughes?" She twisted the knife in his back without mercy.

His face reddened. "That is not the same thing. You know it is not."

"I doubt Mr. Hughes would agree with you."

"You cannot stay here. It is not a proper place for you."

She sat down on the small settee and removed her gloves, an irresistible urge to strike back at him overcoming her better sense. "On the contrary, it seems like a very well-appointed house. I think I shall be very happy here for the week." For once, just for once, she wanted to hurt him as he hurt her every day of her life.

"You know what goes on here?" Running his hands through his immaculate blond hair, he stared at her as though she were mad. "You know what I came here to do? And yet you would stay?"

She shrugged. "I do not see how that concerns me. You cannot keep your prick in your pants wherever we are. It hardly matters to me whether you are fucking Cora Hughes in a manor house in Cornwall or Suzy the underhousemaid in her attic bedroom in our house in London."

"Lillian."

"On the whole, I think I prefer Cornwall. There is less chance of my being humiliated by your behavior."

"*Lillian.*"

"My plain speaking offends you? You will simply have to live with it. Just as I have to live with your infidelity, and the way you flaunt it under my nose every day. Now if you will excuse me, I have some correspondence to write before I retire for the evening. No doubt Mrs. Bertram will be able to find you another bedroom. The house seems very large."

He came to stand in front of her, towering over her, using his height to intimidate her. "That is enough, Lillian. I am your husband, not your bootboy. You cannot dismiss me that easily."

Nobody, but nobody, intimidated Mrs. Lillian Rutherford. "I beg your pardon?" she said in her most quellingly polite tones. The ladies of the Bloomsbury Benevolent Society had been known to wilt when addressed in such a manner.

"You brought Mr. Hughes here to spoil my fun." Low and dangerous, his voice promised retribution for her sins.

"On the contrary, Mr. Hughes brought me here." Though she knew she was playing with fire, she could not help herself. "I suspect he was more concerned with spoiling his wife's fun. I do not believe he thought of you at all."

"What does it matter? You and Mr. Hughes are here now, and my week is spoiled."

"Should I care?"

"You had better care."

"Maybe Mr. Hughes would agree to let you and his wife continue as you had planned." She let a secret smile drift across her face. "I did wonder all the way here in the train whether or not he found me attractive. I suspect he did. And I *did* like him very much."

"You would have an affair with Mr. Hughes?"

His incredulity only fueled her anger. Did he think he had

a monopoly on infidelity? "That would leave you free to be with Cora Hughes to your heart's content. Not that your heart has much to do with it," she added spitefully.

"What makes you think you could hold a man like him?" Cold and cruel, each word bit into her with a serpent's poison. "You don't even like fucking."

She put her hand in her chin and looked wistfully out into the darkness. "Maybe I would with Mr. Hughes. He had the look of a man who could make a woman happy." Her wistfulness was only partly feigned.

"I do not believe you. You are trying to make me jealous, but I know you better than that. You have nothing that would attract a man like him. You would not even want to."

His disbelief was the last straw. All the anger she had suppressed for the six long years of her marriage bubbled to the surface. She stood and replaced her gloves. "If you will excuse me, I will go and test your theory."

"That's right," he said with a mocking laugh. "Put on your gloves and go off and seduce Mr. Hughes."

Her back straight, she glided down the hallway toward Mr. Hughes's room and rapped smartly on the door.

Mr. Hughes answered without delay. His face fell infinitesimally when he saw who was at his door, but he masked it immediately. "Mrs. Rutherford. What can I do for you?"

"Kiss me," she demanded baldly, without preamble.

He looked at her, his eyes gray with shock. "Will you not come in?"

"I do not want to come in. Come out into the hallway and kiss me. Kiss me as if I were your wife, as if you wanted me."

"Your husband is watching?" he asked in a low voice.

"He is. So kiss me."

"With pleasure, my dear Lillian," he said, a good deal louder this time, as he stepped into the hall.

She shuddered with remembered fear as he gathered her into his arms. It had been many months since a man had held her with such gentleness and care.

Holding her against the wall, he bent his head toward hers, brushing his lips against her cheek, then moving to her mouth.

Her body stiffened as he began to kiss her. This was all wrong.

He lifted his head slightly. "Shall I stop?" he whispered.

From out of the corner of her eye she could see Felix lounging against the doorjamb in his usual fashion. He deserved to be taught a lesson. If she backed away now, she would not find the courage again. "No, don't stop."

"Are you sure?"

"Yes, I'm sure."

"In that case . . ." He gathered her more tightly in his arms, stroking down the planes of her back.

She shut her eyes, forcing herself to relax.

"Don't think about it so hard. Stop thinking so hard and concentrate on feeling—concentrate on what your body is telling you," he whispered to her, his breath hot on her cheek. "Let yourself go, and I will catch you."

Enslaved

"Nothing but a kiss," she said quietly. "To make it clear to my husband that he is not the only man in England."

"Just a kiss," he agreed. "I won't hurt you. The minute you say the word, I will release you."

Gareth Hughes was an honorable man—she was confident he would keep his promise. Her posture lost its tightness, and her body started to meld to his.

"That's good," he said softly. "Keep going like that, and your husband will be eating out of your hand in no time."

Eating out of her hand? No, she wanted Felix to suffer. She leaned up and pressed her open mouth to Mr. Hughes's. It was time for the kissing to start again.

His tongue caressed hers, flicking in and out of her mouth with a delicate touch that was never quite enough. She pressed closer to him, deepening their kiss. His touch was waking the sleeping dragon inside of her. It wasn't quite awake yet, but it was definitely stirring in its slumber.

Her sleeping dragon was not the only thing that was stirring. She writhed against the sudden hardness that pressed into her stomach. "Mmmm," she moaned in the back of her throat, making it clear from the waggle of her hips exactly what she was making appreciative noises about. Her moan was only partly for Felix's benefit.

Gareth's hands crept down her back to cup her buttocks and grind her against him even harder.

Her hands drifted up to the back of his neck, pulling him down toward her. Her eyes closed again, not from concentration

125

this time but from abandonment. She had not known kissing to be so pleasant before.

So lost was she in the kiss that the sudden grip on her shoulder made her start. She opened her eyes, straight into the sight of Felix's angry face.

His gaze could have slain an ogre. "Let go of my wife." Though his words were directed at Mr. Hughes and not at her, he did not take his eyes off hers for a second.

Mr. Hughes simply grasped her buttocks tighter. "Now why should I do that?"

"She is my *wife*."

"We could organize a swap, I suppose," Mr. Hughes said evenly. "You take my wife and I take yours. In which case, I suspect I'm already a few fucks behind." He let her go and gestured toward the door to his bedchamber. "What do you say, Lillian? Are you interested?"

She put on a thoughtful face. "Your proposal seems fair to me. And judging by those kisses we just shared, I'd be a fool to not be interested." She turned to her husband, barely able to contain her triumph at his discomfort. "If you will excuse me, Felix, I will see you later this evening. Or not, depending. I may well decide that I would prefer to stay with Mr. Hughes for the rest of the week."

"You will not go with him."

"You cannot stop me."

He grabbed her none too gently and pulled her away from Mr. Hughes's embrace. "I can and I will."

Marching her back to their own room, he turned to glare at Mr. Hughes. "Keep away from my wife, by God, or I will shoot you. Not to kill, but to maim. To turn you into a eunuch."

Mr. Hughes simply grinned back at him. "I will keep my hands off your delectable Lillian for exactly as long as you keep yours off my Cora. You understand?"

A long moment of silence passed as the two men took each other's measure. Finally, Felix nodded. "I understand."

Felix shut the door behind his errant wife and locked it. By God, but she was not going to get out again tonight and make a fool of him with Gareth Hughes. Or with any other man for that matter.

"Felix, you're hurting me."

He forced his fingers to relax enough to let her arm go.

Her back straight, she moved away from him on the instant, rubbing her shoulder ostentatiously.

"You kissed him." His sense of outrage was so great he fought for the power to put it into words.

"How did you expect me to seduce him without kissing him? Or were you expecting me to throw off all my clothes in the hallway and ask him to mount me there and then?"

He took in the flush in her cheeks and on her neck, and the tightness of her nipples thrusting out the fabric of her light summer gown. His wife, his own damn frigid wife, was aroused— and by another man's kiss. "Gareth Hughes kissed you, and you responded to him."

If anything, her back straightened further. "Why should I not? He kisses very proficiently. And he was certainly responding to me most satisfactorily."

"So your coldness to me was just a sham?"

"That was no sham. You are no Gareth Hughes to woo me with gentleness but my own philandering husband. I did not have to pretend that I was indifferent to you. The feeling came naturally enough."

"You have always been cold to me. Even when we were first married." *And when I was still faithful to you*, he added silently, *and had no thought of being otherwise.* It shamed him momentarily that that time had been of such short duration. But what husband alive would have been able to endure such a marriage without taking a lover?

He'd always taken some care to conduct his affairs discreetly. In the social circles in which he moved, it was no good for the reputation of a married man openly to cavort with other women. None of his lovers ever visited him at home—he'd always taken a hotel in a part of town where no one knew him. Most of his lovers were also respectably married and had reputations to uphold. They knew the game as well as he did. Perhaps better, as they had more to lose if they were found out.

With the exception of Suzy, the housemaid. She'd been the first lover he'd taken after his marriage, a sop to his pride that she clearly found him worth bedding when his own wife did not. He'd only had the girl half a dozen times in the house, and only when he had no other lover to entertain him better. Suzy was enthusiastic to be sure, but earthy and uninventive. He liked his lovers to have a little more subtlety and sophistication.

How the hell Lillian had found out about Suzy he didn't know. He'd always thought that even if she suspected him in general, at the very least she had to be blissfully unaware of the particulars. Clearly she had seen more than he had thought.

"What did you expect from me? When I married you, I was a virgin. I had never seen a naked man before, let alone been intimate with one."

What on earth had gotten into Lillian in the last twenty-four hours? Everything about her was different. Her behavior was provocative in the extreme. She had followed him to a naughty house in Cornwall and deliberately kissed another man in front of him. She was even talking differently. Her voice had lost its usual modulated sweetness, and her language was plain and crude. He was not sure that he liked it. "I should hope you were a virgin. I would not have married you otherwise."

"Then you might have had more care for my fears. I was terrified. I did not know what to expect. And our wedding night was not a particularly pleasant experience for me. Certainly not one that I was in any hurry to repeat."

He definitely did not like the new Lillian. She was too plain-spoken for her own good. "You can stand there panting, just having come from the arms of another man, and tell me to my face that you did not enjoy your wedding night?"

She shrugged. "I will not apologize for speaking the truth. You accuse me of being cold to you, and rightly so. But what have you ever done to care for me, to encourage me to show you anything other than coldness? You simply ignore me, unless you are flaunting your lovers in my face. Is there not good reason for my coldness to you? You cannot blame me if I turn to another man for my pleasure when you have turned to so many other women."

Her words struck at his soul. For the first time, he actually believed that she would be unfaithful to him. And with Gareth Hughes, of all men. Gareth Hughes, whose wife he had intended to take as his own lover. If the situation were not so painful, he could almost laugh at the irony of it.

Still, there was hope. Lillian was not as calm and in control as he had thought. She was burning up with rage, rage against him and his treatment of her. A rage that he had never known existed under her quiet demeanor. And she had not yet taken Hughes as her lover. And never would, if he had anything to say about it.

Hughes was a gentleman, and they had reached an agreement between them.

Felix would have to change his plans to take Cora as his lover or risk being abandoned by his own wife. That was not a risk he was willing to take.

Besides, though Cora was an attractive woman, and would no doubt be the kind of sophisticated lover that he preferred, he did not feel anything for her beyond a mild lust. Only a weak regret assailed him at the thought of missing a week's entertainment with her.

Truth to tell, he was far more interested in Lillian than in Cora.

Lillian in a red-hot temper might yet prove to be a woman worth tangling with.

He looked across the room at her as she sat at the dresser brushing her hair, pretending to be unmoved. He'd been a fool to mistake her natural fears for frigidity, and to be hurt when he should have been understanding and taken the time to coax her gently out of her virginity.

It was high time he coaxed her into a better temper with him and helped her to find her natural sensuality. She was no more frigid than he was. By God, any woman who could be turned on by the kisses of Hughes, the bounder, had to be a harlot in her soul.

He watched the brush caress back and forth in a regular rhythm. How he would like to rub his cock through her luxurious mane, to feel its softness caress his balls. After a few lessons, she would beg for him to slide his cock into her mouth, he was sure.

Yes, her warm wet mouth engulfing his cock while he ran his hands through her fine hair. That would make him harder than nails. In fact just thinking about it caused an uncomfortable swelling in his trousers.

Then after a good sucking, he'd get her to lick his ass. Once before one of his playthings had done that, and it had caused him to groan in absolute pleasure each time her tongue ran across his sensitive hole.

Thinking of Lillian's tongue probing his asshole had caused his cock to go completely hard.

Needing some privacy, he moved off to the bathroom and slowly closed the door with a last, lingering look at his wife. Alone, he removed his clothes and looked at himself critically in the mirror. Pulling in his stomach and puffing out his chest, he gazed at his profile, his cock jutting out at an angle.

Squeezing his muscles, he made his cock jump up and down a bit before rubbing a finger over the delicate head.

Watching in the mirror, he wrapped his fist round himself and massaged up and down a few times, then turned his attentions to his nipples. With thumb and forefinger he tweaked them to hard peaks, thinking how much he would enjoy Lillian doing that to him. Moving his hand back to his cock, he continued a slow pump, imagining Lillian bouncing on him, head tossing in ecstasy with him buried deep in her cunt. Yes, she would like that all right. He would teach her to appreciate the feeling of his cock sunk deep into her pussy.

In fact, his thoughts continued, what was he doing in here, in the bathroom, when his dear wife was just in the next room? She was here, and he was ready. Her lessons might as well start right away.

With a growl, Felix stalked out of the room in all his naked glory, his erection preceding him. Walking straight to Lillian, he pulled the brush from her hand and, without a word, grabbed her head and pushed his cock into her mouth. He was too turned on to coax her into a good humor tonight. Let her be an obedient wife for once and kiss him instead of Gareth Hughes. She would learn to like it.

Startled, she pulled away from him and leapt out of the chair with a scream. "Felix! What on earth . . . ?"

Before she could finish her protest, he grabbed her by the arm, pulled her to him, and silenced her with his hand over her mouth. Her eyes went wide, at first with fright, then with anger. So caught up was he with the thought of fucking his wife that he was oblivious to this change of emotion.

He didn't remain oblivious however, when the heel of her slipper came crashing down on his toes. With a yelp, he released her, stepping back.

She gave him a withering stare. Literally withering, his cock rapidly losing the erect state he had admired in the mirror only a few moments ago.

"Just what do you think you are doing?" she hissed. "Parading round the room with your cock in the air. What did you expect of me? To roll over with my legs in the air? To kneel so you could mount me like a couple of dogs rutting in the street?"

He opened his mouth to answer, but she continued her tirade. "And don't you dare answer yes to any of that. I am not one of your fancy pieces to be treated with such disrespect."

His initial shock at her reprisal had turned to anger. She was his wife, dammit, and it was past time she started acting like one. "In fact, my dearest Lillian," he drawled, "that would involve too much work on my part. What I expected was for you too suck on my cock until I spent in your mouth. And indeed, that is what I still expect."

And with that he took two strides forward and grabbed her gown. He pulled her toward him, but she drew back, causing the sleeve to rip at the shoulder.

"Now, now my dear, you are not acting the obedient wife as you should. Come here and kiss me." He would teach her the joys that were to be found in lovemaking even if he had to tie her down and gag her first.

With that he pulled again at her gown, tearing the sleeve even more. The sleeve threatened to give way completely as she retreated.

He moved in to get a good hold on her arm, but she surprised him by stepping toward him and slapping him on the cheek. "Ah, my Lillian has some spark after all. Excellent." Rousing her temper was working even better than coaxing her. In a tempestuous fury, she could not ignore him, or look at him with disdain in her haughty blue eyes.

"I am not your Lillian. Indeed, I am no man's property."

"We can argue the semantics later, but right now I want to fuck you. So be a good girl and lie down on the bed and spread your legs for me," he added, goading her with deliberate vulgarity.

She moved toward the door. "I shall do no such thing!"

He lunged toward her once more, this time managing to get a good handful of gown and the chemise underneath. She struggled to free herself, completely ripping off the sleeves and tearing a long rip down the front of both garments, exposing her breasts to the yellow gaslight.

Incensed with the destruction of her clothes, she made no

attempt to cover herself. Instead, she beat his chest with her fists. "Stop this now, or I shall scream."

Ignoring her lightweight beating, he pulled down on her gown, tearing it further as it fell to the floor. Her chemise and drawers quickly followed, then her slippers and stockings, leaving her naked as the day she was born.

He pushed her away, not so much to avoid her fists but to admire her naked beauty. He could count on the fingers of one hand the number of occasions he had seen her completely naked. His tongue snaked out to lick his lips. "Now we are both naked. You may as well enjoy the inevitable." Admiring her gorgeously naked body had caused his erection to return with a vengeance.

"I shall not!" she fired back. "You cannot make me." She virtually ran at him, tackling him around the midriff. The pair staggered a few paces before falling on the bed in a tangled heap.

She ended up on top of him and proceeded to further her advantage by sitting on his chest, pinning his arms to his sides.

She reached behind and took hold of Felix's hard cock with a firm, menacing grip. "Now, are you going to leave me alone, or shall I make a eunuch out of you?" She reinforced her meaning with a none-too-gentle squeeze.

In reply, he suddenly arched his back, bucking her off onto the floor. Just as quickly, he leapt on top of her, trapping her as she had trapped him, his tumescent cock once again waving in front of her nose.

She was in his power now. Naked and lying underneath him, unable to escape however much she squirmed. Reaching behind to tease her clit, he replied, "Neither, but thank you for asking." With that he ran a finger over the lips of her cunt, which to his surprise were very wet. "Enjoying this, are we?"

"You are a beast," she said, squirming underneath him. "Let me go."

Despite her protests, her wriggling was rubbing her clit against his hand. And she was very, very wet.

"Suck my cock first."

"I'd rather die."

"Suck my cock, or I won't let you up."

"No, I won't—"

Her last words were interrupted with a muffled squeak as he took advantage of her open mouth to slip the tip of his cock into her mouth. "Now suck on it."

She glared at him in silent refusal, her mouth too full to speak.

Her nipples were easy prey. Reaching down, he pulled them into tight buds, then kept on pulling.

A squeak of dismay escaped her. He had to be hurting her, but he would not give in now. To let her get away with her behavior would be to confess his failure. "Suck on my cock, and I'll let them go."

A pleasant suction enveloped his cock as she began to suck on him. Slowly, he took the pressure off her nipples as she increased the pressure of her mouth. He moved in and out of her mouth a few times to help show her what felt good to him. She still had a lot to learn about pleasing a man. Inexpert she might be, but the novelty of his wife, his wife, sucking on him caused him to groan with pleasure.

No sooner had the groan escaped his lips than a cry of pain followed as she bit hard. He pulled out of her mouth and jumped back until he was sitting on her thighs, pinning her down to the bed still.

The little she-wolf. She would pay for that bite. "So, you like it rough? Do you like this?" With that, he inserted two fingers into her dripping cunt, plunging them in and out of her pussy.

"I hate it. And I hate you." But her eyes were glazed with lust, and her cunt was dripping onto the carpet as he held her down and fucked her forcefully with his fingers.

"Do you want my cock in your cunt?" He was more than ready for her.

"No," she spit at him. "I want nothing to do with you."

"You're a poor liar, Lillian. Your nipples are as hard as stones, your cunt is dripping wet, and your chest is blotched with red. You want my cock in your cunt, and you want it there badly. You want me to thrust in and out of you until you come with a scream."

In answer, she scraped her nails down his chest sufficiently hard to leave red marks in his pale skin. "I'll make *you* scream," she said savagely.

He drew in a sharp breath as his cock jumped excitedly with the pain. "Next time I will make you beg before I take you, you little savage. But seeing that it is your first time, tonight I will have pity on you." With that he opened her legs wide, angling her hips so that his cock easily entered her sopping pussy.

He thrust deeply into her tight pussy as she ran her nails down his back, his body tense with his approaching orgasm.

Reaching behind her, he eased a lubricated finger into her ass. As he fucked her hard with his cock in her pussy and his finger in her ass, she cried out in pleasure, at last forgetting her anger and meeting him thrust for thrust.

His orgasm approaching, he quickened the pace, making the strokes deeper. He pulled her to him with his free hand as, without warning, his seed spurted deep into her cunt.

As he spurted into her, he felt the telltale tremors of pleasure take over her pussy as it throbbed around him. Even had he not been able to tell she was orgasming by the contracting of her pussy muscles, he could have told by the strangled gasp she made as her pleasure overtook her, and the lassitude that set it immediately afterward, making her feel boneless in his embrace.

He had given his wife an orgasm. The first one he had given her. And by God, did it feel good.

Two

Felix lay awake for hours, staring at the ceiling. Lillian lay next to him sleeping peacefully, with none of the disturbed twitching and muttering that usually marred her night's rest.

She had taken him by surprise tonight. Who would have known that her calm exterior hid a woman of such passion and fire? Her real nature had been concealed so well he had never known of its existence until now.

Their fucking had been explosive. Utterly explosive. It had left him completely drained, as no other woman had managed to do. And yet, drained as he was, he was already looking forward to the next bout.

Her fury was a useful ally to his desires. Better by far than her calm indifference.

She would not fall calmly in with his plans for her. He had not been married to her for six years without realizing perfectly well that she had a will of steel. Nothing moved her, nothing affected her, nothing had ever broken through the walls she had built around herself before now.

It was his job to make sure those walls stayed broken, to make sure she left herself open to his touch, to his loving.

Cora Hughes was nothing to him anymore. Not that she had ever meant much. His week at Sugar and Spice was proving to be much more interesting than he had imagined. This would be the week he would finally make his mark on the soul of his wife. By the time the week was ended, she would belong to him body and soul as she had never belonged to him.

Lillian buttoned her gown to the neck, hooked up her black boots, tied a cap on over her hair, and donned a brand-new pair of white gloves. Thus armored, she felt almost ready for the day ahead.

Thankfully, Felix had already risen and gone down for breakfast. She did not have to gird herself for battle in the presence of her enemy.

For a battle it was going to be. She had no illusions on that score.

He had thrown down the gauntlet, and she had picked it up.

Well, that was not quite true, she conceded with a slight smile. Despairing of ever finding a gentle knight to do battle on her behalf, she had picked up the gauntlet and smashed it across her husband's face. With such a blow to his pride as she had deliberately dealt him by coming to this bawdy house with another man, battle was inevitable.

The lists were drawn up, the spectators had gathered, and all that remained was for the two of them to fight it out to determine the final victor.

She was not arrogant enough to be confident of winning. Not only was Felix stronger than she, but he was also sneaky. She would need her wits about her to combat him. The proof of that was in his behavior last night—not only had he taken advantage of her, but he had robbed her of the will to fight. Now she knew his tactics, she would not be such an easy target the second time.

Right was on her side—she was confident of that. No matter how strong Felix was, or what tricks and stratagems he could bring to the battlefield, right would always prevail over might.

The memory of the pleasure he had given her against her will was strong in her mind, sowing seeds of doubt. Maybe right would prevail.

Unfortunately, her life was no Arthurian legend, where the good always triumphed over the evil, where even death could be a victory for the just. She had no white knight to fight her battles for her, to rescue her from the man who kept her captive and forced his attentions on her.

Then again, she was no helpless maiden, either. Determined and resourceful, she would no longer suffer and pine away in silence as Felix robbed her of her health, her spirit, her happiness, of her very will to live.

No miracle would come to save her, to give her life the joy it lacked. It was time to end her passive role in her own life and take charge of her destiny.

Her pussy was throbbing at the thought of battling with her husband anew. She turned her mind from the memory of the way he had treated her the previous night and the way she had been helpless in his hands. It meant nothing. Less than nothing. No doubt he treated all his women like that. It was hardly any wonder the poor, weak things kept on going back for more. But she was made of stronger stuff. She would not yield to him for the sake of a moment's pleasure. She would fight to the very end.

Mrs. Bertram had been up since early morning waiting for her latest guest, Mrs. Lillian Rutherford, to appear. When she finally heard the slow, measured tread of her footsteps on the stairs, she hurried out into the passageway to intercept her. "Ah, Mrs. Rutherford. I trust you slept well?"

"Very well, thank you." The pallor of her face and the brittleness of her voice belied the words she spoke.

Her new client was not a happy woman. "I know you must be anxious for your breakfast, but may I beg you for a moment's time? I will not delay you for long." The sooner she knew what Mrs. Rutherford wanted and needed, the sooner she could lay a plan to help her.

Lillian bowed her head graciously, followed Mrs. Bertram into her private parlor, and accepted the offer of a seat on the sofa and a cup of tea from the steaming pot standing on an occasional table.

Mrs. Bertram looked appraisingly at the young matron seated in front of her, her hands clasped in her lap. Outwardly, she was all serenity, but Mrs. Bertram had had long experience in looking beyond outward shows.

This woman was anything but serene. Tension radiated from her body, creating an almost palpable aura of unhappiness and anger around her. She was wound so tight it was a miracle she did not snap under the strain.

Mrs. Bertram offered Lillian a triangle of buttered toast to tide her over until she could have a heartier meal. The poor thing needed fattening up.

Lillian accepted it with a polite nod and nibbled on one corner.

"So," Mrs. Bertram started, gesturing at Lillian with her china teacup. "What brings you to my house?"

"Does one need a reason to come here?" The young woman's tone was perfectly polite, but her intention to avoid the question was clear.

Mrs. Bertram did not rise to the bait so temptingly dangled before her. "Does one need a reason to do anything?" she said in an offhand manner.

Lillian shrugged. "Exactly."

"But I find that nearly everyone who comes here has an agenda of one sort or another."

A small smile played over Lillian's face. "So I am the exception to your rule?"

"No, I don't believe you are." Mrs. Bertram never believed in coincidences or exceptions to rules. Her entire business was based on the premise that life was an ordered pattern of actions and reactions and that it was merely a matter of finding the appropriate action to cause the desired reaction. Her belief had never steered her wrong yet. "I believe you have a definite purpose in coming here. You simply do not choose to tell me what it is."

"Possibly." The indifference Lillian displayed was too calculated to be real.

"Which makes it very difficult for me to help you." Mrs. Bertram sat back in her chair, her shrewd look taking in as much as she could about her latest client. Lillian Rutherford was not going to be an easy nut to crack. The challenge was all the more appealing. "Your husband arrived yesterday with another woman, and you followed him. You clearly had a purpose in doing so. If I knew what it was, I could help you to attain it."

"Maybe I followed him on a whim."

"I might believe that of another woman, but not of you. Even on so short acquaintance as we have, I do not think you are the woman to travel halfway across the country on a whim."

Lillian nodded her head in agreement. "True. I am not."

"Then my question still stands. Why did you come here? What did you hope to gain by it?"

Lillian opened her mouth to speak, then shut it again, an obstinate look on her pretty face.

Mrs. Bertram drank the rest of her tea in silence, then poured herself a second cup, carefully watching Lillian out of the corner of her eye. The younger woman was clearly wrestling with a confession.

Finally, Lillian stood up and walked over to the window, turning her back on Mrs. Bertram. "I want to make him sorry he ever married me," she said in a low voice, talking to herself more than to Mrs. Bertram. "I want to hurt him as he has hurt me."

"He has hurt you badly, then?"

"He has destroyed my life. I want to make him hate me as much as I hate him."

"You do not have the look of a woman who hates. Of a woman who has suffered, yes, but not one who has allowed that suffering to turn into hate. You lack the bitterness, the cruelty, of true hatred."

Lillian turned on Mrs. Bertram with a vicious glare. "I do hate him." The words were almost a shout. Up and down in front of the window she strode, her hands clenched into tight fists, her composure completely shattered. "I despise him for treating me like a cipher, like a chattel with no feelings, no wants, no desires of my own. I hate him for his indifference to me. His unfaithfulness to me with anything that wears a skirt disgusts me." She choked back a sob. "And I hate myself for allowing him to treat me this way, for never having had the courage to challenge him before. I am determined to make up for it now."

Her sudden vehemence would have startled most people, but not Mrs. Bertram. She had been expecting it. No woman could stay stretched so thin with strain without breaking eventually, even in a minor way. "Hate is often close kin to love."

"Hate is, maybe. But not despising. Or disgust." Her back was straight, but her whole body was trembling. "He means nothing to me anymore. Nothing."

Mrs. Bertram noted that telltale tremble. Mrs. Lillian Rutherford might hate her husband right at this moment and want to make him suffer, but one thing was painfully clear. She was not indifferent to him. Not at all.

"Consider the trees we have in our garden." Mrs. Bertram waved in the general direction of the window, where the white morning sun was making a pattern of shadows on the carpet. "The walnut trees are unyielding. They fight and resist whatever nature throws at them, and while they may be fruitful enough, frankly, they aren't much to look at. They grow twisted, their bark is rough and their limbs stout. Eventually their strength is no match for what they have to endure, and they break and snap, dying in their attempt to prevail against irresistible forces.

"Now, in contrast, the willows by the river are beautiful, graceful trees. They flex and move when pushed by the wind, growing with, rather than against, the forces that assail them. They do not fight—they win by yielding.

"Let events flow around you as wind and water flow around the willow. You have tried to fight, and you have failed. Be a willow tree. Win by yielding."

★ ★ ★

Felix was halfway through the morning paper when Lillian finally appeared for breakfast. Her color was high as if her temper had already been roused that morning. Excellent—it would make his job so much the easier. He watched her as she took a seat and helped herself to breakfast, pointedly ignoring him as if she had not trembled with desire under his hands a few short hours before.

"You spoiled my plans for a week with Cora," he began, knowing full well that the mention of Cora's name would be like a red rag to a bull. Especially after the night they had shared, Lillian would have to be a saint not to take offense at his words. And thankfully his dear wife was no saint. "You owe me some recompense for that."

She stopped in the middle of buttering her scone, and a telltale flush of red crept over her cheekbones. "I believe I paid all such debts to you last night."

"You think one quick fuck will make up for missing a week of passion with a new mistress? Think again, my dear Lillian."

"Would you like me to leave again?" She gave a sniff of disdain. "No doubt Mr. Hughes would escort me back home if you do not wish to do so."

He stifled a grin. The little witch was trying to bait him back. "No, I do not wish you to leave. Indeed, I have decided that I will not allow you to leave."

"You can hardly prevent me from leaving if I wish to." Her back was so rigidly straight a draftsman could rule a line by it.

"You are my wife," he reminded her. "I can do exactly as I please with you."

"Not quite. Not if you do not want to cause a scene."

He came to stand behind her, his hands on her shoulders. "I don't give a damn about causing a scene. Indeed, I would rather like it. I find that provoking your temper has certain beneficial side effects."

"I never lose my temper," she lied stiffly, her cheekbones burning.

He reached into his pocket and quietly drew out the pair of handcuffs that Mrs. Bertram had procured for him earlier that morning. "I am glad to hear it," he said, as he leaned over her and slipped the cuffs over her wrists, snapping them shut before she had realized what he was doing. "You will then take having to wear these with equanimity."

"Take them off me," she said, as if he were a bothersome child who needed correction. "I have no interest in playing foolish games with you. Take these off me at once."

He smiled at her now, the smile of a tiger who has his prey firmly in its grasp. "No, I don't think so. I rather like the look of my wife tied up for me, ready and waiting for me to take my pleasure with her."

"I am not ready and waiting to give you anything," she protested, giving up her pretense of indifference and struggling with the heavy metal cuffs that bound her hands together. "I despise you, and I hate you."

Ah, he had succeeded in rousing her temper already. Excellent. "More's the pity. For I will not let you free again until you are as ready and willing as any man could wish his wife to be."

Her struggling stopped as she digested his words. "You are joking," she said finally, her voice betraying her discomfort.

"Not in the least," he replied cheerfully.

"They chafe me." She held out her hands and showed him a tiny patch of red skin on the underside of her wrist. "See, my wrists are being rubbed raw already."

Such a tiny mark as that would not move him to pity. "They would not chafe if you did not fight against them. If you accepted your bonds and ceased your struggling, they would lie lightly on you."

The frost in her look could have made the Thames freeze over. "I am hungry," she said at length. "Take them off so I can finish my breakfast."

"No."

"Be reasonable," she demanded in a most unreasonable tone. "You see I cannot eat with them on."

"Then you will have to ask me to help you." His grin widened, and he stroked her shoulder with one of his hands. A poker was nothing in stiffness to her body. "You will have to ask me very nicely indeed." With the thought of where that could lead, a certain part of his body was starting to take on a distinct resemblance to a poker as well.

Her glare could have shattered boulders to smithereens with its driving fury. "You are despicable."

"Maybe I am, but you are hungry. Will you forgo your breakfast for the sake of your pride?" He picked up her cup of coffee and held it to her lips. "Take a mouthful of this. You know you will feel the better for it."

Her lips were pressed together so tightly that not a drop of the coffee could find its way through.

"A piece of scone, then?" he asked. He buttered one and added a large dollop of strawberry jam on top. "Come now, I know how much you love strawberry jam. Take a bite for my sake."

She shook her head, refusing to open her mouth even to answer him.

"Well, then, my dear wife, if you have finished your breakfast, may I suggest that we retire to our bedroom." He snapped a leash on to the handcuffs and tugged on it until she was forced to rise from the table. "I find we have plenty to discuss, you and I, and I am eager to start."

On the leash, he led her through the hallways and up the stairs to their bedroom. The few servants they passed averted their eyes and made no sign that they noticed anything amiss. No doubt they were well used to all sorts of unusual goings-on and were amply compensated both for their blindness and their silence.

Lillian kept her head high as they passed, no longer struggling with her chains, but her eyes shot daggers at him, and her whole stance promised retribution as soon as they were alone.

As soon as the door shut behind them, she launched into a

tirade of abuse, maligning him, his parentage, and a fair number of his ancestors as well. Interesting. He hadn't been aware she knew such language. She even came up with a few choice terms he hadn't heard before himself.

"Did your mother never teach you that you catch more flies with honey than with vinegar?" he asked, when she finally stopped to catch her breath.

In reply, she swung her tied hands at him, catching him a glancing blow on the shoulder.

"Tut, tut, this will never do," he said, grabbing hold of her hands so she could not try that trick again. "If you continue so vicious, I will have to leave you chained all day. Indeed, I could not risk allowing you to accompany me to dinner when you are in such a temper."

"Release me, and you will find a remarkable improvement in my temper," she ground out between clenched teeth. "After I have shot you in the heart for daring to restrain me in the first place, that is." Her smile was nothing but malice, and ill will spread out over her face. "That would put me in a fine temper for sure."

"You will have to earn your way out of these bonds."

"Earn my way out?" She gave a disparaging scoff, but a spark of interest had flared briefly in her eyes.

He remained silent, waiting to see if the spark would catch.

"So, how do you propose that I earn my way out?" she asked eventually, her voice dripping with scorn.

"Nothing too onerous, I assure you, dear wife. You can earn your way out quite easily—by being the good, obedient wife you swore to be on our wedding day."

Her only reply to his suggestion was another oath—and one that had nothing to do with obedience.

He took a chair opposite her and settled down to wait. Ten pounds to a farthing he could hold out longer than she could. After all, he was not the one in bonds.

And she had something he wanted. Something he wanted very badly. Until now, he had never realized just how badly. Well, it was worth waiting for, and wait is what he would do, by God.

The morning wore on, the shadows moved around the room as the sun rose toward noon. Still, Lillian sat primly on the chair in the window, her hands in her lap, ignoring the restraint of her handcuffs as best as she could. Her mouth was dry, and her stomach rumbled with hunger, but her determination to outwait him sustained her. She would not give Felix the satisfaction of simply giving in. Starving was preferable to that. Passive resistance would be her best strategy. It was not fighting, but neither was it yielding.

Just then her stomach gave an extraloud gurgle. A creeping heat spread over her face at the unladylike position she was forced to assume. One more sin to chalk up to Felix's account.

Felix made an exasperated noise and tugged the bellpull. "A pot of coffee and a plate of scones, if you please," he asked the maid who answered his call.

The maid bobbed into a curtsy. "Right away, sir."

In just a few minutes she was back again, a laden tray in her hands.

Lillian's mouth watered at the aroma of the coffee, but she steadfastly looked away from the tray. Mere food could not break her spirit.

The coffee gurgled as Felix poured it into a cup. "Here," he said, handing it to her. "I have no wish to starve you."

She turned her head away without a word.

"A scone, then?"

He deserved no answer. She would give him none.

"I see I will have to resort to desperate measures."

The anticipation in his voice should have given her pause, but she was too focused on remaining calm to think straight.

"If you will not eat your lunch, I will have to eat it for you."

She wanted that coffee. She hated him for drinking it. *I hope it is poisoned. I hope it gives you a stomachache and makes you die in screaming agony.*

She was so busy both hating and ignoring him that she hardly noticed when he took a blob of clotted cream on his forefinger, until he dabbed it on her nose. "What do you think you are doing?" she spit out, startled, reaching up awkwardly with her bound hands to wipe it away.

He held the leash down low so she could not reach her face. "Ah, so the lady deigns to speak." He scooped up another blob of cream and dabbed a bit on each of her cheeks, and then another blob on her tightly closed lips. "Since you ask me so politely, I am preparing my lunch."

There was nothing she could do to stop him as he bent over her and licked the cream from the tip of her nose and her cheeks. By the time his tongue reached her lips to lick the cream from her there, her whole body was trembling.

So this was how he seduced his lovers, was it? Clamping her legs together to stop them from drifting open, she tried to concentrate on ignoring him. She tried to think of the willows by the riverbank, not about the growing desire she was feeling at the touch of his mouth against hers. If she once let go of her focus, she would be lost.

Rocking back on his heels, he licked his lips. "That was a pleasant start to lunch."

"I trust you have finished now." His nearness, the very male scent of him, was playing havoc with her good intentions.

"Goodness no. I have barely begun." His gaze raked her body from head to toe. "I still have the rest of your body to lick cream from. And strawberry jam. I think I will start with your breasts. Yes, definitely your breasts. I will cover them all in cream, except for your nipples, which I will cover with strawberry jam. And then I will make a trail of jam and cream across your belly and down to your mound of Venus." His eyes closed with a fair imitation of rapture. "I will cover your mound with cream, and then I will lick it all off again. My tongue will search out every last drop from every crevice, licking you until even the memory of cream has gone and the taste of you fills my mouth instead."

Her breasts tingled at the thought of being covered in jam and cream and being licked clean again. Bringing her arms up to her chest to hide the peaking of her nipples, she glared at him. "No."

"You cannot stop me, wife. Despite your cold temper, I do not believe you would want to stop me once I had started."

"I want nothing to do with you." How she hated the weakness in her that made her words a lie.

"Is that a challenge?"

"No, a mere statement of fact."

"Ah, I love a challenge." He moved behind her, and she felt first the brush of his fingers, then an unaccustomed draft, on the back of her neck.

He held her leash too tightly to allow her either to stand up or move away from him. Leaning firmly back in her chair to forbid him access was her only choice. With any luck she would break one of his fingers with the force. "Leave my bodice alone."

"I intend to drop cream on your breasts and lick it off again. I cannot do that without first removing your bodice." Prodding her in the ribs to make her squirm, he succeeded in undoing her buttons faster than her maid did of an evening. Clearly he had had far too much practice in undoing ladies' bodices.

A ripping sound followed. She winced at the noise and felt the coldness of steel on her bare shoulder.

"Hold still."

The terse command was quite unnecessary. At the touch of the blade on her shoulder, she had frozen in place. She did not move again until her entire bodice had fallen away, cut from her body with his small pocket blade.

How dare he take a knife to her bodice! "That gown cost me nearly three guineas. You have completely ruined it." She could not believe what he had done.

"I have always hated that dress. It doesn't suit you. You should wear bright jewel colors, lush velvets, and shimmering satins. They would suit you better than dull brown serge."

He sliced through the waistband of her skirt, then, pulling her to her feet with a tug on her leash, he pushed it over her hips until it pooled at her feet.

Wrapping the leash around the bedpost, he secured her so she could not escape and sliced through her corset strings with his blade. Her spoiled corset joined her ruined gown on the floor.

Tied to the bedpost wearing only a fine linen shift, silk stockings tied above her knees with garters, and indoor slippers, she felt as vulnerable as if she were completely naked.

It was, she was finding, surprisingly hard to hold on to her aloofness when all her dignity was stripped away with her clothes.

Behind her, he was panting far more than the effort of stripping her required.

He had enjoyed her resistance, she realized with a flash. He was using her noncompliance as an excuse to get her into his power. If she had simply given in to him right away, he would have been disappointed, not having an excuse to mistreat her, to strip her nearly naked and tie her up.

Now that she knew what his intentions clearly were, she would play his game with a vengeance. "I would like my lunch now," she said coolly.

"You want what?" he asked, clearly taken aback at her apparent capitulation.

"I would like a cup of coffee and a scone. With plenty of strawberry jam."

That took the wind right out of his sails. "If you insist."

He poured her a cup of coffee and brought the steaming liquid over to her. She managed an awkward swallow, but the way she was tied made it difficult for her to drink. Several drops of the coffee spilled over the rim of the cup and splashed on to her breasts. "It would be a good deal easier for me to eat my breakfast if I were not tied up," she remarked, to no one in particular.

"I will untie you."

In reply, she merely looked at the bonds that held her. Words spoke louder than deeds.

"I will untie you from the bedpost," he continued, "if you will take off your shift."

A devil's bargain, indeed, but one that she could make use of. "I agree."

Keeping a wary eye on her, he untied her from the bedpost.

"Do you want me naked before or after I finish eating?" she asked, as if neither the question nor the answer bothered her much one way or the other.

"Before. Definitely before."

Though her hands were tied awkwardly together, she managed to pull the shift over her head until its way was blocked by the handcuffs.

She looked at Felix and shrugged helplessly. "I cannot get it any farther."

He approached her, knife in hand. "Allow me."

"Please, do not cut my shift."

"Any particular reason why I should not?" His voice was silky smooth, as if he suspected her of all kinds of trickery.

"I am fond of it. It was a present from my grandmama."

"Hold still. I will have to undo your cuffs one at a time."

He stooped over her, drew a small silver key from his waist-coat pocket, and unlocked one of the cuffs that bound her hands together. The cuff clicked open and came away from her wrist.

The instant her hands were no longer tied together, she gave Felix a hearty shove and ran toward the connecting door that led into the next room, shaking off her chemise as she ran. Once in there, with the door firmly locked behind her, he would find himself alone with his hard cock. Ha! What would he do then without her around?

The door was a scant inch away from being closed when it stopped short, against Felix's foot. Try as she might, she could not close it the rest of the way.

She cursed volubly. Her goal was so close and yet so unattainable. Another half a second would have been sufficient. If only she had pushed him just a tiny bit harder, or run a fraction faster.

Though she pushed against the door with all her strength, panting aloud with the effort, inexorably it opened. Felix stood there in the opening, his face a picture of outrage. "You tried to trick me."

Naked and defiant, with her handcuffs dangling from one wrist, she glared at him as he stood in the doorway. She would not be cowed by her failure or by his superior strength. "Any slave will try to escape if she can. I did no more or less than any other woman in my situation would have attempted."

"You were disobedient. You deserve to be punished."

As Felix advanced, so she retreated, staying out of his reach, until she came up against the high back of the sofa.

Thinking he had her trapped, he made a lunge for her. Just before he reached her, she hopped up on the back of the sofa and used her weight to topple over onto the seat on the other side, where she landed facedown in the cushions.

A heartbeat later, before she even had time to gloat over her clever escape, she was slammed into the cushions once again as Felix followed her example.

Caught.

She pounded her fists over and over again on the cushions in a helpless rage. Damn Felix. Damn every goddam inch of his body.

Every goddam inch that was plastered all over her, pushing her into the cushions so she could hardly breathe. She just didn't have the weight or strength to fight Felix on equal terms. Perhaps Mrs. Bertram had been wise in her advice to bend like the willow.

There would be no escaping him again. Now that she had lost his trust, she would not be able to regain it in a hurry. Certainly not soon enough for her purposes.

His body moved on top of hers, sliding up over her. He reached out and grabbed her hands, snapping the handcuffs shut once more. Her wrists once again firmly tied together, he clicked the leash on to them and tied the other end around his own wrist, all the time lying full length on top of her. "I dare not take the risk that you will try to escape again."

"You gave me an opportunity," she growled into the cushions. "I took it."

"Then I will have to take care not to give you another such." His breath ruffled the tiny hairs on the back of her neck, tickling and teasing her.

With some effort, she raised her head. "I can make my own opportunities. I do not need you to hand them to me." Her words were sheer bravado. Not a single possible avenue of escape had occurred to her. And, despite her best intentions, her body was reacting to him, to his closeness, to the weight of him against her. The memory of last night, of the pleasure he had forced her to take in his embrace, vibrated strongly within her still. She wanted to let her thighs open for him, to buck up against the erection she could feel pressing against her buttocks, to rub herself against him like a hungry cat. Though she wanted her freedom from the chains that bound her and revenge for the punishment he was inflicting on her, a tiny part of her reveled in the helpless position she was in. If he wanted to unbutton his trousers and take her here, on the couch, she would not be able to stop him. She would have to lie there, bound to him, and suffer his hands on her naked body, his strong thighs pushing hers apart, his fingers and maybe even his tongue exploring her pussy, his cock entering her, thrusting inside her until he shot his seed deep into her.

She squirmed uncomfortably on the couch. God, just thinking about it was making her whole body flush with heat. Her pussy was practically throbbing with anticipation.

It really wasn't fair. However much her brain told her that Felix was a worthless, good-for-nothing, cheater of a husband who deserved to be thrown out on his ear, her body told her something different. Her body did not care how many other women he had touched as long as he touched her, too. Her body hungered for him and refused to let its demands be ignored. Though her brain knew he should be thrown out with the morning refuse, her body, her damned stupid body, insisted that he was a keeper. Deliberately, she focused her mind on more mundane matters. "I suppose I will have to drink cold coffee now."

"Do you deserve anything else? Indeed, do you deserve anything at all?"

"I removed my shift for you."

He ran his hands over her naked flanks with slow and studied appreciation. "For which I am duly grateful."

"So, show your gratitude in a way that will please me, instead of mauling me. Let me up."

"Will you try to escape again?"

"If I can."

He gave a bark of laughter. "You are honest, at any rate." Slowly he got up from the sofa, leaving her there wishing he was still lying on top of her between her thighs. It had felt so right to have him on top of her, his body pressed to hers.

She sat up awkwardly, her movements once again constrained by the cuffs fastened around her wrists. "I am always honest."

"Disobedient, but honest."

"You have to take what you can get."

"That, my dear wife, is the best advice I have heard all day." He tugged at the leash. "Come with me."

Having no choice, she rose and followed him through into the connecting room.

The coffee was still lukewarm. Cradling the cup in both hands, she managed, albeit rather clumsily, to drink it, then hold it out to be refilled.

He poured another cup for her, but did not hand it over. "If you want another cup, you will have to let me feed you."

If she wanted another cup? The first one had hardly taken the edge off her thirst. "If you insist." Fighting against the inevitable was losing its charm. And everything about Felix, and the effect he had on her even when he was tormenting her, meant that her defeat was looking more and more inevitable. Though her inner demons made her fight him every inch of the way, she was afraid that secretly she wanted him to win the battle between them, to possess her and own her utterly.

Pulling his chair up close to hers, he held the cup to her lips. "Drink."

Her breasts were tingling at his nearness, her nipples hardening into tight buds. Obediently, she drank.

"Having to chase after you has made me hungry," he said, looking at her rather than at the food on the table. "I will be sharing your breakfast."

Her nipples tightened even further at the memory of the threat he had made to eat it off her body. "There is plenty for two," she said far more casually than she felt.

"Indeed there is." He took a scoop of cream on his fingers and spread it over both her breasts. "There is enough for both of them."

The cream slid over her skin like a caress. "Don't."

His fingers massaged it into her skin. "Why not?"

"It will make a mess." A lame excuse, but the best she could come up with on short notice.

He continued to cover her breasts with whipped cream. "What are maids for but to clean up messes made by their mistresses?"

The image of Suzy flashed through her brain. "I suppose that depends on your point of view," she said acerbically. "Cleaning up messes or fucking in the attic bedroom."

The flush of red that suffused his face gave her a small measure of satisfaction. She hoped his conscience was tormenting him over that little escapade. It was nothing less than he deserved.

He leaned over and took a lick of the cream that covered her. "Mmm—cream with the scent of a woman."

If his fingers had tormented her, his tongue was a thousand times worse. She could not resist thrusting her breasts forward into his mouth, smearing whipped cream all around his lips.

He drew his head back and gave her an admonishing glance. "Keep still, or I shall have to punish you again."

The cream was making her hungry. Not for food, but for him. Sad, but true. She could not help herself, but neither would she give in to her desire. "Are you threatening me, Felix?"

His hands were on her breasts, massaging the cream into her skin. "Do not call me Felix. I want you to call me master."

"Master?" The thought of openly acknowledging his power over her secretly thrilled her to the core. "No. I will not." *Willow tree be damned!*

"Then you leave me no choice. I will have to punish you." He unbuttoned his trousers, took a glob of whipped cream, and rubbed it over his semihard cock until it was standing up straight and stiff.

He took her by the shoulders and forced her down on to the floor until she was kneeling at his feet.

His erection thrust into the air right in front of her eyes. She stared at it greedily. He was going to make her suck his cock again.

Parting her lips slightly, she allowed him to force his cock into her mouth.

His hands in her hair, he moved her mouth backward and forward along his cock, making her fuck him with her mouth.

"Suck me," he commanded her. "Like you did last night."

Obediently she started to suckle on him, the cream making him slick and slippery.

Leaving one hand tangled in her hair to guide her movements, he reached down with his other to play with her breasts.

Her mouth was stretched with his cock. She stopped for a moment to rest, but he urged her on. "Keep sucking me."

His movements grew sharper and more urgent as he thrust in and out of her mouth until with a grunt he spurted his cum into her mouth.

Letting it dribble out of the corners of her mouth, she continued to suck on him, milking him of every last drop, until finally he pulled away, his cock limp with satisfaction.

He rebuttoned his trousers and hauled her to her feet. "Now that you have tasted my cream, I want to taste yours. Lie on the bed and spread your legs for me."

Moving slowly, she made her way over to the bed and lay on her back, her legs together. If he wanted her legs spread, he would have to make her spread them.

Slipping his hands between her thighs, he found her clit and tickled it, until her legs opened of their own accord.

The last of the whipped cream was soon spread all over her pussy. Then, with the very tip of his tongue, he proceeded to lick it off.

Her tied hands moved to her breasts, pinching first one nipple and then the other until they were hard, as his tongue swirled around her clit and her cunt.

Tickling and teasing her, he brought her to the edge of an orgasm.

Her eyes drifted shut, and she felt herself on the brink. Just one more lick, and she would fall over the edge.

At that exact moment she knew she would die if she didn't come right away, he raised his head. "Get up. It's time to dress for dinner."

Her eyes flew open. "You cannot stop now."

"I owed you a punishment." His smile was pure evil. "Leaving your pussy wet and wanting all the way through dinner will be a suitable chastisement, I believe. Now hurry along or we will be late for dinner." He patted her flanks. "You have already missed breakfast and lunch. I cannot have you miss dinner, too."

How she hated him at that moment. "I will not go to dinner."

"You will go down to dinner if I have to drag you down in your handcuffs."

"You could not do that."

"I can and I will."

"You would shame me in front of Mr. Hughes?"

His face grew dark. "You care so much for what Mr. Hughes thinks of you?"

It was one thing to be tied up and forced to do Felix's bidding in the privacy of their bedroom, but she could not parade out in company in her handcuffs. The humiliation would kill her. "Please, do not make me go down to dinner in my handcuffs," she begged him. "I will do anything you want me to do, I will swear to be as obedient as you want me to be. I will be your slave. I will even call you master, as you have ordered me to. Just do not make me do this."

"I do not trust you."

She gazed into his eyes. "Please. I swear to you that I will not embarrass you in any way during dinner. I will do everything you ask me to do."

"And if you do not? What then?"

"Then you may punish me in whatever way you think fit, and I will not complain."

"If you do not behave tonight, and do exactly as I command, then I have the perfect punishment for you."

She bowed her head. Whatever it was, she would accept it.

"If you shame me tonight, I will shame you tomorrow night. I will bring you down to have dinner with the company in your handcuffs and tied to me so you cannot move from my side. Everyone will know that you have been disobedient and that I have had to take such a drastic step to curb your naughtiness."

Though she did not like it, she had expected nothing less.

"Not only that, you will be naked as well."

That did shock her. "You would parade me naked in front of the rest of the company?"

"I will do whatever it takes to ensure your obedience, dear wife."

"You would parade my nakedness in front of Mr. Hughes?" She gave a small smile, as if she were keeping a delicious secret all to herself. Let him have a taste of his own medicine once in a while. "Mmm—that does not sound so much like a punishment to me."

"I do not mind if he looks, so long as he does not touch. And I would be there to make sure he did not lay a finger on you. He would be in no doubt at all that you belonged to me—body and soul." He took hold of her tied hands and pulled her to her feet. "Come, let me help you wash before you put on your fine gown."

The bathroom adjoining their rooms had a clawfoot tub, and hot, or at least warm, running water. He ran a shallow bath and made her sit in it.

The washing was nothing but an excuse to torture her some more.

Lathering up the washcloth, he smoothed the soapy cloth over her body, lingering on her breasts and thighs until her pussy was screaming out for him to touch her there.

She arched her body up into his hands, spreading her legs in a wordless invitation, in a wordless plea. But no, he would give her no relief from the desires he had stoked in her.

By the time the soap was all rinsed from her body, the bathwater was lukewarm, but she was fiery hot.

With her hands still tied, she could not dry herself. He patted her dry with the towel with as much care and attention as he had bathed her. Standing stock-still on the bath mat, she closed her eyes and tried to think of anything other than the touch of his hands on her body, the rough fibers of the cotton towel as he stroked her, the need that he awakened in her.

No wonder he had women falling over themselves to become his lover. If the need he awakened in them was half as strong as that which she felt, she could only pity, not hate, them. Indeed, she was weaker than any of them, for her husband could rouse such desires in her even though she knew full well that he was a rapscallion who would never remain faithful to her. His faithful-

Enslaved

ness, or lack of it, could not diminish the heat that consumed her entire body at his touch. She wanted him to take her on the cold-tiled floor of the bathroom, to bend her over the rim of the tub and enter her roughly from behind. She would not be able to form a single coherent wish or desire until he had slaked her frantic need of him.

Every inch of her was dried, several times over, by the time he pronounced himself finished, and she dared to open her eyes again. Her body was trembling with the effort of sustaining an impression of indifference to his caresses when inwardly she was screaming and begging for release. He would not give it to her. Not yet. And she would not humble herself in front of him when she had no chance of success.

Once she was dry, he unlocked the handcuffs and removed them with a warning look. "Let us get you dressed."

She donned her chemise and her corset, with her husband serving as her maid. When she reached into the wardrobe and chose herself an evening gown, a demure matronly dress of dark green, he took it from her hands and tossed it onto the floor. "I have something else for you to wear."

While she had been in the bath, a gown of leaf green silk had been laid out on her bed. "I told Mrs. Bertram you liked to wear green, and she chose this from her wardrobe to accommodate you."

Somewhat hesitantly, she allowed Felix to help her first into the profusion of lace petticoats, then into the gown that went on top.

She knew at once why Felix had chosen it. The gown had no sleeves and left her arms quite bare. Not as bare as her breasts, though. The fabric only just skimmed the top of her nipples. She tugged the top a little higher. She was sure that a hint of pink still showed through.

"Leave it," he ordered her. "I like it the way it is."

Reluctantly, she let it fall back again. Yes, there was definitely a hint of nipple to round off the cleavage it showed. If there was any justice in the world, the tantalizing sight would drive Felix as mad as he had driven her.

He played lady's maid with her hair, too, dressing it in a simple style that looked very well on her. Finally, he tied on her garters and slipped a pair of embroidered slippers on to her feet. "There," he said, stepping back to admire his handiwork. "You have never looked better. Now sit there and wait until I am ready."

In just a few minutes, Felix, impeccably dressed in an evening suit, was handing her downstairs and in to dinner.

She ate and drank mechanically, murmuring responses to the conversation that went on around her, barely knowing what she was saying. All her attention was focused on Felix; her wants and desires were centered on him to the exclusion of everything else.

When Mrs. Bertram stood at the conclusion of the dinner and invited the women to retire with her, she looked at Felix for a guide.

He nodded his permission, and she followed Mrs. Bertram

and the other women out of the dining room and down the hall to a pleasant sitting room.

Mrs. Bertram gestured at them to sit down in a circle around her. "Tonight," she said with a smile, "you are going to learn how to drive your husbands totally wild with desire for you."

Her ears pricked up. A new weapon in the war against her husband was exactly what she needed. If she had known how to drive Felix totally wild this afternoon so that he had not been able to hold back as he had, she would not be in such a sorry state.

One of the other women, a flashy redhead with a gown cut as low as her own, pouted. "My own husband doesn't interest me—he is already wild with desire for me. It's such a bore. I would rather learn how to drive other women's husbands wild with desire for me."

Of course, that would be Cora Hughes. It was funny how completely she had forgotten about the woman her husband had intended to make his mistress. Cora Hughes. A sudden burst of anger seized her at the woman's confidence, her lack of subtlety. "That's funny," she said, pretending to be confused. "I thought by the way Gareth kissed me last night, that he was pretty wild with desire for me at the time."

Cora's eyes narrowed. "Gareth kissed you?" She made a scoffing noise. "I don't believe you."

"Believe it or not, as you like, it doesn't worry me." She gave a smile that did not reach her eyes. "But if I were you, I would not be quite so confident that your husband is wild for you. Or at least not for you exclusively."

Her gibe hit home, silencing Cora for long enough that Mrs. Bertram could explain what she had in store for them. "Men like variety and new experiences. I am here to help you give them some. Tonight, you are to be Turkish slave girls and will offer your master a Turkish massage. The combination of a sexy costume and your hands on his naked body will be guaranteed to drive him wild. I have your costumes here—get into them, and we will practice on each other until your husbands arrive."

The costumes were even briefer than the gown she was wearing. Diaphanous pants, a short bodice that covered only her breasts, leaving her stomach bare, and a veil of golden coins that hung over her face and clanked musically as she moved. The costume made her feel exotic—and brave. Tonight she would drive Felix wild—she was sure of it.

Once they were changed into their harem-girl costumes, Mrs. Bertram led them into another room done out in Turkish carpets and low long sofas and cushion and lamps, just like a Turkish harem.

Mrs. Bertram beckoned the third one of the company—a young woman called Gwendolyn—to join her. Lillian had already discounted Gwendolyn as a rival. All through dinner she had only had eyes for her own husband, a rather stiff-looking banker. She was disposed to like Gwendolyn. Felix would have no chance with her even if he tried.

"The trick to a good Turkish massage is all in the setup," Mrs. Bertram explained, as she gestured at the Turkish accoutrements around her. "Set the scene well, let them know what to expect. Make your husbands think they are getting an exotic treat, and that is what they will get. The next thing you must do is to get them naked as soon as possible. A naked man is an expectant man, and an expectant man is putty in your hands. The last thing is the massage itself. This is actually the least important part of all. Still, as it is the part with which you will be the least familiar, it is worth some practice."

She gestured at Gwendolyn to lie on one of the sofas, and she knelt on the ground beside her. "A firm pressure is called for, but not roughness. Knead the muscles as if you were kneading a loaf of bread."

Cora snorted. "I was brought up as a lady, not as a cook. I have never kneaded dough in my life."

"Then you will have the most to learn," Mrs. Bertram replied equably. "Watch me, and you will see how it is done." She knelt beside Gwendolyn and began to knead the muscles in the younger woman's back and shoulders. "How does that feel?"

Gwendolyn gave a little sigh of appreciation. "It feels marvelous."

"Just think how your husbands will feel with your hands on them, massaging them. I guarantee that not a one of them will be able to resist. Now, let me lie down, and you try it out on my back. Cora and Lillian, please try it out on each other. There is time for a few minutes practice before the gentlemen join us."

As Lillian hesitated, Cora lay facedown on one of the sofas with a languid air. "Go on, then," she challenged Lillian. "Let's see how irresistible those hands of yours are."

Lillian knelt beside her and started to knead Cora's back as she had seen Mrs. Bertram do it. "How does that feel?"

"Well enough, I suppose," Cora said grudgingly. She reached back and grabbed one of Lillian's hands in a firm grip. "But I suggest that if you want to keep your face unmarked," she hissed, "that you keep your pretty white hands off my husband in future."

Lillian felt a surge of exaltation. Cora, man-eating Cora, who tried to run off with her own husband, was jealous of her. "I did not have my hands on him—he had his on me."

"Then I suggest you do not encourage him to put his hands on you again. I am not a woman who makes a comfortable enemy."

"Or a comfortable friend either, I have no doubt," Lillian replied. "However, I am prepared to oblige you on one condition—that you keep your harpy's talons off my husband in the future."

"Are you calling me a harpy?" Cora rose halfway off the sofa, her voice high with anger.

"If the cap fits," Lillian said with a shrug, as Cora stood up in a towering rage. "I see you have had enough of my massaging. Come, try it out on me." She lay down on the sofa that Cora had just vacated.

Cora hesitated and then, with a scowl, knelt at Lillian's side and put her hands tentatively on her back.

The touch of another woman's hands on her back was strange, but not unpleasant. Even though Cora made no effort to be gentle, indeed, she seemed deliberately to be as rough as she could get away with, the very roughness made her muscles feel good. Five years and more of stress and tension seemed to melt away into nothing under Cora's impersonal touch.

Before she had had half enough, Cora sat back on her heels, letting her hands flop back down at her sides. "I'm sick of this." Her voice, high and clear, carrying across the room like a bell.

"Indeed, it is about time I fetched the gentlemen," Mrs. Bertram said in an even tone. "Arrange yourselves on the sofas, ladies, and we will be back in a moment."

"Are you always this rude?" Lillian asked Cora, as the three women gathered together in one end of the room, offended on Mrs. Bertram's behalf by Cora's behavior. "Or does this company in particular bring out the worst in you? Are we not worth your politeness?"

"Rude?" Cora looked genuinely taken aback. "I was merely being honest. I was tired of kneading your back. Why shouldn't I say so?"

"You live your life by that?" Lillian was offended on her own behalf now as only a self-effacing woman could be. "Everything is to bow down to your pleasure, to your convenience?"

"Why should I care for what anyone else wants? No one cares about what I want. If I did not attend to my own desires, no one else would. So I see what I want, and I take it if I can."

"I see." And indeed, she did see. Cora was as selfish as a man and proud of it. She had not a whit of the self-sacrificing generosity that a woman ought to have.

"What has your politeness ever gotten you?"

Lillian quailed at the abruptness of the attack. "I beg your pardon?"

"I asked what your politeness"—Cora positively sneered the word—"has ever gotten you. A husband who takes off for a week to fuck another woman. If that is what politeness gets you, then I would rather be rude any day. At least Gareth knows what I want. If he chooses not to give it to me, that is his loss, not mine."

"A woman ought to attend to her husband's needs, not to her own," Lillian replied doubtfully, a little shaken in her beliefs by Cora's outspoken attitude.

"Stuff and nonsense. A woman has a duty to herself, first and foremost. If she does not look after herself, no one else will."

Certainly Felix had never shown much solicitude for her feelings before this weekend. Before she had uncovered the rage that lay within her soul and demanded his attention and his respect. Maybe Cora had a point. "You treat Gareth like a beggar at your gate even though he loves you."

Cora shrugged. "So he claims. And speaking of the devil, here he comes."

As the men walked into the sitting room, Cora turned one last time to Lillian. "Just remember what I told you before," she hissed. "Keep your hands off my husband or face the consequences."

"As long as you keep your talons out of mine," Lillian replied out of the corner of her mouth, taking delight in taunting Cora one more time.

There was no time to trade any more insults as the men were

fast approaching. Lillian rose from the sofa and approached Felix, keeping a wary eye out for Cora. No way was she going to let the harpy snaffle her husband under her very nose. Cora, she was relieved to see, was making a beeline for Gareth. Good.

Felix was looking at her with interest in his eyes. "Good evening, sir," she said, in the best Turkish accent she could muster. "I am your Turkish slave for the evening. I should like to offer you my services as a masseuse, if it would please you. I am well trained in the fine art of a specialty of my homeland, the Turkish massage."

He leaned forward and brushed her veil aside for a moment before letting it drop again. "Lillian. I thought by the way you moved that it could only be you."

A wave of gladness swept through her at the knowledge that he had known it was her and wanted her still. A wave of gladness that had nothing to do with the punishment he had threatened her if she did not behave herself exactly as he wanted her to do tonight. Fear of punishment could only take her so far. No, what she felt was a genuine gladness that he found her attractive, that he was watching her, hoping that it was her.

"Mrs. Bertram says that a Turkish massage is best when the man is naked," she whispered. "Or at least when a man is not wearing uncomfortable English clothes, but a soft Turkish robe instead." She held out one of the soft dark red robes Mrs. Bertram had left for the gentlemen. "May I undress you?"

"I can hardly refuse such an offer from my obliging slave girl, now, can I?" He held out his arms. "Come then, slave, swap my clothes for your Turkish robe."

He stood still as she took off his jacket and unbuttoned his shirt, slipping it off his shoulders. His naked chest gleamed in the candlelight. She could not resist running her hands over it, over the planes and hollows of his torso. It was as smooth and free of hair as her own, and positively rippling with strength and virility. God, how she loved his chest.

"My trousers?" he prompted her. To anyone else in the room, his voice held a world of laughter. Only she would be able to detect the element of warning that lay under his amusement.

Hurrying to do his bidding, she sat at his feet and slipped off his shoes, then his socks. Reaching up, she unbuttoned his trousers and slid them over his hips, together with his linen undergarments.

Standing there, proud and tall, unashamedly naked, he looked like one of King Arthur's legendary knights, ready to take on whatever challenges should come his way.

It was a shame to cover up his glorious body with the Turkish robe. Until she caught Cora looking at Felix's nakedness out of the corner of her eyes and licking her lips. Her anger boiled at the woman's insolent hypocrisy—warning her off Gareth, then eyeing Felix when her own husband wasn't looking. She shot Cora an evil glare while helping Felix on with his robe.

In the other woman's defense, Gareth wasn't nearly as worth staring at as Felix was. From the back view, Gareth was tall and solidly built, with a body as strong and hard as though he worked as a navvy, but he lacked Felix's fine-boned elegance and grace.

As Lillian's glance lingered on Gareth's nakedness, Cora

returned her glare and turned her attention back to her own husband, claiming him for her own.

Lillian smiled to herself. All she had to do to scare Cora away from Felix was to look a little too long at Gareth. The knowledge gave her power—power that she would not shy away from using. All was fair in love and war.

The dark red of the robe suited Felix's dark blond good looks. She spent a moment admiring him before gesturing to the long, low sofa. "If you would please to lie down, Master, I will give you a Turkish massage as you have been promised." The word of submission came easily to her tongue. In these clothes, she felt like his slave.

He lay down as she requested, and she knelt by his side. "If you slip out of your robe, Master, you will enjoy the massage far more." His nakedness was as much for her benefit as it was for his. Besides, the back of the sofa would hide his naked body from Cora's sight.

He slipped his arms out and let the robe lie on his back, covering his backside.

"Mmmm, much better," she murmured, rubbing a small amount of scented oil on her hands as Mrs. Bertram had shown them how, and running her hands over his back, gently at first, then more strongly as she gained confidence.

When every inch of his back had been kneaded and pummeled and was covered in a fine sheen of scented oil, she sat back on her heels and shut her eyes for a moment's rest. Massaging was hard work.

"I liked that." Felix's gravelly voice broke in on her thoughts.

Her eyes opened, her attention immediately focused utterly on him once more. "I'm glad that I pleased you, Master."

"I want to fuck you, slave."

She looked around doubtfully. The other couples were still engaged in their Turkish massage. A sensual massage for sure, but not outright lovemaking. "Here? Now?" Surely that would be going just a bit too far.

"Are you refusing to do as you are bid?"

Her shake of the head came in immediate denial. "I am your obedient slave tonight. You know that." The stakes were too high for her to be anything else. He would have no mercy on her if she did not fulfill his every wish and cater to his every whim.

"A wise move." Tossing his gown aside, he sat up on the edge of the sofa, his knees wide apart. "Massage my cock."

She moved closer to him and laid her hands on his cock, which was already standing proudly to attention. "Yes, Master."

"With your mouth."

Hands were one thing, but her mouth? In company? Her throat went dry, and she swallowed convulsively. "Yes, Master."

His skin was smooth and tasted slightly salty. She took him into her mouth, pleasuring him with her tongue and lips while massaging his back with her hands—not exactly roughly, but with firm and deliberate strokes and suckles.

His breathing grew loud and labored as she worked on him, her oiled hands caressing his balls as she massaged him with her mouth. His cock twitched and grew under her ministrations, until it was harder than stone. From deep in his throat came a guttural moan of pleasure, and he reached down and took her breasts in his hands, kneading them in his turn.

A jolt of pure lust shot through her at his touch, settling into her pussy, where it burned hot and wet. Oh God, she had longed for him to reach out for her with desire. Her thighs were clamped together to stop her legs from trembling, but it was no use. Her entire body was on fire for him.

Just as she was on the verge of spontaneously combusting with desire, he let go her breasts. "Bend over the sofa for me. I want to take you from behind."

So far gone was she that she did not care who else was in the room with her, who else might be watching them. Panting with desire, she got to her feet and leaned over at the waist, her legs spread wide.

His hands snaked their way through a slit in the crotch of her baggy silk pants to fondle her pussy. "Ahh, how convenient."

The gentle touch of his fingers was not enough for her. She wanted him to fuck her, she needed to feel his cock thrusting home inside her, pounding her roughly, bringing her to an orgasm that took her to Heaven and back again. Wriggling her ass in invitation, she reached back and took his cock in her hands, guiding it to her cunt.

Still he tormented her, holding himself back and just allowing the tip of his cock to touch her. "Beg me for it."

"Please."

"Please what."

"Please fuck me." The crude words tasted strange on her tongue.

"Fuck you? How do you want me to fuck you?" He drew back and teased her with one finger. "Do you want me to fuck you with my finger?"

"Not with your finger."

"Then what?"

If he didn't take her soon, she would explode. "Please, Master, please put your cock inside me. In my cunt."

He entered her with one long, slow stroke, pausing only when he was so deeply embedded in her he could go no farther. Then slowly he withdrew, and just as slowly entered her again. "Like this?"

Such slowness, such gentleness was not for her. She wanted to feel, to really feel that he was taking her, branding her as his own. She wanted to feel him dominate her, to know that he was more powerful than she was and that she was helpless to resist him. "Please, no." Pain mixed with her pleasure made the pleasure all the greater. Knowing that he was in control of her, being made to obey his every desire, made her completely helpless with desire.

"No?" He paused, holding himself still, halfway inside her. "You don't like it?"

She thrust her ass hard up against him, enveloping him inside her cunt. "Fuck me faster, please. I'm begging you. Fuck me hard, punish me for my insolence and my disobedience. Spank me and bite me. Do not be gentle with me. Fight me. Dominate me. Overpower me and force me to do your bidding."

At last he gave in to her entreaties and started to fuck her in earnest, pounding in and out of her with energetic thrusts. It was what she had been craving ever since he had tormented her with the whipped cream and strawberry jam earlier that day.

Then came a slap on her haunches, so hard and sharp that it made her cry out. She thrust back harder, the pleasure of his cock taking away the pain of his slap.

Again he slapped her, and again, slapping and thrusing until the two sensations mingled together in her brain, and she could not tell the pleasure from the pain. All she knew was that the feelings were overpowering her. She was a mass of sensation, able to do nothing but ride out the storm.

When he leaned over and bit her on the shoulder, she lost all control. A rush of pleasure swept over her, a pleasure so intense that the world went black in front of her eyes.

When she came to her senses once more, Felix was buried in her up to the hilt, his cock pulsing with his own release and his hot, sticky cum spurting deep into her cunt.

Lillian awoke the next morning with the first pale fingers of dawn, as the birds were sleepily beginning their early-morning chorus. Lying there as the sky turned from black to gray and then to palest blue as the sun rose on the new day, she knew that she did not hate and despise her husband any longer. Indeed, she never had. Jealousy had eaten her up from the inside, gnawing away at her like a canker, until her love for him had been poisoned. And this poisoned love had felt very much like hate.

For she did love him. She always had. Mrs. Bertram had been right when she said that love and hate were close kin. And the best way to deal with a force that cannot be opposed is to bend with it, not to meet it head-on. More like tail-on, she thought with a silent giggle.

His treatment of her fulfilled some deep need inside of her, a need that she had never known or understood before now. In some dark place in her heart, she wanted him to be her master and her lord, to use his physical strength and the unbending steel of his will to force her to do his bidding. Feeling helpless in his arms, knowing she was his slave and must submit to his every whim, shook her out of her passive unhappiness and made her come alive. Bound and naked and waiting for his pleasure, she could not maintain the protective walls she had built around herself. He could see through her, right to the very heart of her, and there was no way she could escape his eagle eye or pretend to be anything other than what she was. A wife who loved her husband with such passion that it had nearly killed her.

Still, she fought against the impulse in her that demanded her total surrender to his mastery. He had proven to be unfaithful before. She could not relinquish all her power, all her self-respect, and be nothing but his sex slave. Not without trust.

She felt her walls slowly build up around her heart again. Brick by brick, she must wall herself off from human feelings again. Only by keeping him out could she protect herself from certain heartbreak.

Slowly, carefully, she pushed away the covers and rose from the bed they shared. Felix was still sleeping soundly, his breathing regular, his face untroubled. Tenderly, so as not to wake him, she brushed away the lock of hair that had fallen over his face. He muttered in his sleep and stirred restlessly, but did not wake.

The breath she had been holding escaped with a whoosh. Before he woke, she must escape from his presence, just for a short while. She needed to come to terms with what had been happening to her, with all the new sensations she was feeling. Most of all, she needed time away from him to rebuild the walls around her heart. She could not do that when he was with her.

He would miss her as soon as he woke and come looking for her, angry that she had left him while he was sleeping. Certainly he would punish her when he found her again.

Her nipples peaked into tight buds at the thought of the punishment he would mete out to her. It was worth it to disobey him once in a while just to deserve a punishment from his hands. She pulled on a loose robe and tiptoed out of the room on legs that shook just a little.

What would her punishment be when he found her? She would make sure she was very bad indeed, so that she deserved every torment he could devise for her.

Felix pushed open the door of the pool-room and scanned it quickly. Empty. Not a sign of Lillian. Dammit all, he should have tied her to the bed last night, made her sleep in her bonds. His indulgence had allowed her to escape.

But not far and not, he hoped, for long.

Mrs. Bertram had informed him that she had not left the grounds. She must be here somewhere, hiding from him. The contrary wench. He'd lay a wager that she had escaped him solely for the spanking he would have to administer to her.

His cock twitched into semihardness at the idea. Despite her cool exterior and her pretense that nothing in the world could shake her composure, Lillian had the soul of a true submissive, who longed to be dominated and mastered.

He wanted to be the one to dominate her, to make her into his willing slave. It turned him on more than he could ever admit to have her bound and helpless in front of him, to know that she was his to do with as he pleased, to deal her pain or pleasure depending on his fancy.

Most of all, he adored her utter abandonment to her role. She wanted to be his plaything, his toy. She welcomed his attention, whether it be a fucking or a spanking he dealt to her. If he liked mastering her, she liked being mastered just as much, if not more. And her enjoyment spurred his on.

Never before had he known such pleasure from a woman. A week ago, he would never have thought his frigid wife capable of such passion and fire.

He carried on down the hallway, peeking into each room as he went. In one room, he disturbed a trio of saucy housemaids at their work. They giggled at his interruption and made eyes at him, inviting his attentions.

They were a good-looking trio, and even just a few short days ago, he would have eagerly taken them up on their blatant offer, kissing them, groping inside their bodices to feel their breasts and under the skirts to fondle their pussies. If he could have pushed them far enough, he would have taken all three of them one after the other in the room they were cleaning, just because he could.

But that was then, and this was now. What did he care for serving girls and their silly giggles when somewhere in the house his Lillian was waiting for him? Lillian, whose dark desires so neatly meshed with his own.

So he ignored the three of them and continued with his search.

The sunroom was at the end of the hallway. Opening this door and walking several paces into the room, he was hit with a sight he had not expected—even in this house of Sugar and Spice.

Cora Hughes was lying on her back in the sun, stark naked, running her hands lazily over her own body. One hand was on her breasts, moving backward and forward between them, caressing her nipples into peaks one after the other. The other was sliding in and out between her thighs, stroking her mound. Her head was flung back, her eyes were half-shut, and her mouth was slightly parted as she breathed in and out with audible effort. She looked and sounded like a woman on the edge of an orgasm.

Hoping she hadn't noticed his intrusion into her very private moment, he backed away immediately and put one hand on the door to shut it behind him.

"Don't go."

Those were the very last words he expected to hear. He stopped stock-still, his hand frozen on the door. "I b . . . beg your pardon?"

"Don't go. Stay and watch me. Look at my naked body. Watch the way I run my hands over my breasts. Look at me, with my finger in my cunt, pleasuring myself." She opened her eyes, projecting him another invitation. "And if you get tired of watching, come and join me. Put on a show with me for everyone out in the garden to watch."

Felix stayed in the doorway, making no move toward her. Though she put on a sensual show, he had no desire to join her in it. Fucking in a room of other couples all engaged in the same activity was one thing, but to display himself for others simply to watch was not his cup of tea. He did not fuck for the entertainment of others.

"Lie next to me on the floor and run your hands where mine have been. Lick my pussy and taste how wet I am for you. Thrust your hard cock deep into my cunt and fuck me until I scream. Fuck me until you spend all your seed deep inside me." She shot him a knowing glance. "Your cock is hard right now, isn't it? You like looking at me, spread out on the floor like this, touching myself. You want me."

Certainly his cock was trying to burst out of his trousers, but that was hardly a surprise with Cora lying naked and touching herself in front of him. His arousal simply proved that he was a man with a pulse—it did not mean that he had to take the woman. He was perfectly capable of resisting his urges. Besides, he had no particular desire for Cora herself. What he really wanted was to find Lillian and to spend his lusts with her. "I'm afraid I can't stay. I'm rather busy right now."

She sat up and twisted around, indignation written in her eyes. "You would turn me down for a matter of business?"

"Certainly, when the business involves my wife."

"Your wife." She positively spit the words. "Your precious Lillian, who is probably upstairs spreading her legs for my husband right at this moment."

He wanted to kill Cora at that moment. "You lie."

"Do I?" She shrugged her shoulders, her pink-tipped breasts bouncing with the movement. "Believe what you like then. Believe if you can that I am a faithful wife and my husband is not cuckolding you as we speak." She turned away from him with a moue of disgust. "Some people will not see the truth even when it lies right under their nose."

"Lillian is not like you are."

"Fiddlesticks. Every woman wants the same as I do underneath—the power to control her own destiny. We merely go about fulfilling our desires in different ways."

"I am afraid that I cannot help you by fulfilling your desires this morning. You will have to finish what you so ably started by yourself." With that, he retreated back through the door and shut it on Cora's peal of malicious laughter.

Her words had left him uneasy. Would Lillian really have run from his bed to that of Gareth Hughes? Though he did not think it likely, still the thought rankled within him. Heaven knows, she had found pleasure in his arms last night—he had touched her desire, tasted it on her body, and heard the cries of pleasure that she could not repress or deny escape from her lips. She liked being his slave, his mistress, his plaything. Naked and bound in chains, she had found a freedom from her inner censor that she could not achieve when she was free.

Or had he badly mistaken the matter? Did she hate and despise him even more now that she had plumbed the depth of his desire for her? Did the chains secretly repulse her, even as they helped to bring her pleasure?

What could Gareth Hughes offer her that he could not? Gareth did not love her as he loved her. Gareth was not obsessed with her, completely obsessed with her, as he was. She had to know that. Besides, Gareth was married already, as was she. He could never be anything more to her than a quick romp in the hay.

No, Lillian was no fool. Now that they had discovered each other's deepest desires, she would be truer to her marriage vows than he had been, as true as he would be from now on. She was a better person than he was. He would not suspect her of a single misplaced thought.

Still, his feet had a mind of their own. Without him willing it, they made their way up the stairs toward the bedrooms. Lillian would not be with Gareth, he knew she would not be. But there was no harm in making absolutely sure.

His own room was as empty as he had left it a few minutes ago, she had not returned. He stood in the hallway, listening.

From behind one door came the muted sound of voices, interspersed with bursts of laughter. Moving quietly closer to the noise, he tuned his ear to the sound of Lillian's voice. No, it was not Lillian—her voice was softer and more mellifluous than the woman's voice behind the door.

No sound, not even a whisper, came from behind Gareth Hughes's door. Felix hesitated. If she was not in there, he would look like a fool. But if she was inside with Gareth . . .

On a sudden impulse, he pushed open the door.

The room was empty. He could breathe again.

"Are you looking for my wife?" Gareth's voice came from behind him, making him jump. "Or for your own?"

"I don't need to inquire where your wife is," Felix replied belligerently, whirling around to face him and hiding his embarrassment under the guise of an attack. "I left her naked in the sunroom not two minutes ago. She has been enjoying herself greatly this morning."

Gareth's eyes narrowed at the intelligence. "Indeed. You must be looking for your own wife then. It might interest you to know that I have just come from your pretty Lillian. It will please you to know, I'm sure, that she was not naked, but then again, one does not always need to take one's clothes off to find pleasure. No doubt you will find her still in the garden, recovering from her endeavors."

"Did you put your hands on my wife?" Felix stepped forward threateningly. "By God, I will kill you if you touched a single hair of her head."

Gareth stood his ground. "Did you lay your hands on mine?"

"Your wife is of no interest to me." Felix dismissed her with a gesture. Cora Hughes was the lowest kind of woman, the type of woman who would take a lover simply to spite a good man who loved her. He did not know why he had even bothered to give her the time of day. She was less than worthless. "Naked and willing though she was, I did not touch her. The only woman who interests me is Lillian. And no man touches my wife and lives to tell the tale."

"Is this the same Felix Rutherford, the man who has made a career out of fucking the wives and sisters and daughters of every respectable merchant in the City?" Gareth asked with a mocking laugh. "The man whose reputation as a lecher is known all over London? Whose wife is openly pitied as being wed to a rampant whoremonger? Why do I not believe you?"

"Believe me or not, I do not care," Felix said stiffly. He had been careful in his amours and owned no such reputation; he would stake half his fortune on it. "Though Mrs. Hughes could confirm my story if she pleased."

"Believe me, I shall ask her side of the story. She may deserve many names, but 'liar' is not one of them. And if I find you have taken advantage of her despite your denials, I will repay you in kind. Lillian will be my willing mistress before the day is out."

"I have every confidence in my wife," Felix said stiffly, striding out of the room and down the hallway. "If you ever try to lay a hand on her again, she will scratch your eyes out." As for the ridiculous story about Gareth pleasuring her in the garden, that was a transparent pack of lies. He would not dignify it with another moment's thought.

Lillian sank down onto the stone seat in the garden, her head in her hands and her heart racing. She could not bear to look, and yet she could not bear not to look, either.

The sight of Cora touching herself had first caught her attention as she wandered past the window of the sunroom. Cora's mocking laugh filtered out of the open window as she hurried by, her eyes averted.

She would have kept going if she had not suddenly heard Felix's voice. Hiding behind the shrubberies so as not to be seen, she peeked back into the room. Cora was still touching herself, now watched hungrily by Felix, who had entered the room from the hallway. Listening intently, she heard Cora offer herself to Felix, practically begging him to take her.

It was like a bad dream that kept recurring, watching Felix in the arms of another woman.

That was when she closed her eyes and sank down on the stone seat. The sight of Suzy riding atop her husband was still seared on her memory—she did not need to brand her memory with such another sight.

And yet she could not bear not to know. She had suffered his unfaithfulness for five years and more of wedded sorrow—what was another lover to add to the long list that had gone before?

And yet it was different this time. Over the past few days, she and Felix had shared a new bond, one that was new to both of them. He had enslaved her, and she had thrown her caution to the wind and become his willing slave.

Her face burned as she recalled how she had humbled herself before him and begged him to fuck her. Was he turning his back on her already? Was she no more than a passing fancy, to be discarded when a new, shinier plaything caught his eye?

Slowly she stood up again, her eyes still half-closed, and peeked through the shrubberies into the sunroom.

Cora was sitting on the floor still, stark naked, her face a picture of fury. Felix was nowhere to be seen.

A cry of exaltation resounded in her heart. The old Felix would never have passed over such an opportunity for a quick tumble. To have a woman, a naked woman whom he desired, in front of him asking him to take her, and to turn her down? If she hadn't seen it with her own eyes, she would never have believed it possible.

There was only one explanation for his actions. He was the old Felix no longer. Their time together, exploring the boundaries of each other's desires, had changed him as much as it had changed her. Though she was the one who wore the chains, he belonged to her body and soul as she belonged to him. The chains bound them both together, master and slave, in an unbreakable bond. Though she wore them on her body, he wore them on his soul.

Her heart lightened with every step she took back toward the house. There was no need for her to hide herself away from him and rebuild those walls around her heart that had kept her so safe, and so lonely, for so long. She could give herself to him in the knowledge that he would not break her as she had feared.

She must abase herself in front of him for daring to doubt his sincerity, for daring to leave him without his express permission and hiding herself away from him in the garden.

If she begged to be punished for her temerity, and again for her disobedience, and a third time for her willful disregard of his wishes, and if she took all her punishments in good part without a word of complaint, in time he might forgive her.

She hoped he did not forgive her too soon.

Their bedroom was empty when she finally reached it. No matter, she would wait patiently for him to come to her. If she waited all day by herself, it was no more than she deserved.

Quickly undressing and binding the cuffs around her wrists, she made herself ready for him. He liked her to be naked for him, naked and ready for his pleasure.

She arranged herself on the coverlet, her legs spread apart. When he found her here, his anger would be assuaged at her obvious obedience, at her readiness to fulfill his every desire.

She did not have long to wait. Almost as soon as she was splayed on the bed, counting the minutes until he arrived, Felix walked into the room.

He stopped and stared at her, drinking in the sight as if he was dying of thirst and she was a long cool, glass of water. "Lillian." He breathed her name as if it were the most precious sound in all of England.

"Yes, Master?"

"Where have you been this morning, Lillian? I was most upset that you left our room this morning without my permission."

"I am sorry, Master. Truly I am. It was very wicked of me, and I deserve to be punished for it."

"We will see to your punishment later. Tell me first, where were you?"

"I could not sleep, and I wanted fresh air, so I went for a walk in the garden. Nothing more."

"In the garden." His brow furrowed. "And who did you see there?"

Had he seen her hiding in the shrubberies, watching Cora? She felt a tide of heat creep up her neck. "I saw nobody," she lied.

"You are not telling me the truth, Lillian."

She turned her head to the side so she did not have to look at his accusing eyes. "No, Master, I am not telling you the truth."

"Who did you see in the garden?"

"I saw Cora Hughes," she whispered.

"Cora Hughes? Not Gareth?"

"I have not seen Mr. Hughes since the night I arrived here, but Cora was in the sunroom, touching herself. She knew I had seen her, but that did not stop her. I think she liked it, I think she wanted me to stop and stare at her, but I could not. I was hastening away from her when I saw you walk into the room where she was, naked and wanting you, then I saw you leave again." All her wonderment and her love shone in her voice. "You walked out and left her there alone and came to me."

"Did you think I would neglect you for such a woman as Cora Hughes?"

"For an evil moment I did think so, Master, but I was mistaken. I am sorry for my lack of faith in you."

"No, I am sorry, my love. My behavior has been poor in the past, but no longer. I am your slave as you are mine."

"I know you are. When you turned away from Cora, I could see it in your heart. I knew you belonged to me. Utterly. Just as I belong to you."

"What have you done to me, Lillian?" He came to sit beside her on the bed, his hands idly stroking her stomach. "You have spoiled me for other women. I cannot look at another woman now without comparing her to you and finding her wanting. No other woman holds any charm for me. The only one I want is you. The only woman I ever really wanted was you, all the others were only substitutes for what I believed you did not want to give me. I believed you were deliberately holding back on me, refusing what I wanted most of all just to spite me. Or even worse, because I was not worth your love, because you hated and despised me."

"I did not know myself until you forced me to look deep into my heart."

His hands moved to stroke her breasts. "It was time for desperate measures. I knew I was taking a hideous risk that I would alienate you forever. But there was always a slim chance that my gamble would work, that I would succeed where I had failed for so many years, that I would touch your heart at last."

"You did more than touch my heart. You touched my soul." She let a small smile play over her face as his hands moved over her breasts, across her belly, and down to her mound. "Not to mention the rest of me."

"I will never get tired of touching you. I will be touching you for as long as I live."

"I am glad of it, Master." His fingers were stroking her gently, making her shiver with need. "I want to belong to you always."

"Do you, now?"

"Yes, Master. If it pleases you."

"You will not run away from me at the first sign of adversity."

"I could not run from you even if I wanted to." As she spoke the words, she knew how true they were. "You are a part of me, you are with me wherever I go."

He took her hands in his and brought them to his lips, kissing them with all the love he felt in his heart. "As you are a part of me, Lillian, and always will be."

Exposed

One

Cora Hughes lay on her back in the sunroom, quite naked, her forefinger idly teasing her clit and brushing at her wiry red hair. In the days she had been at Sugar and Spice, the sunroom had become her favorite place. The bay windows afforded her an expansive view of the garden, a cluster of shrubs and well-tended flower beds leading down to a grove of stately oak trees.

But Cora wasn't the type to find pleasure in such a view—she found pleasure in being the view. And so here she was, once again, her legs spread wide and her knees bent, exposed to whoever might chance by. It aroused her to imagine an audience on the other side of the window as she slicked her fingers with her juices.

With her knees back near her shoulders, she plunged a finger into her wet pussy while her other hand rubbed at her clit. Withdrawing her finger, she watched as strands of her juices glistened in the sunlight before dripping onto her belly. She returned her fingers briefly to her pussy, then moved her attentions to her sensitive ass, flicking at her tight opening with a light touch and causing the wickedest of sensations to shiver through her body.

She strained her head up to look out the window, hoping for an audience, but none of the other couples staying at the house were in evidence. No gardeners either. Not even an ostler to gawp openmouthed at the sight of a naked woman, legs splayed and pussy exposed to the sun.

She sighed, and her hand movements slowed, then stopped altogether. Her solitude took a lot of the fun out of displaying herself. There was nothing she liked better than an audience.

Behind her, she heard the door open. "Cora, my dear. I thought I might find you here."

At the first words from that deep voice, her whole body stiffened. She loved an audience—of anyone but the man who had just discovered her. Resisting the temptation to curl into a ball and hide her body from her husband's sight, she merely replied in as casual a voice as she could. "Evidently."

He grabbed a cushion from one of the long, low sofas in the room and came to sit beside her, his big hands stroking her hair. "Are you still in a foul temper?"

The affectionate caress and the kindness in his voice withered her soul. She did not deserve affection from this man. The sooner he realized it, the easier it would be for him to forget her and move on with his life. Without her. She would not let the thought depress her. It would be for the best. "Why should you care what kind of temper I am in?" she said, cutting into him with an experience born of long practice. "I'm not in the mood for fucking you. I imagine that's all you care to know."

His hands did not stop their long, slow stroke of her hair. "You have a very dull imagination in that case."

Her teeth clenched together. How did Gareth always manage to find that chink in her armor, the few words that would pierce her soul? "No one has ever called me dull before." How dare he accuse her of such heavy stupidity. She was popular among her circle of friends—even if she was slightly feared for her sharp tongue and acerbic wit. "Many other things, maybe, but never dull."

"Then you apparently do not associate with the right people."

She glared at him. His words were a far cry from the apology she had a right to expect. "Clearly not." Sitting up, she reached for her Chinese silk dressing gown. "Please excuse me. I suddenly find that I have had enough sun for one day."

His hand reached out and grabbed her wrist, pulling her gently off-balance so that she needed to lean on him to stop herself from sprawling onto the floor. "Don't go." His voice was soft, but the tone of command was clear. He was giving her an order, not making a request.

"Why should you care whether I stay or go?" She could almost feel the beat of his heart against her back as she leaned against him. "You find me dull, remember."

"Not you." The amusement in his voice was almost palpable. If she turned around to look, she knew she would see a smile spread out over his face. "Just your imagination."

"It's the same thing."

"Not at all. I would never have married you if I had thought you dull."

She raised an unbelieving eyebrow. "Now that I find hard to believe," she drawled in her most supercilious tones. "You wanted an aristocratic wife, a wife with all the right connections to get you an entrée into society. My family was impoverished enough to overlook your lack of breeding and desperate enough to get me married off to sell me for a pittance." Pulling away from him, she lounged back on the floor. "You would have married me if I had been as dull as ditchwater."

He ran an awkward hand around his collar as if it were strangling him. Ah, finally she had hit a nerve. "There was more to our marriage than that," he said, his manner unusually stiff. "You fulfilled all my requirements for a wife."

"I believe I just enumerated them." She ticked them off on her fingers. "I was well-bred and I was available."

"And young," he added easily, the amusement back in his voice. "I would not have married an old crone, even a well-bred available one."

"Twenty-three is hardly in the first blush of youth, but young enough for your purposes, I suppose," she admitted grudgingly.

"Not to mention elegant."

"What would a man like you know of elegance?" she scoffed, wanting to hurt him even as the compliment warmed her from the inside out. "I thought the bottom of coal mines was more your sphere."

"I knew enough to recognize it when I saw it," he replied equably. "And you were emphatically not dull. When I first saw the red of your hair, I knew I would be taking on a fiery handful if I were to marry you."

"Fiery?" Her lips pursed. That was nothing more than a polite way of calling her a bad-tempered shrew. "You've seen nothing yet."

"Explosive handful," he amended.

Explosive was worse than fiery. Explosive meant *seriously* ill-tempered shrew. "And you married me anyway?" She shook her head. "The more fool you."

"You met all my requirements," he said casually. "And you seemed happy enough with the match. Why should I not have married you?"

Not even someone as obtuse as he was could have mistaken her reluctant capitulation with happiness. "I was not happy with it." Their marriage was a mistake from start to finish. She should have been brave enough to refuse him. There had to have been another way out. "I have never been happy with it."

His face was somber, serious, as he drummed out a tattoo on the bare floor with the fingers of his hand. "It is too late now, my dear wife. You have married me already. You should have spoken out earlier if you did not want me."

"Would you have changed your mind if I had?" Her curiosity surprised her. Though it could not matter now, she still wanted to know whether he would have wanted her if she had adamantly refused him. "Would you have gone off to court another woman?"

Telling him the truth about her would have frightened him off, for sure, but she had not been able to do that. Putting her fears into words would have made them too real. It was easier to hide from the world behind her tough facade so that no one could see the brittleness and the hurt that lay underneath. And, unwittingly, he had offered her the protection she so badly needed.

"Not until you had irrevocably refused me. I wanted you from the moment I met you." His eyes, so dark and gray, were fired from within by passion. Then, as she watched, it was as if a shutter came down over them, blanking all expression from them. "As I said, you met all my requirements."

He was keeping secrets from her, too. She could sense it. "Then what would have been the use of speaking out?"

His eyes bored into hers, seeing through to her very soul. "You could have refused me."

Her temper, never far from the surface, rose again, threatening to swallow her whole. He did not understand the situation she had been in. A man like him could never understand. "No, I could not have refused you," she snapped. "Not if you had been Blackbeard himself. I had no choice but to marry you."

Reaching out for her, he lay back on the floor and took her in his arms. "Well, we are married now, for better or for worse. We shall have to make the best of it or be miserable."

For all his hard upbringing and rough manners, he was such an innocent in the ways of the world. Stiff as a board, she refused to melt into his warmth and his strength. Only by keeping aloof from him could she retain her sanity. "I have long since resigned myself to misery."

Gareth Hughes held his naked wife in his arms, trying to concentrate on her words rather than on the satiny feel of her skin and the way her breasts rose and fell with every breath she took.

Fully dressed, she could take him to the pinnacle of desire with just one smoldering look from her jade green eyes. Naked as she was now, he could barely function in her company. He wanted only to hold her close to him, to rain kisses down on her, to worship her body with his own.

From the moment he'd first met her, he'd desired her with an overwhelming need that he could neither fight nor ignore. True, she had met his short list of requirements in a wife, but so had a good many other young women he had met over the past few years. Though any of them would have made him a perfectly adequate, if unexceptional, bride, he'd put off making a choice among them. Making a marriage in cold blood to some aristocratic young woman with ice in her veins, though it had seemed a good idea when he had first thought of it, was simply too distasteful to go through with.

Then he had come across Cora. The instant he'd met her, his mind was made up. He would have her and no one else. No other woman had come close to matching her vivacity, her spark, and the terrible vulnerability that she tried to keep so closely hidden but broke out of her at the oddest moments. She was irresistible, and he had no will even to try to struggle against her lure. Henceforth she would belong to him and to no other man.

So intent had he been on the match that he hadn't noticed her disinterest. Or rather he hadn't wanted to admit that a lack of interest rather than maidenly nerves was driving her coolness to him.

Now that they were wed, there was no mistaking her coldness. His wife did not love or desire him. She did not even like him very much.

He did not want coolness and a calm detachment from his wife—he wanted fiery passion, the sort of passion that Cora could give him if only she chose. He knew she could. It was why he had chosen her.

Now that he had married her, he would have to win her heart as she had won his. Nothing else would content him. And what better way to win her heart than through passion and desire?

His arms tightened around her. Making love to his wife wouldn't exactly be a hardship.

Unfortunately, she had made it quite clear to him that she wasn't interested right now.

It was doubly a shame, given that she was already naked and he was as hard as nails. As indeed he always seemed to be when he was around his wife. It was only a pity she was not so predictable.

No other woman he'd ever met had blown so hot, then so cold. Just a few nights ago she had dressed as a Turkish slave girl and ridden him hard and fast, driving him until he could hold out no longer.

He'd orgasmed explosively, and as his seed had spurted out

from him, he had felt the convulsive contractions that signaled her pleasure.

Ever since then, however, she had been as skittish as a virgin. And heaven knows how long it had been since she had been one. Certainly she had not come to their marriage bed untouched.

Not that that had mattered to him. In the Welsh pit town in which he'd grown up, girls walked out with their fellows from the age of fifteen or earlier. He'd walked out with a few himself before he'd left the mines and come to the city of London to make his fortune.

Now that he was married to her, he expected fidelity, but any amours she had indulged in before their wedding night were her own affair. Indeed, if she had fancied herself in love and given herself to some scoundrel who did not deserve her, he'd rather not know. Ignorance in cases like this was, if not bliss, then at least preferable to knowing all the gory details.

He had no wish to make her miserable over so little a thing as a maidenhead. "Is being married to me as bad as that?"

Her shoulders rose and fell against his chest. "Why did you follow me here?"

"Because you are my wife. I am not the sort of man to look on with indifference when my new wife informs me she is about to start an affair."

"Why should you care who I fuck?" Unhappiness made her voice hard. "I was not a virgin when I married you. I was honest about that at least." The last words she added under her breath so softly that he barely caught them.

"Now that you are my wife, your fidelity reflects on my honor."

She gave a disbelieving sniff. "You mean you would not want your entrée barred into the society you married me to gain."

"No, I would not." Not that he cared for the society itself, except for the opportunities of enriching himself that moving in such circles entailed. Rich men were happiest dealing with other rich men, the sort of men they met at grand London dinners and talked business with over the turtle soup. If he wanted their business, he needed invitations to such dinners.

But that was not the reason he cared about Cora's fidelity. She was his now, and he did not share what belonged to him. "Neither would I want you to cause a scandal and be barred on your own account."

"There would be no scandal in an affair. Nobody cares about that sort of thing anymore."

"There would be a great scandal in a divorce," he replied bluntly. Cora might as well know just where she stood and what would push him over the edge.

"Divorce?" The surprise in her voice was telling.

"Did you think I would turn a blind eye if you took a lover?" He may be an ex-miner, but he was also a man, and he had as much pride as any gentleman born. "Or welcome another man's child into my house and home?"

"A mutual agreement to separate." She waved one hand airily. "Separate houses. Separate lives. No scandal."

"That is what you were counting on?" He gave a harsh bark of laughter, his arms still held tight around her naked body. "Then let me enlighten you. I have no wish to enter into such a marriage. If we cannot live together amicably, I will brave a divorce, though it cause the biggest scandal of the century." Though it would kill him to live without her, he would do so rather than accept her cold indifference or her carelessness over the pain she caused him.

"Then you will marry again?"

"Naturally," he replied, although the thought of any wife but Cora was like a red-hot knife in his stomach. "I want a wife and children to carry my name on after I am gone."

A frown crossed her face. "A bad marriage to me would not put you off the wedded state?"

"One mistake does not necessarily lead to another one," he said more coolly than he felt. "I would hope to choose more wisely the second time around."

Her laugh was rather shaky. "Then you must be glad that Felix Rutherford made up with that poker-backed wife of his instead of chasing after my skirts. Though for the life of me I cannot see what he saw in her."

She did not like the thought of his marrying again. That was the first hopeful sign he had seen from her all day. "Yes, I am glad of that. More for the sake of Lillian, his wife, than for my own. She adored him, and he was making her life a misery."

"It was as much her fault as his. She had no idea how to handle a man like him."

"And you do?"

Her eyes were limpid with confidence. "I can handle any man. Even a bounder like Felix Rutherford."

"As you are handling me right now?"

"I wasn't handling you before. But now you mention the idea . . ." She wriggled around in his arms until she was sitting next to him rather than in his embrace, and her hands moved to caress his groin. "Maybe I am in the mood for handling you after all."

He shot a glance toward the full-length windows that looked out on to the garden. Much as he hated to stop her when she was in an affectionate mood, the sunroom was not the place for privacy. Anyone walking by would be able to see them in plain view. "Put on your dressing gown and come up to our bedchamber," he suggested. "Then you will be able to handle me as much as you like."

She pouted. "By the time I reach the bedchamber I will not feel like handling you anymore. I want to touch you right now. Right here. Or not at all."

"Even though anyone could see us?"

"*Especially* though anyone could see us."

Though he hesitated for a moment, he really didn't have a choice. He would sell his soul for a chance to make Cora feel kindly toward him. It was a weakness in him, but a weakness he could not easily overcome. Shrugging off his jacket, he leaned back on one elbow, determined to call her bluff. If she didn't mind an audience, neither did he. In fact, the exposed windows of the sunroom and the possibility that someone would walk by and watch him fucking his wife merely added an extra fillip of spice to their encounter. "Go ahead. I am all yours."

* * *

Cora eyed him briefly, torn between wanting to fuck her husband in the warm sun streaming through the large windows, and keeping herself aloof from him as she had intended to do.

But really there was no contest—she enjoyed the bacchanalian pleasures of fucking where she could be seen far too much. Her earlier caresses had left her wet and wanting, and Gareth, for all that he had once been a coal miner, was all man where it mattered most.

Leaving him reclining on the floor where he rested comfortably on large cushions, she stood above him and stretched like a cat, arms over her head, on tiptoe with her legs slightly apart. She knew he had a fine view up her smooth legs to her cunt, and her breasts beyond. "Do you like to see me naked in the sun?"

The sun gave her skin a white glow, the bright light showing off her body like gaslight never could. She looked down at the reddish hair that framed her pussy, glinting in the sun. Dropping her hands to her sides she spread her legs farther apart and ran a finger over her now wet pussy lips. Her juices glistened on her fingers as she bent down to offer her husband a taste. He accepted the proffered fingers gladly, straining his head up and licking her fingers clean.

"How do you prefer me? Covered head to toe in linen and silk like a good society wife ought to be, or naked and free, a true wanton?" As she spoke she emphasized her words by slowly turning around, displaying herself to her husband below.

Wordlessly he began to remove his own clothes. Starting with his trousers and shorts, he released his hard cock to the warmth of the sun.

She couldn't help but giggle at the sight of him sitting on the floor in jacket and tie but with his cock standing so proud.

Scrambling to complete the job of undressing, he was oblivious to her amusement. His mixed state of properness and wantonness didn't last long as the last of his clothes were quickly cast aside.

She stood before the large full-length windows, her body on display to anyone who might wander past. How she hoped that someone would wander past and stop to watch.

If she wanted an audience, she had better give them something to watch. Standing directly over Gareth's head where she knew he had a perfect view of her pussy, she bent at the waist to flick her tongue over the tip of the hard cock below her.

It had been some years since she had sucked a man's cock, but she had not forgotten all the tricks she had learned. His reaction to her gentle licking showed his pleasure. Stretching out for her, he placed his hands on her knees. She shivered as he ran his hands up her legs to caress her inner thighs.

Wrapping her lips over his cock, she plunged her head down to the base, completely engulfing him with her mouth. Withdrawing slowly, she encircled the base of his cock with her hand. He moaned audibly as she stroked him with her hand while licking around the purplish head with her eager tongue.

She reached up and tweaked her nipples with her free hand as she looked into the bright sun pouring through the windows. Gareth's cock jerked spasmodically in front of her as she sucked and stroked on it, her eyes closing in pleasure. He was getting so big and hard. Any moment now he would slip into her pussy and fuck her until she screamed.

All of a sudden the sun stopped streaming through her eyelids as if it had been eclipsed in some way. Opening her eyes and standing straight she looked directly at a very skinny and dirty young man in a tall stovepipe hat. He carried a handful of large brushes, his sooty clothes and black face marking him as a master chimney sweep.

The man gaped at her for a moment before lowering his eyes, only to be confronted with the sight of Gareth's cock bobbing in excitement, waiting for her to resume her moist caress. His gaze returned to Cora, lingering over her golden pussy, flat stomach, and full breasts, staring amazed as she squeezed her nipples while looking him in the eye.

She could feel his lustful stare on her tingling nipples, making her more anxious to be fucked than ever. Raising one hand over her head as she pumped Gareth's cock with the other, she made her breasts lift, affording the sweep an unrestricted view of her hard nipples.

She watched as the sooty voyeur's eyes slowly moved up from her breasts until his smudgy face looked at hers. To her surprise he held her gaze, evidently not in a hurry to leave.

She grinned back at the sweep, then reached down to once again caress her nipples before continuing the downward journey to run her hand over her pussy.

The combination of the sun on her naked body, her fingers on her pussy, and the young man at the window watching her was just too much for Cora. Suddenly she climaxed, her stomach muscles tightening visibly as the powerful orgasm coursed through her body. Unable to maintain eye contact with her audience, her eyes closed as she cried out in supreme pleasure. After an immeasurable time, she regained control of her senses and opened her eyes to find the sweep had fled, leaving a barely visible dusting of soot on the grass outside to show where he had stood.

On fire and wanting more, Cora crawled around to kneel between Gareth's legs, where she cupped his balls with one hand while gently stroking his cock with the other. Bending down, she brought her mouth to his straining cock and proceeded to lick him with full warm strokes from his balls to the tip of his cock. Each time she reached the sensitive head, she gave him an extra little flick over his glans, causing his cock to stiffen and jump while he groaned in pleasure.

Bending down with her ass high in the air, she could feel the wonderful sun on her back and pussy. She wondered if the sweep had returned to stare hungrily at her open pussy and exposed asshole. She thought of being watched by the sweep, with his thin pale body and contrasting face and hands, blackened from the ingrained soot that could never be washed out, even if he had access to a bath and hot water every week.

She imagined him standing behind her, rubbing his cock while wanting to taste her pussy, to plunge his cock deep into her cunt while his sooty black hands gripped her creamy white buttocks.

The thought made her instantly ready for more. Judging by Gareth's straining cock, he was ready, too. She wriggled up his body and, holding his gaze with her own, lowered her dripping cunt onto his cock.

When his cock was buried deep inside, she slid back slightly, giving her exquisite sensations as she slowly rode up and down on his shaft. She lowered her breasts to his mouth, where he greedily sucked at her nipples.

His hands on her ass pulled her deeper, spreading her cheeks and causing her ass to open slightly. She thought of the sweep, imagining him standing behind rubbing his cock while looking at her pussy lips wrapped around her husband's cock and her ass open to his stare.

She wondered what it would be like to have two hard cocks to play with at the same time. Maybe she could ride Gareth while the sweep thrust his cock into her mouth. Or perhaps he could slide into her cunt, along with her husband. As one cock slid out, another could slide in. She imagined the fullness having two cocks deep in her pussy, a thought that brought her close to her second orgasm.

Then she remembered a story she had read in a journal in the house. *The Pearl*, it was called, and it had nothing in it but stories of people fucking. There were even risqué drawings. In one story a woman rode a man, as she was riding Gareth, then another man approached the woman from behind and eased his cock into her ass. That would be a new experience! With that thought she sat up straight on his cock, reached around behind her, grabbed one of his hands, and guided one of his fingers up her ass.

Getting the idea, he pulled her closer, straining to get as much of his cock into her pussy as he could. With one hand he pulled her ass open wide, while the other gently slid two fingers into her other tight hole.

The feeling of such an intimate embrace finally caused the orgasm that had been building for so long to peak, and with a cry she collapsed onto him, arms and legs quivering with the intensity of the powerful waves rippling through her body.

Gareth, still hard inside her, continued to move slowly as her breathing subsided. "I know you like to watch and to be watched," he murmured as her breathing returned to normal. "Lie down on your back and let me put on a show for you."

She did as she was bid and rolled off him onto the cushions.

He straddled her belly and looked down at her. "Watch me come, watch me as I stroke my cock until my seed erupts onto your breasts."

As he spoke he placed his hand around his cock and with full strokes moved his hand up and down his shaft. As he rubbed his slick cock, she reached up and grabbed his buttocks, pulling him closer to her as his climax approached.

Then without warning he gave a cry of his own as he spurted over her breasts and face. His body convulsed, the several streams of cum he spurted out leaving sticky trails over her body.

She rubbed his cum into her breasts until all that was left was a trace of tacky wetness, wishing that she could erase the memory of his lovemaking so easily. Though she was fully satisfied, still she wanted to weep. Lovemaking was supposed to be nothing more than scratching an itch—she was not supposed to feel any emotional connection to her husband. Even less was she supposed to feel this bone-deep contentment, this lassitude and pleasure.

She should not allow herself to be distracted by sex so easily as that. Her happiness, her very survival, depended on keeping herself strong.

Two

Gareth drew the curtains of their bedchamber, letting the sunlight stream into the room.

Snuggled deep in the bedclothes, Cora grumbled at the light and pulled a pillow over her head in protest.

The open window let in a breeze scented with summer. "Come for a walk with me this morning, wife."

Briefly taking away the pillow, she looked at him through eyes hooded with sleep. "It's too early."

He tugged playfully at the covers. "It is nearly noon. And a glorious sunny morning to boot. You are nothing but a lazy slugabed."

"I am not used to keeping miners' hours."

Her words pricked at him. She took every opportunity to needle him about his lack of birth and the poverty of his childhood. As if working his way up from nothing to his current state of riches was something to be ashamed of. "Too bad," he

220

retorted. "If your family had been a little more industrious instead of lying in bed all day, they would not be hanging on your apron strings now, hoping for a handout from your hardworking and very wealthy husband."

To his surprise, she laughed out loud at his ill-natured description of her impoverished clan and put the pillow aside. "Very true." With a yawn, she threw back the bedclothes and got gracefully to her feet. "Be my lady's maid and help me to dress, and I will come for a walk with you. Though not too long a walk, or too energetic," she amended. "I am no sturdy miner's wife to be dragged over hill and dale trotting like a pony." Her words were sharp enough, but this time there was no malice in her tone.

"You are no miner's wife," he agreed as he helped her off with her nightgown and on with her shift. "You're an ex-miner's wife."

Her aristocratic nose turned up, and she gave him a supercilious stare. "I may be the wife of an ex-miner, but I am also the daughter of an earl. Pray do not forget it."

"I will not forget it," he promised her, unable to repress the urge to tease her. She was so very teasable when she got into one of her haughty moods. "I will remember it long after the rest of the world has forgotten."

The look she gave him could have cut glass. Tossing her gown to one side, she sat back down on the bed. "I do not feel like taking a walk anymore. You will have to go without me."

"You gave me a promise. You cannot go back on your word now, my dear wife."

She did not move. "Have miners' wives so much honor?"

"The wife of an ex-miner might break her word on the odd occasion, but the daughter of an earl never would." He picked up the gown and held it out to her. "Come, put on your clothes."

Though her face was black, she obediently stepped into the gown. "You are enjoying this, aren't you?" she said, as she held still for him to fasten the row of buttons down her back.

"Dressing you? Of course I am. It's not every day I get to play lady's maid for a beautiful woman."

"Not dressing me, you dolt." Her foot stamped hard on the floor, hazardously close to his own. "Teasing me."

"You finally realized I was teasing you? Congratulations. I wasn't sure how long it would take for you to catch on. Of course, you are far more intelligent than the average earl's daughter."

"And you are far more presumptuous than the average miner."

Damn, but the buttons down her back were small and fiddly. "Ex-miner."

"Whichever. It hardly matters."

"Ex-miners are cleaner." Nearly there. Only a couple of buttons at her waist to go. "No more coal dust."

"Thank Heaven for small mercies."

The last button slid into the buttonhole. With a pat to her slender hips, he twirled her around to face him. "There we are, my dear wife, you are buttoned at last."

Her face was flushed a pretty pink. "Do not ever ask me for a reference. You are a particularly ham-fisted lady's maid."

He held out his hands, huge plates of meat more at home with

222

a pick and shovel than with the delicate fabric of a lady's gown, and made a wry face. "I can't imagine why that would be."

"Lack of practice?" she suggested.

"That, too."

Their good-natured bantering continued as they strolled out into the extensive gardens. He enjoyed the idle chatter, the intimacy of being married and being able to trade quips with his wife on a fine sunny morning.

His wife. He may have married her, but he was well aware that he had not won her over yet. The icy shell she kept around her had barely a crack in it.

Cora stopped to sniff appreciatively at an apricot rose. "Mmm, beautiful."

"Worth getting out of bed for?"

"Almost."

He did not push it any further. It was the closest he would ever get to an admission that she was enjoying the walk.

They wandered on in silence through the gardens until they came to the entrance of a small maze. Tucked away at the bottom of the garden, it lay out of the way of the rest of the house. A perfect place for the talk that he needed to have with Cora. No one would be likely to disturb them there.

He pushed open the small wicket gate and motioned her inside. "Shall we?"

A shrug of her elegant shoulders signaled her agreement.

The tall hedged walls gave an impression both of safety and complete privacy. There was something comforting about being surrounded on all sides by hedges of green that blocked out everything but the blue sky overhead.

Arm in arm they strolled on toward the center. Finally, he brought up what had been weighing on his mind for days. "Why did you come here, Cora?"

"I told you already." Her voice was airy and unapologetic. "I came to spend a week with Mr. Rutherford. As much of it as possible in bed."

"Why?"

"I thought it might be tolerably amusing."

"Why did you run away from me when we had been married for barely a fortnight?" He ran his hand through his hair in frustration. Though he had puzzled over it for hour after sleepless hour, he was no closer to an answer than he had been at the beginning. "Had I been cruel to you, or beaten you, I could've understood your actions. But I have never laid a hand on you in anger, never spoken so much as an impatient word to you. I have been nothing but kindness. And you repaid me with the greatest insult that a wife can offer her husband. If you hated me that much, why did you marry me? For I can think of nothing I have done since our wedding day to give you such a disgust of me."

Her steps faltered briefly. "I thought this was to be a morning walk in the sunshine, not a lecture."

"Do not put me off with foolishness, Cora," he said sternly, angered at her levity. "I married you in good faith, expecting to build a life with you. You have not treated me with the good faith I had a right to expect. I want answers, Cora."

Her steps grew quicker, as if she wanted to get to the end of the walk and of the conversation. "I married you because you asked me to. Because the alternative was worse."

Her words held the ring of truth. A sudden suspicion crossed his mind. "You are with child to another man? Is that why you felt forced to agree to my suit?"

"Nothing so dramatic." She waved her free hand airily, clearly not in the least insulted by his suspicion. "My family decided they had better marry me off before I became a hopeless spinster. Three-and-twenty, and in their eyes I was already in dire danger of languishing forever on the shelf. Given their combined forces, I could not be bothered mustering the energy to stay unwed. Especially when you offered them such a tantalizing prospect of an alliance to a wealthy man. They care deeply about such things."

He looked pointedly at her dress, bustled in the latest fashion, and her expensively trimmed bonnet. "Whereas you do not?" Although they had been married scarcely a fortnight, he had already laid out more money on clothes for her than he did for himself in a full year and more, and he had done so gladly. A beautiful woman like she was deserved to have only the very best of everything. Until she had used her fine new feathers to snare Felix Rutherford in her net. That, he had to confess, rankled.

Her eyebrows raised at the curtness of his voice. "Every woman likes to be well dressed if she can. I am no exception. But I did not marry you for the sake of a wardrobe full of new gowns. The purchase price would be too dear."

"Why did you wed me, then, if not for my money? Clearly you have no great liking for me."

"You will not like the truth if I tell it to you." All traces of lightness had left her face. "It does not reflect well on either of us."

"I would rather have an unpalatable truth than a pleasant lie."

She shrugged. "On your own head be it, then. I married you because you were in trade." Her voice was curt, as if she scorned varnishing the plain truth in any way. "An ex-miner. Because I thought you would be rude and uncouth, unsophisticated, ill educated, uninteresting, even boorish. If I were lucky, you might even beat me. And then I would be able to hate you without feeling guilty." She gave a mirthless laugh. "I always intended to hate you."

He did not understand her. "You married me hoping I would be an easy man to hate?"

"I never expected to find happiness in marriage. That would be far too much to ask of Fate. But a simple existence not troubled overmuch by a guilty conscience that I thought I could manage. Until you married me."

"Do you hate me, then?" The thought was like a sharp knife slicing into his soul. Cora could not, must not, hate him. He could not bear to go back to his lonely bachelor existence, driven only by the desire to make enough money to drag himself out of the mining pits forever. His life had been one of constant toil and risk, never knowing if one false step would plunge him back into the world of poverty and despair out of which he had so slowly and painfully crawled. Investing time in friendships had been a luxury he had not been able to afford. The resultant loneliness had eaten into his soul, driving him into his desultory search for an aristocratic wife who could bring him joy and acceptance into society both at once.

Then he had found Cora, and his world, once so gray and mirthless, had exploded into a rainbow of colors. He could not go back to how he had been before.

His marriage was supposed to be a Heaven on Earth, not another form of hell.

A flush crept over her cheekbones. "You are a harder man to hate than I expected. I have had to chart another course. I have had to make you hate and despise me instead."

"There should be love between a husband and wife, not hate. What is wrong with love?" *What is wrong with you?* he wanted to shout, *that you hold such warped ideas about marriage?* He clenched his fists at his sides, resisting the temptation to take hold of her and shake her foolish ideas right out of her head, and some good sense in.

"I cannot love anyone. Least of all the man who has had to take me as his wife. It would not be fair to either of us."

"It is not just me, then? You would feel the same about any man who married you?"

"It has never been about you. Just about me. I have been broken, and I will never be whole again."

He had suffered through many hardships in his life but so far had survived them all. The human heart, he had discovered through sheer necessity, was hardier than it might appear to be. "There is nothing so broken that it cannot be mended."

"I am beyond mending," she said, matter-of-factly, with as much emotion as she would use to talk about the weather. "Besides, I would not care to be mended, even if I could be. I would merely break again, and that would be worse than never being whole."

By now they had reached the center of the maze. An ornately decorated gazebo stood in the very center, offering some welcome shade.

He guided her over to the gazebo and heaped a pile of Indian cotton cushions, the only furniture in sight, on the bare wooden floor as a makeshift seat.

She sank down on to them with a sigh of sybaritic pleasure, her dark mood forgotten for the moment. "Ah, this is divine."

He did not understand, and yet he knew that hidden somewhere in her words was the key to her erratic behavior. "What is so beyond mending in you, Cora, that you feel you must try to hate me?" If only he knew what troubled her, he was sure he could make it right for her again.

"Do I need to spell it out for you?" Her mood had changed like quicksilver again, darkening into a temper. "I was no virgin when I married you. My maidenhead was broken beyond mending—and long before I met you."

"You were not a virgin when you married me." His forehead creased in puzzlement. "Is that all that is worrying you?"

"Is that not enough to shame me?" she retorted. "Or should I add more sins to my account?"

"Neither was I."

"You are a man," she said dismissively. "Such matters are different for a man."

"A virgin is a virgin, whatever sex they may be."

"I do not care a jot about your sexual experience or lack of it. I was not expecting much from a miner. I am merely grateful that I did not have to teach you everything."

"As am I."

That quietened her, if only for a moment. "You are teasing me again."

"Not at all." He sat down beside her and took hold of her hand. "To my great joy, I found myself possessed of a beautiful, desirable wife, who takes a healthy enjoyment in sex and possesses the skill to turn my knees to jelly with a single touch. What man could want more than that?"

"Most men want to marry a virgin."

"I am not most men."

"Most men I know would have cast me off with disgust, quietly put me aside, when they discovered that I was not as pure as they had thought."

"I did not want to marry a virgin. I wanted to marry you."

"You are different from most men." It sounded as though in her eyes, at least, different was not a good thing to be.

"Not that very different inside. I want the same as any other man would want."

"Which is?"

He reached out and stroked her beautiful red hair. "I am here in a secluded part of the garden with a beautiful woman, and you have to ask me what most men would want in my situation?" She was all woman, and the most desirable one he had ever known, virgin or no. If only she could see herself through his eyes just for a moment and realize how deeply he cared for her. Her eyes were too clouded to see herself clearly. "Have you no imagination?"

"I do not pretend to read minds."

"Most men would want a kiss. I am no exception."

She sniffed. "Then most men would want so little that they would likely get nothing at all."

"The more you want, the more you get? Is that your philosophy?"

"If you don't ask for what you want, how will anyone know to give it to you?"

"We are in the garden. Anyone walking into the maze will have a clear view of us."

"Just as anyone walking by the windows of the sunroom yesterday would have had a clear view of us, too. But no one came. No one but the sweep, and he was not worth much. Too sooty for my taste."

A chimney sweep had seen them making love? He had not known at the time. "You sound disappointed."

"I was. I am."

"Were you hoping that anyone in particular would stop by?" Jealousy of Felix Rutherford still burned in his soul. She had better not have been hoping for that bounder to step by. There was still plenty of time to rearrange Rutherford's face and send him packing.

"A guest. A gardener. It doesn't matter who, as long as they were suitably surprised. And entertained." A smile lingered on her face. "Have you never secretly wanted to throw off all the restraints that we live under and do something shocking? Something that would cause an immense scandal?"

"Something like making love in public?"

"That would be a good start."

"I am a miner who has made good in railway speculation. Is that not shocking enough? There are plenty who consider me to be a great scandal already." Including his own wife, if the pointed barbs she continually threw at him were anything to go by.

She shrugged. "That is nothing."

"Nothing? You are too cruel."

Lying down on the cushion, she crossed her hands behind her head and stared up at the painted ceiling of the gazebo. "I have been ruled by proprieties all my life. Since childhood, before I was even a woman grown, I have lived in constant fear of scandal. I am tired of being afraid of causing a scene."

"So you want to cause a scene to get over your fear?"

She reached for him, her hands going straight for his groin. "I just want to cause a little scandal. Just for starters."

He smiled to himself. Cora really did have a thing about being watched while she was making love. Now that he thought about it, the best sex they had ever had had been with an audience. First as a Turkish slave girl, when she had ridden him into oblivion, and then yesterday in front of the full-length windows of the sunroom. Each time she'd been hot enough to spontaneously go up in flames—and to take him with her.

Being caught in the gardens making love to his wife would not be such a bad thing. To be stared at by a couple of young gardeners as he fucked his wife, to know they were wishing they were in his place. To have a couple of the pretty young house-maids stumble across them and stare at his huge, hard cock and wish that it was thrusting into their pussies instead of into Cora's. And then for the gardeners to take the housemaids and strip their dresses off them and lay them on their backs in the grass and fuck them, too, until the center of the maze was covered in writhing bodies. He was stiff as a poker just with the thought. "This gazebo is not so sheltered after all. The chances of being discovered are really quite high."

"Are you a coward, then?" Her voice was half-taunting, half-disappointed as she stroked him through his trousers. "Too scared of being caught to make love to me in the gardens?"

"Not at all." He reinforced his words by stripping off his jacket, then his shirt. If Cora wanted a public fucking, then he was the man to give it to her. It didn't matter how many men saw Cora naked and writhing beneath him, as long as they knew that although they might be able to look, they could not touch. He didn't even care if Rutherford was one of them. He'd already seen them fucking anyway, in the Turkish harem room. Except that Rutherford's attention had all been on his own poor neglected wife, for once, instead of on every other man's wife. Gareth wasn't sure if he had even noticed there were two other couples in the room.

Cora had slipped off her shoes. As he watched, she hiked her skirts up above her waist and opened her legs in invitation. Her pussy, pink and glistening with invitation, beckoned him closer.

His trousers were soon unbuttoned and cast aside, letting his erect cock spring free into the sunshine. He was naked in the sunshine. Let whoever wanted look at his naked body—he was not ashamed of the way God had made him.

She held out her arms to him, wordlessly inviting him to join her on the pile of cushions. "I was thinking . . ." Her voice tailed off in what in any other woman he would have sworn was embarrassment.

"You were thinking what?" he asked, as he lay beside her on the cushions, his fingers grazing her mound.

"I was thinking how delicious it would be," she said with a shiver, as his caresses grew more intimate, "if we made so much noise that we attracted the attention of the others and they came to see what we were about."

Winking at her, he gave a loud groan. A very loud groan. What was a husband for but to turn his wife's secret fantasies into reality. The thought of attracting an audience was making his cock pulse with need. "Like that?"

The light of mischief kindled in her eyes. "Or maybe like this." The shriek that followed was almost enough to pierce his eardrums, after which came a giggle of nearly equal volume.

He tickled her under the ribs to give her something to giggle about. "They won't know if I'm killing you or kissing you."

Helpless to escape him, she squirmed under his merciless fingers. "With any luck they'll come running to find out," she gasped, between giggles.

Her neck was soft and sweet, just made for nuzzling into. "Then we'd better make sure they have something worth coming to see."

"This is one of my favorite dresses. I would not like to ruin it." Finally managing to escape him, she scrambled to her feet and turned her back to him. "You will have to play lady's maid again and unbutton me."

His fingers fumbled far less when engaged in undoing rather than doing up. In no time at all, her dress was pooled around her feet, and she was standing before him in nothing but her shift.

Her breasts, as large and round as the finest Seville oranges, tantalized him, the hard nubs of her nipples pushing out the thin cotton. He wanted to taste them, to test the hardness with his tongue, to suckle on them and make her moan with pleasure.

He would show her that though he used to be a miner, he could pleasure a woman as well as any gentleman. "Lift your shift up for me. I want to see your pussy." Seeing as she liked to expose herself so much, she could expose herself to him. First he would drink in the sight of her, then he would enjoy the touch, the taste, the smell of her.

She raised her shift up to her thighs, giving him the merest glimpse of the auburn triangle of hair at the top of her legs.

The little witch was nothing but a cock-teaser. He wanted more. "Higher."

Obediently, she pulled her shift up around her waist. Her eyes were large with desire as she showed herself to him. "Is that high enough?"

His cock grew longer and thicker than ever at the sight of her mound, covered with fine auburn curls. He gave himself an idle stroke, teasing himself with the gentle pressure. "Spread your legs apart. I want to see your pussy, pink and glistening with juices. I want to see your wetness and know that you are wet for me."

As she moved her legs apart a trickle of juice began to run down her leg.

Sinking down to his knees in front of her, he touched it with the tip of his tongue. She tasted musky, but sweet, the very essence of womanhood.

A gasp escaped her, and she tried to close her legs. "What are you doing?"

He raised his head, holding her thighs apart with his hands so she could not deny him access to her parts. "Right now I am kissing your thighs." He suited his actions to his words, planting a row of kisses up her thigh, along the path of her juices. "And in a very short moment, I will be kissing your sex."

"Kissing my . . . ?" Her words trailed off into a startled squeak as his tongue flicked out and touched her clit, teasing it lightly with his tongue. "You can't do that."

His tongue flicked out again, licking her harder, more intently, swirling around her clit until every fraction of it was tasted. "You have never been kissed here before?"

Her hands were tangled in his hair, and her breath was coming in short pants. "Never." Her voice was strangled, as if she could not quite get the words out.

"Then I do not think much of your previous lovers," he said to her pussy, his breath setting her soft curls in motion. "What selfish beasts they must have been never to have kissed you there. And how foolish they were, too, not to taste one of the delights of woman."

"I did not know . . ." Her voice tailed off into a moan.

She tasted of Heaven in the shape of a woman. "Surely you know that a man likes to have his cock sucked?" He put his mouth to her clit and sucked on it gently, as a woman might suck on her lover's cock.

"Of course I do," she panted, sounding almost insulted that he could question her experience in such matters. "Every man wants his cock sucked."

His own cock was certainly keen to savor the experience. "And it never occurred to you that a man might reciprocate the delights you were giving him?"

"I never thought about it before."

"Then think about it now." He applied himself to her clit

again, licking and sucking on it until her panting told him that she was nearly ready to come.

Anchoring himself firmly with one hand on her naked buttocks, he plunged one finger firmly into her cunt as he licked her clit.

She gave a cry of pure lust and thrust herself down on his finger, urging him on to fuck her harder. A second finger joined the first, opening and stretching her, caressing deep inside her.

Harder and harder she rode his fingers as he licked her clit, giving her no rest from the sensations that were beginning to rule her. He wanted to feel her come for him in the garden, to feel the throbbing in her cunt as she convulsed around his fingers. Her pleasure was not far off. The trembling of her body, the stranglehold her hands had on his hair, the tension in her legs all told him that she was on the brink of coming.

Then her eyes closed, and a cry of pure delight burst from her as her pussy muscles contracted around his fingers, and a burst of wetness flooded her.

He sucked her clit harder, holding his fingers deep inside her as she orgasmed noisily around him, panting and crying and moaning as if she were on the stage.

It was several minutes before the effects of her orgasm subsided, and her pussy stopped contracting around his fingers.

She untangled her hands from his hair with a sigh. "No wonder men like having their cocks sucked so much," she said, her voice shaking, "if that is what it feels like. Heaven on Earth, with a touch of the devil thrown in to spice things up a little."

He slid out of her cunt, threads of her juices coating his fingers. God, she was wet, and his cock was so thick and long that he felt about to burst. "That is pretty much what it feels like."

She tugged him to his feet. "Then stand up and let me suck on you."

As he stood up she sank down to her knees in front of him and took him into her mouth, licking him and sucking on him with the expertise of a trained courtesan. She might not have received oral sex before, but she had certainly given it. Every touch that could drive him wild with desire, every pressure point that sent his blood surging through his veins, she knew them all. And she proceeded to demonstrate her knowledge until he was gasping on the brink.

He didn't want to come in her mouth this morning. Not yet. There was still too much he wanted to explore with her here, naked in the garden.

Reluctantly, he pulled away from the sweet suction of her mouth.

Just then he saw a couple of the bushes move and heard a rustling in the leaves that had nothing to do with the wind. From out of the corner of his eye he caught a glimpse of russet brown, the color of the jackets that he had seen the men working in the garden wearing. Cora would be pleased. Their noise had attracted one, maybe two, spectators to watch her sucking on his cock.

He pulled her to her feet and took her into his arms. "You have your wish," he whispered into her ear as he hugged her naked body close to his, his cock pressed firmly against her rounded belly. "We have an audience. A shy audience, over there hiding in the bushes. A gardener, by the look of him."

Cora wriggled her body against his, her wet pussy rubbing against his thigh. "Then I think we should show him what he has come to see."

He turned her around so that she was facing in the direction of the hidden audience, and stood behind her, his cock nestled between her buttocks. "Come on out," he called softly, as he played with her breasts, teasing the nipples to attention. "Come and admire my wife's naked body. See how her nipples are hard as little pebbles and her neck and chest are flushed red and hot with desire."

Running his hands over her stomach, he tempted them further. "Gaze at the roundness of her belly and the swell of her hips."

Then moving to the juncture of her thighs, he pulled her legs apart and with his fingers he spread out her cunt lips so her pussy could be clearly seen. "See how her pussy is wet and glistening, just ready for a cock to be thrust into it. And I have got a cock here, hard as nails, itching to find a warm, wet welcome in her pussy." He was enjoying flaunting her body, showing off what a prize he had won. "In fact, I'm going to fuck her now. Come out and watch me fuck her."

A shuffling in the bushes and not one or two, but three young gardeners stepped out from behind the bushes. Judging by the state of their trousers, they had all seen Cora's nakedness and liked what they had seen. Their pants were tented out with erections almost as big as his own.

They ought to be worshipping at Cora's shrine just as he did. He wanted to see them worshipping her, loving her with their hands and their mouths as well as with their eyes. "Do you want them to touch you?" he whispered in Cora's ear. "Or just to watch as I fuck you?"

Her whole body shivered at the offer he made her. "I don't mind if they touch me," she whispered back. "If you don't."

He didn't mind. They posed no threat to him. "Come closer," he called out to the young men. "Cora wants you to come closer and look at her."

Their faces red, they shuffled closer until they were almost near enough to touch her.

He ran his hands over her breasts. "She's beautiful, isn't she?"

The middle one of the three, a dark-haired young man, nodded eagerly, and the other two followed suit a second later. "Aye, sir. Your woman's a fine piece."

Nudging her toward them, he offered her up to them. "Touch her. Feel her breasts."

They shuffled their feet, unwilling to take him up on his offer. Then the middle one came out with what was clearly on all of their minds. "You mean it, sir? You want us to touch your woman?"

Cora reached out and took the wrist of the young man closest to her and laid it on one of her breasts. "Touch me," she begged. "Touch me while my husband watches."

"Go on, touch her." His cock was so hard nestled in between her buttocks that a few strokes and he would come. With a great force of will he held himself still, not allowing himself to orgasm as he desperately needed to. He wanted to see her adored as she deserved to be adored first. "Taste her. Suck on her breasts. Touch her all over with your hands, your tongue. Lick her pussy."

He held her with his hands on her hips as the three of them, tentatively at first, and then growing bolder by the second, started to explore her body with their hands, then their mouths.

The middle one, the boldest of the three, even sank to his knees and started to lick her pussy. Judging by the shudders of pleasure she made in his arms, she was enjoying this licking almost as much as she had enjoyed her first.

The other two were fastened on her breasts, their hands on her belly and thighs, teasing her nipples with their tongues. Little whimpering noises were escaping from the back of her throat as they played with her.

He couldn't stand it for another moment. If he didn't fuck her right now, he was going to die.

With a growl of pure animal lust he swiped at her other admirers, dislodging them all from their posts at her breasts and her pussy. Then bending her over at the waist, he entered her with one hard thrust, until he was buried up to the hilt in the wetness of her pussy.

He held himself there, embedded deep within her, for a long, glorious moment. She was his, all his. He had claimed his rights over her as her husband and her lover. She belonged to him and to no one else.

This was the closest any man on Earth could get to Heaven.

Anchoring himself with his hands on her hips, he thrust into her with a long, slow thrust.

The three young gardeners were watching him with envious eyes as he fucked her. One of them had a dribble of wet on his pants where his still-bulging cock was leaking its load of semen. They hadn't finished worshipping his Cora yet. Not by any means. He wouldn't be happy until they had paid her homage with their seed. "Come on her breasts," he ordered them, holding himself deep inside her. "Come on her while I'm fucking her."

All around him, Cora shuddered with pleasure at the thought. "Yes, please," she murmured. "Watch me being fucked and let me watch you stroking yourselves. Make me come while I'm watching you."

"Take your cocks out and stroke them until you come on her breasts," he ordered them. "Make her swim in your cum. Cover every inch of her with your sticky fluids. Drown her in it."

One by one, the three of them unbuttoned their trousers and took their erect cocks in their hands, pumping them up and down with eager fists.

His own cock was bursting with the need to thrust into her hard and fast, riding her until a wave of pleasure overtook him, and he spurted his seed into her body. But he wanted more than just his own pleasure. He wanted to tie her to him with chains so firm they could not be broken, to give her more than she had ever been given before. He wanted to win her over with his loving and make it impossible for her ever to leave him. He needed to give her the loving that would heal her wounded spirit and make her turn to him with love, not hatred in her heart.

So he thrust in and out of her with a slow, steady rhythm, slowly building her up to a peak.

The three gardeners were pumping their cocks furiously now, the purple heads straining toward her breasts.

The first one gave a guttural cry as his semen splattered over her breasts and stomach, a white wave of cum on her nakedness.

He felt the first tremblings of her orgasm start to build inside her. Reaching around with one hand, he touched her clit, pinching it lightly between his finger and thumb. The tremblings grew into a full-blown shudder.

The second gardener splattered his seed on her breasts with a grunt of pleasure, then the third followed suit with a strangled yell. Dripping with their seed, she cried out his name, and her pussy convulsed around him.

Her contractions were so strong that they pushed him over the edge. Furiously, he pumped into her, his cock spurting out his seed as her pussy sucked every last drop out of him. She was his now. With this fuck, he had claimed her.

Cora stood up straight and nestled into Gareth's chest, watching the trio of gardeners as they tucked their cocks back into their trousers and scurried away out of sight again behind the bushes. "Thank you," she called out softly after them.

One of them, the dark-haired one who had licked her pussy, turned briefly and tipped his cap to her before he disappeared.

Their cum was slowly drying on her breasts and stomach. She rubbed it into her skin with one hand, loving the thought that they had come all over her at the sight of her fucking, loving that Gareth had brought one of her fantasies to life.

"That was naughty of you," she said to him, feeling as full of contentment as a cat who'd just licked a saucer of cream. She could forgive him anything, anything, for the pleasure he had just given her. "Inviting them to join us like that. Inviting them to touch me and to taste me, to spill their seed on me."

Gareth's seed, though shot into her so forcefully she knew it had reached the very top of her womb, was now dribbling out of her pussy and down her legs. She scooped it up in her fingers, touched it to her tongue, then added it to the mix of semen on her breasts. She wanted his seed all over her, inside and out.

She could feel his eyes on her, watching her intently. "You wanted them to," he said carefully. "It turned you on, having them touch you all over while I watched them."

His words flowed over her skin like warm honey. It was enough to make her want to call them back again to touch and lick her some more.

"You liked being licked again," he said, warming to his subject now. "You liked having one of them on each breast and the third lap at your pussy juices while I held you in my arms. Watching them stroke their cocks as I fucked you made you orgasm so powerfully that your pussy milked my cock of every drop of cum in my balls. You loved every minute of it."

"So, I get turned on by having people watch me when I am fucking," she said defensively. "I liked seeing their cocks hard in their hand. I liked having them spurt all over me while you were thrusting deep into my pussy. You should not have invited them if you didn't want them."

"I invited them on purpose. I liked knowing they were watching us, wishing they were the ones with their cock in your pussy." He placed one possessive hand on her stomach. "I liked fucking you while they were watching us both. It made me feel like a king among men."

"And it made me feel like a queen." Her rough miner husband was turning out to be more of a catch than she had ever imagined. "Like the most beautiful, desirable, best-loved queen that has ever lived."

Three

Cora's good temper lasted for the rest of the day and into the night. For those blissful hours, she did not make a single nasty comment about his lack of breeding or turn away from him with coldness and dislike. Her step was jaunty and her spirits glad. For the first time since their marriage, she looked and acted as if she were genuinely happy.

His lovemaking had won her over, he was sure of it. Now that she had tasted his desire for her, his delight in making her fantasies come true, she would be the wife he had always dreamed of. The wife he wanted her to be.

So it was all the more of a shock when he woke the next morning to find her sullen and cross all over again. Turning away from his embrace, she buried her head in the pillows and refused to face him.

He was sure she was weeping silently, but he could not comfort her. She would not let herself be comforted.

Exposed

In desperation, he sought out their hostess, Mrs. Bertram. If anyone would know how to win over an unwilling wife, surely she would.

Mrs. Bertram was sitting behind her desk in a pleasant, light-colored study that looked out over the front garden. Putting down her pen, she looked steadily at him, her gray eyes seeming to see right through to his soul. "What can I do to help you?"

"My wife is not happy."

She merely looked at him, waiting for him to continue.

"Sometimes she seems content enough, almost happy, but other times . . ." He put his head in his hands and sighed. "Other times she lies in her bed, weeping, and will not tell me what the matter is."

"And this is one of those times?"

"She lies upstairs now, as miserable as I have ever seen her."

Mrs. Bertram frowned. "Has she a melancholy temper? I confess I would not have thought so, but I have been wrong before."

"She told me yesterday that she married me hoping I would be an easy man to hate."

Mrs. Bertram's face cleared. "That sounds like a woman with a guilty conscience, not a woman suffering from melancholia. She fears she has done you a great wrong, and her only solace would be to believe that you deserve it."

"She has done me no wrong." He paced up and down the room, unable to sit still. "True, she came here with the intention of having an affair with another man, but in the end she did not go through with her plans. Nothing came of it. Besides, her ill temper is not a new development. It began with our marriage. Maybe even before."

Mrs. Bertram sat back in her chair, her hands steepled together in thought. "Think back to the time you have spent with her, in her company. Is there nothing else? Nothing she has said that would give you a clue to what is bothering her?"

He stopped pacing, her words bringing back a memory. "She was not a virgin when I married her. That seems to matter somewhat to her, though it does not matter to me."

"She has mentioned this to you?"

"Only yesterday."

Mrs. Bertram was silent for a moment, considering her words carefully. "There is something eating into her from the inside. It may be this, or it may be something else altogether—I cannot tell. But what I do know is that she will need time. You must give her that time. Encourage her to talk to you, but do not press her into giving more than she wants to give you. If you pressure her, you will lose her forever."

"Can I do nothing else?" He resumed his pacing, striding up and down the room as if he was thinking with his feet. He hated feeling so helpless in the face of Cora's pain. "Nothing but wait?"

"She enjoyed the gardeners?"

That brought him up short. "I beg your pardon?" He had no idea that Mrs. Bertram knew anything at all about their adventures in the garden the previous day. He felt his face grow hot. Had they told her of their adventures in the maze, or had she spied them from her window? Either way, he did not altogether like Mrs. Bertram being privy to his secrets.

"There is not much that goes on here that I do not know about," she replied with a knowing smile. "While you are waiting for your wife to come to terms with her conscience, you may as well enjoy yourself and help her to enjoy herself as well. It may well assist in the process. And if there is anything that I can provide for you, anything you would like from me, you have only to ask. I pride myself on catering to all tastes here."

What the hell. He needed every weapon in his arsenal if he was to win Cora over for good. "Cora liked the gardeners," he confessed. "She likes being watched while I fuck her."

"Would she enjoy having another woman join you?"

His mouth fell open in surprise. "I s-suppose she might," he stammered. He knew he certainly would like it.

"The local vicar has a pretty young wife who might suit you well. She enjoys playing games with my guests. Shall I ask her to come up to you this afternoon?"

Another woman watching them? Joining in their lovemaking? If Cora's fantasy was to have three young men come all over her while she was being fucked, his was to have two women at once at his beck and call. What man could resist the offer of having two women in his bed at once?

Cora would like watching the vicar's wife fondle him as much as he had liked watching her being fondled by the gardeners. It might even help her temper. At any rate, it was well worth a try. "Yes," he said, his mouth dry. "Send her up to us."

★ ★ ★

Cora lay on her bed, the covers pulled up to her chin, pretending that it was still night. Refusing to have the curtains pulled back helped her pretense—the heavy velvet drapes kept most of the sun out of her room, turning it into a gloomy cavern. The darkness suited her mood.

Her conscience pricked her so she could not rest or sleep, could not even muster the energy to get out of bed. All she wanted was to hide away from the light of the day, seeing nobody and nothing.

She should never have married Gareth Hughes. Anyone, even the fat old parson in the village church who leered after the young married women and licked his fat lips until they glistened with saliva, would have been better than Gareth.

Slowly but surely he was breaking down the walls she had constructed around her heart, around the very essence of what made her Cora.

The very worst had happened, the very thing she had tried to guard against. She was falling in love with her husband.

And because she was beginning to care for him, because she could not hate and ignore him and believe he was unworthy of her, she would have to tell him the truth.

He was no different from any other man. Once he knew the truth, he would turn from her in disgust, and her heart would be broken all over again.

She had sworn to herself that she would never put herself through such pain again, that she would keep her secret until the day she died. But she could not bear to live with a lie, not even to save herself.

Though she had to tell him, she couldn't tell him yet. Not now they had forged such a sensual bond with each other. His touch was precious to her, every caress bringing tears of joy to her eyes. He was precious to her. Somehow he had weaseled his way past her defenses and made himself part of her life.

Even if his love for her was only temporary, he still loved her. She would treasure the memories until the day she died.

It was too much to ask of her to spoil her newfound happiness before it had hardly started.

Until the end of their week here she would pretend everything was all right, pretend she did not harbor a secret that corroded her soul. Their days at Sugar and Spice would be her refuge from the world.

She did not know how she could bear it if he were to break her heart.

Her first plan was still the only way out. Marry a man whom she could hate and protect herself that way.

Only she could not hate Gareth. Heaven knows, she had tried.

Then she had tried to make him hate her, but she had lost the will to do even that.

She had no choice left but to resign herself to heartbreak.

Reluctantly, she dragged herself out of bed and down to the hot pool-room. A soak in the steaming-hot water might restore her soul.

The pool-room was deserted. Much as she usually liked an audience to admire her nakedness, today she was glad of the solitude. After throwing off all her clothes and tossing them onto a strategically placed chair, and tieing up her long hair on top of her head to keep it dry, she stepped into the steaming water.

Even though she was expecting it, the heat still made her gasp.

She immersed herself up to her neck, enjoying the feeling of weightlessness that came from being cushioned on all sides by deliciously warm water.

Made sleepy by the heat, she allowed her eyes to drift shut. Despite all the pain in her past, and all the pain that she could see in her future, life was still worth living just for these perfect moments of utter comfort.

Half an hour or more she stayed in the hot pool until her mind was calmed, and her body felt utterly boneless. Maybe Gareth would build her a pool like this in their house. From what she'd seen, he certainly had enough money for it.

Of course, as soon as she 'fessed up to the truth of her past, he would not be in a particularly indulgent mood toward her. He'd claimed that her life before her marriage was her own affair, but there were some things that not even he would be able to forgive. She'd be lucky if he didn't divorce her on the spot. A sigh escaped her. All in all, her chances of a hot pool were pretty damn slim.

On that depressing thought, she climbed out of the water, wrapped herself in a towel, and shook her hair out again. Maybe she would go and find Gareth and take refuge in his arms again. He seemed to want her despite her sharp tongue and the perversity of her nature that impelled her to exercise it on the man who deserved it least.

Besides, the hot water had heated more than her body—it had heated her blood. Gareth would brave the worst her tongue could dish out if it meant he got a good fuck out of it. She liked that about him. In everything to do with making love, he was a man after her own heart. Rather than being turned off by her more unusual desires, he'd enjoyed having the gardeners join them as much as she had.

She owed him a gift for that. Surely the woman who owned this place would know where to find a young woman to join them for a romp. Gareth would like that for sure. Didn't every man want two women at the same time?

She would like that, too. Her pussy started to tingle at the thought of having another woman join them, actively making love with both of them at once.

It was too hot to get dressed again after her bath. Wrapping the towel firmly around herself, she picked up her clothes and wandered off through the hallways to her bedroom.

If nothing else, she was a survivor, and she was not beaten yet. Whatever happened, she would hold her head high and take it like a woman.

Gareth was not in their room. No doubt he was sick and tired of her sulking. She didn't blame him—she was sick of it herself.

Tossing the towel aside, she reached instead for her silk peignoir and threw it on over her shoulders. She liked the fluid feel of it, the cool smoothness against her skin.

A soft knock at the door interrupted her, and a well-dressed young woman popped her head around the door. "May I come in?"

Cora nodded regally. Given that the young woman was already inside, it seemed she had no choice in the matter.

The young woman flopped down on the bed. "I'm Esther. Mrs. Bertram sent me up here. She thought you might like my company."

Cora raised her eyebrows. "She did?"

"I'm very skilled. And always enthusiastic. That counts for a lot, Mrs. Bertram says."

"Just what is it that you do?"

Esther giggled as she took off her bonnet and tossed it on to the chair next to Cora. "I'll do whatever you want me to do. I'm always up for a bit of experimenting." She looked around the room curiously. "Where's your husband? Mrs. Bertram said there would be two of you. Not that I mind if it's just you," she added hastily. "As I said, I'm ready for anything. It's just I thought I would be with a couple this afternoon."

"Gareth has gone out," Cora replied, finally getting an inkling as to what Esther would be offering. Suddenly she wanted him back again. Badly. "I'm not sure where."

"Shall we start without him?" Esther asked with a naughty twinkle in her eye. "Give him a little surprise when he returns?"

What a great trick to play on Gareth to have him walk in on

the pair of them already engaged in an amorous embrace. Especially since he must have arranged this little surprise for her in the first place. She smiled to herself. Her husband was no stiff-necked, pompous tradesman who thought that sex should only take place in the dark behind closed doors. She and Gareth really did think alike. "I'm not sure where to start," she said a little hesitantly. She'd never been intimate with a woman before, had never really thought of being intimate with one except in the presence of a man. If it were to be just the two of them, she wasn't confident about what to do. Still, no doubt Esther had plenty of experience in the matter. "But I'm open to experimenting as well."

Esther bounced off the bed with a giggle. "Help me off with my gown. That'll be a good start."

Carefully, Cora unbuttoned Esther's gown. Beautifully made of silk and in the latest fashion, it must have cost her a small fortune. Her profession must pay better than Cora had ever imagined.

Esther, however, treated the expensive garment with contempt, simply tossing it over the back of the chair with no regard for how it would wrinkle.

Cora grimaced. Not even she would treat her favorite dress like that. Of course, she had only been able to afford expensive dresses like that since her marriage, and the novelty hadn't yet worn off.

The fine linen shift and drawers fared no better. "Ah, that's better," Esther exclaimed, when she was finally quite bare. "Clothes are so restricting. I like to go without them whenever I can."

Esther could certainly afford to go without her clothes, Cora decided. Her body was young and firm, her skin white and unblemished bar a few light brown freckles sprinkled here and there, and her waist was small but her hips and breasts nicely rounded. Her nipples were peaked into tight buds though it was not cold in the room, and the bush on her mound was neatly trimmed and so blond that it was barely visible.

"Take off your peignoir and see what I mean," Esther urged her.

Slowly Cora slipped the peignoir off her shoulders, letting it pool on the ground at her feet. Though it was strange to have a woman stare at her rather than a man, she liked it. She wanted Esther to desire her and to make love to her body just as much as she had wanted the gardeners to desire her and stroke themselves into coming on her.

A greedy look came into Esther's eyes as Cora's nakedness was revealed, and she licked her lips. "Mmm. You have a nice body."

Cora reached out to the other woman, running her hands over the roundness of her hips. "So do you." It was not merely politeness speaking. She wanted to feel Esther's curves under her hands, to touch the satin smoothness of her skin, to breathe in the scent of her arousal. And she wanted Esther to do the same to her.

Esther reached out and cupped Cora's breasts in her hands. "I love the feel of a woman's breasts," she murmured. "So soft and full."

Cora felt her own nipples harden under Esther's gentle touch. She thrust her breasts forward and, her hands on Esther's ass, tugged her closer.

Their first tentative contact turned into a full embrace. Esther's breath was on her cheek, and then Esther's mouth was on her mouth, and Esther's tongue was on her tongue. Wrapped around each other, they kissed, exploring each other's mouth, as their breasts and their pussies rubbed together in a futile effort to slake the fire that was building in them both.

A deep voice interrupted their growing passion. "Well, my love, I see you have already discovered the new playmate I procured for you." So intent had Cora been on savoring every inch of Esther's body that she did not know Gareth has walked into the room until he spoke.

Lifting her head, she gave him a saucy smile. "I was just testing the wares. Come and play with us if you please."

"He's still dressed," Esther squealed, "while we are naked. We can't have that, now, can we?"

"Indeed no," Cora agreed gravely, as they disentangled themselves from their embrace and advanced on him with naughty intent. "Prepare to divest yourself of your clothes."

Gareth stood unprotesting as they came to stand, one on each side of him. Working quickly, it was only a moment before they had removed his jacket and shirt, his socks and shoes, then his trousers.

"What a man," Esther squeaked, as between them they removed his drawers, letting his cock spring free. She reached out and stroked him, moving her hand from his balls to his shaft with noisy appreciation as his cock grew thicker and longer under the attention. "He's as fat and thick as any woman could want. Ooooh, I wish I could have a cock like that inside me all day and night."

Cora watched as the other woman stroked her husband's cock, then got down on her knees and took it in her mouth. Strangely, she felt no jealousy, only a burning desire to join in the fun.

She crouched down behind Esther, reaching forward and taking Esther's breasts in her hands, rubbing her palms over her large, red nipples.

Esther moaned with appreciation, and her sucking increased in tempo.

Cora's pussy was burning with the excitement of watching Esther suck on her husband. His face was screwed up as if in concentration, and his body was already covered with a fine sheen of sweat. Breathing fast and shallow, he was clearly trying to hold on to his self-control.

She wanted him to lose all control. She wanted to see him shudder with pleasure as his release came and his seed spurted out into Esther's mouth. Then the pair of them could tease and stroke each other and do the same to him until they made him rise into another erection and he could fuck them both.

She moved her hands over Esther's belly and down to her mound. "Look at me touching her," she whispered, watching the look on Gareth's face intently. "Look at me stroking her pussy as she is sucking you." Her fingers moved down to between Esther's legs, touching her clit and then moving down to explore the wetness of her cunt. Her fingers came away again, dripping. "She likes sucking on you. She's wet with it." She held her fingers up as evidence. "Look at that. Soaking wet."

"Touch her again." Gareth's voice was hoarse. "Touch her so I can see you."

"You like watching me touch her?" Cora's own pussy was starting to drip down her legs. Putting on a show for him while he was putting on one for her was turning her on more than she had imagined possible. She wanted him, God, she wanted him so badly that it hurt.

With one hand she continued to stroke Esther's pussy, dipping her finger in and out and stroking the short fine hairs that covered her. Giving in to the demands of her body for attention, she let her other hand creep down between her own legs. She stroked Esther just as she stroked herself, hoping that what made her feel good would also turn Esther on.

Was it her imagination, or was the air in the room growing thick with steam?

Esther's hands were cupping Gareth's balls, stroking them. Breaking the suction, she moved her tongue up and down his shaft, licking each protruded vein and sucking on his engorged head.

He was huge, bigger than she had ever seen him before. His legs, wide apart, were trembling with desire.

Esther took him back into her mouth. Her hands on his hips encouraged him to buck into her.

His thrusts grew more and more urgent, and his face beaded with sweat. Then he gave a cry, his cock jumped, and he shot his seed into Esther's mouth.

She continued to suck on him as his seed dribbled out of the corners of her mouth, until he pulled away from her, limp and sated.

Cora got to her feet and pulled Esther with her. A glob of semen was stuck to her chin. Cora touched it with the tip of her tongue. It was salty and tasted of man. Of him.

"Kiss me," she demanded of Esther, wanting to taste more of him.

Esther leaned into her and kissed her, their tongues twining together like a pair of lovers. Cora searched out the taste of him in Esther's mouth.

Gareth had sunk back into a chair, his hands flopped at his sides. At the sight of them kissing each other, his eyes lit up with interest again. One hand moved to cup his balls and play with his cock, which was starting to twitch again.

"Play with each other's breasts," he ordered them, from his seat on the chair. "I want to see you touch each other's breasts."

Not breaking the kiss, Cora moved her hands to Esther's breasts. Esther did the same, kneading and squeezing until Cora's nipples were tiny buds of desire.

The room was so hot she felt as if she were going to explode. Her skin prickled with desire, and her eyes drifted shut.

She felt Esther tugging on her. "Come over to the bed with me. Then we can lie down and love each other all over."

The bed was soft under her, and the sheets cool on her over-heated skin. Rolling over onto her side, she moved to take Esther in her arms again, but the girl had moved so they were topping and tailing in the bed.

The touch of Esther's mouth on her pussy, and Cora instantly realized why. This position had definite advantages, not the least of which was the tickling of the girl's tongue on her pussy.

Tentatively, she reached out with her own tongue to Esther's clit. Wet with juice, it tasted musky but not unpleasant, and Esther's whimper of pleasure and redoubling of efforts made it even more worthwhile. Lightly she licked, and was licked in return.

Gareth had risen out of his chair and was pumping his cock furiously in his hand as he watched them, clearly hard again already.

She wanted to watch him make love to Esther. Though she was hungry for him herself, she wanted to hang back and see him pleasure Esther first.

Rolling away from Esther, she came up onto her knees at the head of the bed. "Let him fuck you," she whispered into Esther's ear. "Get up on your hands and knees and let him fuck you from behind."

Her eyes glazed with lust, Esther clambered onto her hands and knees, her ass thrust invitingly into the air.

Cora spread Esther's pussy lips apart with her fingers. Esther's pussy was wet with her desire. Cora thrust two fingers inside and drew them out again, soaking wet. With the same hand she took hold of Gareth's cock, massaging the juice into him until he was slippery all over.

Then, with one hand spreading Esther's pussy lips apart and the other on Gareth's cock, she guided him right to the entrance of her cunt and nudged his swollen purple head inside. "Fuck her, Gareth," she pleaded, as he hesitated. "Thrust your cock deep into her pussy while I watch you."

He could not resist her entreaty, but sank his cock inside Esther. Ignoring the squeals of pleasure she made and the bucking of her hips that urged him to thrust into her harder and faster, he held himself still inside her. "Let her lick you," he commanded Cora. "I want to watch her licking your pussy while I'm fucking her."

Cora scooted up to the other end of the bed, positioning herself strategically where Esther could suck on her pussy.

The sight of Gareth thrusting into Esther combined with the delicate sucking on her clit was almost enough to drive Cora right over the edge.

Before she could orgasm, though, Esther cried out, and her whole body shuddered.

Gareth held himself still as Esther noisily enjoyed her orgasm, and then pulled out, his cock still as hard as nails. "Get on your hands and knees, now," he instructed Cora. "It's your turn for a good fucking."

It felt as though she had been waiting for this moment all her life. His cock slipped into her until she felt as full as she could possibly feel.

As Esther looked on in sleepy satisfaction, Gareth rode Cora hard, thrusting into her with vigor.

It was not long before she was on the brink again, desperately holding herself back, clinging to the edge with her fingernails to stop herself from falling over until Gareth was ready to fall with her.

He slapped her buttocks—hard.

The pain mingled with the pleasure until she could not tell where the one stopped and the other started. Again he slapped her, and again, and she thrust herself back on his cock and begged him for more.

Just as she knew she could not stop herself from coming for another second, Gareth pulled out of her. She twisted her head around to look at him. "What are you doing?"

He parted her buttocks with one hand, and she knew with a shiver of delight what he was going to do even before he told her. "I'm going to fuck you in the ass."

Slowly he pushed the head of his cock into her ass as she struggled and panted to relax and receive him.

Once the fat head of his cock had forced its way into her tight hole, he paused for breath, holding his cock still. "Am I hurting you?" The strangled tones of his voice showed how close he was to another orgasm, his second for the day.

She shook her head, not wanting him to stop. The hurt felt

good. He was taking possession of her in every way that he could, branding her soul with his ownership. There was nothing she could do but accept his dominance, his mastery over her, and to welcome both the pleasure and the pain.

With her permission, inexorably he pushed farther, until he was buried deep in her ass. The sensation of having him inside her there added a new dimension to her desire, teasing pleasure points she had never found before.

With one hand he reached around her hips and found her pussy, rubbing it in rhythmic circles. As he did so, he withdrew from her ass and then plunged in again, fucking her hard and fast.

It was too much for her. Thrusting herself back to meet him, she exploded in a rush of pleasure. On and on her muscles throbbed with release as he fucked her hard in the ass until at last she felt a rush of warm liquid deep inside her. His seed spurted out of him, flooding her passageway with the proof of his pleasure, and his deflating cock slid out of her on the tide.

Unable to hold herself up any longer, she collapsed, boneless, onto the bed.

He lay on top of her, his head resting on her back, taking his weight on his elbows so as not to crush her. "Christ, Cora, that was the best sex I've ever had. It was so damn good I thought I was going to die."

"I did die," Cora murmured back, utterly sated. "And went to Heaven."

"I liked it, too," Esther piped up next to them on the bed. Cora had forgotten she was even there in the room with them. "Any time you want to play again, please, ask Mrs. Bertram to bring me over. I'd love to get naked with you anytime you feel the urge."

Having Esther join them to make a threesome had been fun, but now all Cora wanted was to be alone with Gareth and luxuriate in his tenderness for her.

Gareth evidently felt the same way. "We'll be sure to ask Mrs. Bertram for you again by name," he said. "You were wonderful, and I thank you for your time and efforts."

It was a dismissal. A polite one, to be sure, but a dismissal nonetheless. Esther took the hint. "Thank you, too, but I really must be going now. I would not like to keep my husband waiting for his dinner. Sermon-writing makes him ferociously hungry." Rising from the bed, she clambered into her gown and threw a shawl on over the top to disguise the lack of buttoning. "Good night."

"Good night. And thank you," Cora said, her thankfulness genuine. Even before Gareth had arrived and stoked the fires to a fever pitch, Esther had been a wonderful playmate, unusually inventive and adventurous. She wouldn't have minded a few more minutes alone with her. Maybe Gareth would organize that for her one day if she asked him to.

Esther threw a wistful look over her shoulder as she left. "Maybe I will see you again soon."

"I hope so," Cora replied fervently. Just one night of sex like this would not be enough for her. Now that she had tasted just how good it could be, she would want to experience it again. Not every night, or even every time that she and Gareth made love, but once in a while for a special treat. A very special treat.

Gareth gave a deep belly laugh at the tone of her voice. "What my wife wants, my wife usually gets. Good night for now. I have no doubt we shall be seeing you again soon."

Four

Inviting Esther to join them had done the trick. Cora's good humor lasted through the rest of the day and well into the next evening. Gareth started to hope that his technique of winning her heart through passion was working. Certainly she had been much less snappish than usual, and was now lying peacefully next to him on the bed in the darkening light of late evening.

Just then she rolled over and gave a lazy yawn. "Mrs. Bertram has asked me if I would like to entertain the company one night we are here. Dancing maybe, or singing, she suggested. Or even playing the piano." She pulled a face. "She has never heard me play the piano, or she would not have suggested that particular form of amusement."

"Be careful or the wind will change and you will be left looking like that for the rest of your days." He traced lazy circles on her naked back. "And what did you reply?"

"I said I would dance."

"You will dance a waltz?" He failed to see the entertainment in watching a woman, even his wife, waltz. The only reason for dancing was to hold a woman close in your arms until the peaks of her breasts brushed across your shirtfront as you moved, to breathe in the scent of her, to torment yourself with the thought of pleasures to come.

"Don't be silly. Of course I will not. I will do a belly dance. Just like the Turkish women do when they want to entertain their men."

"You can dance like a Turk?" For the first time in their marriage she had truly surprised him. "Where on earth did you learn such an unusual pastime? There could not have been much call for belly dancing in the aristocratic circles in which you moved."

"I can also japan tables, net screens, and make elaborate cutouts to paste on greeting cards. I hardly know which is the most useless occupation."

He liked the notion of her dancing like a Turk. An acquaintance of his who had fought alongside the Turks in the recent Crimean War, Captain Robert Carrick, was full of the sinuous sensuality of the Turkish women and their bare-breasted dances that were more invitation to sin than anything else. Her body was made for such dancing. "Show me."

"It looks better when I wear a costume," she protested, not getting up from the cushions.

"Show me."

With a grumble, she rose from the cushions and struck a

graceful pose, one hip jutting out and her bent arms in the air above her head. "You will have to imagine the rest."

"The rest?" His imagination didn't go much further than Cora dancing for him, naked.

Her hips swayed, and her breasts bounced up and down as she danced for him. "The tassels strung low across my belly. The bells on my wrists and ankles that tinkle whenever I move, and the tassels on my nipples that shake as my breasts shake."

On and on she danced, moving her body in seductive rhythmic movements as she softly hummed an exotic-sounding tune under her breath. His cock rose again as he watched her, displaying her body for him, every movement designed to seduce and entice. As he watched, he stroked himself, enjoying the desire she was rekindling in his body.

He could have watched her all night by gaslight until the sun rose once more in the east, but eventually she stopped, out of breath, and flopped down beside him once again.

"That was beautiful."

She nudged his still-erect cock with her bare knee. "Evidently."

"Would you rather I had no courage in me?"

She looked suddenly unsure of herself. "I have never danced for anyone but my old nurse before."

"You look as if you have been belly dancing from the cradle. I will be proud of you when you dance for the company and everyone can see what a beautiful, talented wife I have managed to snare."

"I must look very silly. Maybe I will tell Mrs. Bertram I will not dance after all. She can find some other entertainment for everyone."

"You would make all the women jealous and all the men poker-stiff."

"I cannot dance. I have no costume."

"The Turkish slave girl outfit you wore a few nights ago? Would that do?"

She shook her head doubtfully. "Maybe, though it was not made for belly dancing. It needed more tassels, and I should have bells around my wrists and ankles. The tinkling music is all part of the allure."

He grabbed her peignoir off its hook and tossed it over her shoulders. "Mrs. Bertram is nothing if she cannot procure a proper costume for you by tomorrow evening, tassels and bells and all. Come, we will see what she can beg, borrow, or steal for us."

She came with him unprotesting, though her feet moved slowly along the floor as if against her will.

"And if you are very good and dance very well," he whispered in her ear as they were going down to stairs in search of Mrs. Bertram, "then I will come up to you while you are dancing in front of all the company and fuck you while they all watch. You'd like that, wouldn't you?"

By the shiver that his words elicited and the way her feet picked up their pace, he knew she would like that very much indeed.

* * *

Exposed

The costume that Mrs. Bertram managed to produce on such short notice was perfect. Even Cora declared it so as she made herself ready for her performance.

The skirt was a shimmering ice green silk that billowed and flowed about her legs as she walked, showing more than a glimpse of thigh from the slit that stretched from the hem up to the tasseled waist. Tassels hung from her waist all around, accentuating the graceful length of her legs, while the tiny bells sewn on the jade green wrist and ankle bands tinkled with every movement.

Her bodice, if you could call it a bodice, was simply stunning. It was nothing more than two tiny scraps of fabric that barely covered her nipples, hung with tassels and tied behind her neck and around her back. The shape of her breasts could be clearly seen—there was not the least attempt to hide them. The iridescent scarf that she twirled around her shoulders only brought more attention to her near nakedness.

With a dark green sequined headdress and her long red hair flowing down her naked back, she looked completely irresistible.

Catching one end of the scarf, he tugged her toward him and ran his hands up her smooth thigh until he reached her mound. "You are not wearing anything else?"

She held the sides of her skirt apart so he could clearly see her nakedness underneath. "If you are very lucky, you will be able to see my pussy when I dance."

He pulled her down on to his lap, the beginnings of an erection already tenting out his trousers. He nudged it into her nakedness. "Maybe we should just forget about the dancing. You can sit on my lap and dance there instead."

Pushing him away, she got to her feet again. "First you have to watch me dancing." She shot him a saucy smile. "And I hope you have not forgotten what you promised me if I danced very well indeed. For my part, I remember every word."

How could he forget his promise? When it came to Cora and fucking, he would never forget a single thing he had promised her. He was too anxious to experience every new thing with her.

With a final pat on her bottom for good luck, he took his place back in the parlor, where the rest of the company had gathered after dinner. It was showtime.

With the jangle of an exotic percussion instrument, Cora moved fluidly into the room, the tassels around her hips flicking around as she swayed to the rhythm.

There was a sharp intake of breath from around the room as the other couples in residence recognized her.

Adam Farrell was staring at her as if his eyes would pop out of his head. Even Felix Rutherford, newly besotted as he appeared to be with his own wife, could hardly take his eyes off her. As for the women, they were staring at her openmouthed, openly goggling at her movements.

As sinuous as a snake, she moved through the room, pausing in front of each person in turn to give them an individual view, shaking the tassels on her breasts and making her hips sway back and forth in a seductive rhythm.

One by one she was making love to the entire room, though she never touched a single one of them.

Finally, it was his turn. She stood in front of him, swaying slightly to the music and gave him a sleepy half smile. "Imagine that I'm sitting on your cock," she murmured softly, so that no one else could hear her words, "moving my pussy muscles around your cock just as I am moving my stomach now. Imagine how good that would feel." She swayed a little harder. "Imagine the tension starting to build in you as you get closer and closer to coming as I squeeze you intimately. And then imagine taking my breasts in your mouth, these breasts that you see here jiggling in front of you, and sucking on them until my nipples are tight. Imagine me riding you up and down, harder and faster with every stroke, until you come deep inside me." She stopped her swaying and looked him right in the eye. "Are you imagining that?"

He was ready to come in his pants before she had even touched him. "You're trying to kill me. I know you are."

"Just seeing if you will keep your word." She lifted her skirts to her knees, letting them gape open so he could see her pussy. "If you like my dancing, come and show me just how much. Pull out that hard cock of yours and let me ride it till I come. Turn me around and fuck me from behind. Use me like you would use a real Turkish belly dancer, without any thought or care for my pleasure, just for your own."

She turned her back to him for a moment, addressing the rest of the company. "My husband is going to fuck me now as a reward for my dancing," she announced. "Come and watch us. Do."

He had no qualms about performing in front of the other couples, not with Cora waggling her ass so enticingly at him. With a growl he bent her over at the waist, forcing her to grab hold of a chair to stop herself from toppling over. Flipping her skirts up over her waist with one hand, he unbuttoned his trousers with the other.

Cora's teasing had already made him stiff. Without a thought in his head beyond the moment, he took his cock in his hand and guided it directly to her cunt.

No foreplay. No sophistication. Just one hard thrust, and he was buried in her.

As she had promised, she squeezed him with her pussy, welcoming him inside her and dragging on him when he went to withdraw, showing how much she wanted him to stay inside her.

The other two couples sidled closer, fascinated at this wanton display of loving. Adam was surreptitiously touching his wife's breasts as she, flustered, tried to pretend she did not notice. Felix, on the other hand, had his hands well and truly up his wife's skirts. Judging by the rapid heaving of Lillian's chest and the redness of her face, he had a couple of his fingers thrusting in her pussy for sure.

And all of them were watching him as he fucked his wife, getting turned on at the sight of his cock moving in and out of her pussy.

He slowed the pace for a while, drawing himself right out of her pussy, stroking down the length of his cock with his fist, then plunging back into her with force. Proud of the girth and the length of his engorged member, he wanted the other women to admire him, too, and to wish he had *them* up against the chair. When they went to bed that night, he wanted them to fantasize that it was him on top of them, pleasuring them until they screamed.

Cora liked the change of pace. Each time he thrust into her, she gave a tiny cry, and her pussy shuddered around him with pleasure. One last time he pulled right out, then thrust into her hard, holding himself deep inside her.

She gave a gasp, louder than the others, and thrust herself back against him, once, twice, then he felt her muscles contract all around him as she came.

He was close himself. A couple of fast-paced thrusts, and he felt his seed shoot to the top of his cock. Her pussy gave one last contraction, and that was enough. With an incoherent cry, he pushed deep into her again and again, spurting his seed into her with every thrust.

Her hungry pussy milked him until he was dry, wringing out every last drop of semen from his balls.

Only then did he let her get up from the chair. "Good dancing," he said with a satisfied grin, as he tucked his dripping cock back into his pants. "You should dance in public more often."

As she slowly straightened up again, a smile of satisfaction on her face, the door to the parlor opened.

He knew something was wrong the moment the man appeared in the doorway. At the merest glimpse of his tall figure standing there, Cora gasped, and her whole body stiffened. The lassitude of satisfaction was instantly gone, replaced with a wary, frightened tension so thick he could almost taste it in the air around her. She looked as if she had seen a ghost.

The strange man, on the other hand, strode toward them with his arms outstretched, the look on his face strangely predatory. "Cora Hamilton. My own dear niece. How delightful to meet you here. And how very unexpected of you to hide away in a place like this when you knew I was coming back to England. Thankfully, your housekeeper knew where you had gone and was able to give me directions." He looked her up and down in a way that Gareth found highly offensive. "And may I say what delightful taste in clothes you have developed."

Instead of greeting her uncle with a smile, Cora frowned and sidestepped away from his embrace, putting her arm through Gareth's instead. He held her tight, fiercely glad that instinctively she had run to him for protection.

Twitching her skirts around her so that the slit gave no hint of her legs, her free hand moved to cover her breasts. "Uncle Ralph," she said curtly, and pulled a slight face as if his name left a nasty taste in her mouth.

The smile on her uncle Ralph's face slipped a fraction. "Is that any way to greet your favorite uncle?" he boomed. "When I have only just now returned from India, where I have been stationed for seven long years? Do you not recognize me? Are you not glad to see me?"

"You have not changed," Cora said stiffly. "You are the same man you always were." Gareth got the decided impression that her words were not meant as a compliment.

"You have changed, Cora." His words were low and ominous. "Once upon a time you would have greeted me with open arms and kissed me warmly out of sheer joy to see me."

"You have not met my husband yet, I believe," Cora said, drawing him smoothly into the conversation. "Gareth, this is my uncle Ralph. Uncle, this is my husband, Gareth Hughes."

"So you are married now. I had forgotten. To a coal miner, I believe?" His face was screwed up in distaste, and he made no move toward a handshake or to directly acknowledge Gareth's presence.

The cold disdain in his voice sent tendrils of unease snaking down Gareth's spine. Unlike the rest of Cora's family, who had been delighted to welcome his money into their family, Cora's uncle did not wish him well.

Before he could open his mouth to reply, Cora stepped into the breach. "Gareth is a businessman. A spectacularly success-ful businessman." The coldness in her uncle's voice was nothing to the pure ice and fury in Cora's. "A banker. Given our family's lack of funds, it would be wiser not to antagonize him."

"No offense meant," her uncle said, his voice patently false. The coldness in his eyes remained, and he continued to watch

Cora as if she were a rabbit, and he was a hungry poacher with a wire snare in his hands.

"None taken." The words came out even curter than he had intended them to. Even though the man was Cora's uncle, he made Gareth's flesh crawl.

"I'm sure your husband will excuse you for just a moment to take a walk on the terrace with your uncle." The man's smile did not reach his eyes.

Cora went as still as a statue, her face as pale as marble. The only color was the red of her hair, standing out in stark contrast to the white of her face. "If you will excuse me for just a moment," she said to Gareth through bloodless lips, as she disengaged herself from his arm. "This will not take long."

Placing her hand gingerly on the arm her uncle offered her, she walked, stiff-backed, to the double doors that led to the garden.

Gareth watched her go, troubled to the bottom of his soul. His Cora was a fearless Amazon, not afraid of anything. Except, it appeared, of her uncle. She was seemingly terrified of him.

He had not grown up on the streets for nothing. For all his size, he could move as silently as a mouse when the occasion warranted. As soon as they had gone onto the terrace, he slipped out of the parlor and down the hallway. The next room also opened onto the garden. He would slip unseen out of those doors to keep an eye on Cora's uncle and make sure that he did not trouble or threaten her in any way.

She was his wife, and it was his duty to protect her, even from her own family if need be.

Exposed

The night was dark, with a bank of clouds covering the moon. The gaslight, so bright in the house, could not penetrate the gloom of the garden.

A couple of figures were standing at the edge of the terrace, their voices dull and muffled in the muggy heat of the evening. He stole closer, straining his ears to catch their conversation.

"Come for a walk in the garden with me, Cora."

"I prefer to stay on the terrace." Her voice held no warmth in it.

"You have turned shy." Her uncle's words were sly and coaxing. "Before I left for India you would have jumped at the chance to go strolling in the gardens with me at night, when no one could see what we were doing or where my hands were straying."

Gareth held himself still as her uncle's words assaulted his ears, making him feel sick to the stomach. What had she suffered at her uncle's perverted hands?

She edged away from him, farther down the terrace. "I was a green girl then. I knew no better."

"You were hungry for me then, Cora. You would beg me to put my hands on your breasts and squeeze them hard, the way you liked it. You wanted my hands up your skirts, my fingers dabbling in your pussy. Your hands were never happier than when they were wrapped around my cock, milking me. Why have you changed?"

"You are my uncle." Her voice was laden with disgust.

"I was your uncle then, too, and you did not care. You were hot for me."

"It was wrong then, and it would be even more wrong now."

"How can love ever be wrong?"

"I never loved you, even then, and I am a married woman now. I will not shame my husband by taking a lover."

"You are married to a miner. A nothing. He need not come between us."

"There is no us. You are my uncle. My mother's brother. Nothing more."

"You did not use to be so cold."

"I have changed, Uncle Ralph." Her voice, trembling with emotion, carried through the night air. "I am no longer the frightened young girl you twisted to serve your disgusting purposes. I have grown up. And I have grown stronger. You will not break me so easily now. Indeed, I suggest you do not even try if you value your life."

"My life? Pah, what melodramatic nonsense is this. You are still my niece and, grown-up or no, you will still do as I say. Now be quiet and kiss me the way you used to. The way you kissed me before I was exiled to India for your sake."

"You were sent there for your own misdeeds, not for mine. And I will not kiss you. I will never touch you again."

"If I tell you that you will kiss me, you will kiss me." He took her by the arm, his fingers digging into her flesh. "A soldier's life in India was no bed of roses. You owe me for what I suffered there. And believe me, I will collect on every hardship. You will repay me everything."

The sight of her uncle's bruising grip on Cora's arm roused

Gareth from his state of horror. He stumbled toward them, making no effort to conceal himself, but so intent were they on their quarrel they did not hear his approach.

"Let go of me."

"I am not going to take no for an answer."

At that instant, Gareth's fist shot out and struck her uncle Ralph on the side of his head with a satisfying crunch. "Take that for an answer, then, and let go of my wife."

Her uncle sank to his knees, blinking in the dim light. "What was that for?" He shook his head from side to side as if to clear his vision. "Why did you hit me?"

His fists were itching to pound the man again, but he could not hit a man when he was down. Even miners fought fair. "You threatened my wife."

"Your wife?" Her uncle gave an ugly laugh as he staggered to his feet. "She was my whore long before she was your wife. How does that feel, to be married to my leavings?"

Insulting Cora was her uncle's second mistake. Getting to his feet was his third. Gareth's fist shot out again, with twice the power in it as before. Her uncle swayed, then toppled over on to the ground. He did not get up again.

Cora nudged him with the toe of her boot. "Is he dead?" Her voice, though brittle, was laced with hope. "Can the body snatchers come and take him away now, and cut him up for medical experiments so that I never have to see him again?"

The man's chest was rising and falling as he breathed. He was not dead. "Unfortunately not."

Leda Swann

"Hit him again then," she said viciously, and burst into violent tears. "Hit him until he cannot get up again. Ever."

He put his arm around his weeping wife and led her inside, through the back rooms, and up the stairs until they were closeted safely in their bedroom. "You are safe now," he crooned to her, pillowing her head against his chest. "He cannot hurt you again. Not while I am with you."

Her tears subsided into hiccups, then stopped altogether. "You heard what he said to you."

Yes, he had heard. Every word her uncle had spoken had dripped into his ears like poison. "It was nothing but the ravings of a madman."

Slowly she shook her head from side to side. "He was not raving." Her voice was muffled in his chest. "It was true. All of it."

"Your uncle was once your lover?" Such things were not uncommon in the rough society in which he had grown up, where extended families lived cheek by jowl squashed into tiny living quarters. But even then it was only whispered of, never openly talked of. The taboo against incest was powerful.

"My uncle was the reason that I married you. My uncle and no other."

Cora stood in her bedchamber, rooted to the spot, unable to look her husband in the face as she made her confession.

This was the end, the end she had always known would come. Now that Gareth knew the truth, he would discard her for sure. No man would ever be able to accept what had been done to her,

282

what she had done. Still she clung to him, wanting to spin her last minutes out to the end.

"Your uncle." The disgust in his voice told her everything she needed to know, trampling her last faint hopes that he would be able to overlook what she had never been able to forgive herself.

"He was always so kind to me when I was little. Whenever he came to visit us, he'd bring me presents. A new dress, a doll, some trifle or other. I used to look forward to him coming to visit. I treasured the affection he lavished on me. And then, when I was a little older, he'd ask for a present in return. A little gift, he said, that would cost me nothing to give him, but would mean so much to him. And then he would kiss me with great slobbering kisses and put his hands up my skirt." She shuddered with the memory. "When he was finished he would make me swear on my grandmother's grave not to tell, and he would promise me another present for being a good girl."

Her words were spilling out of her in a torrent, the confession long overdue. Now that she had started talking, telling of the horror of her childhood, she could not stop. "By the time I was twelve, he wasn't content with just touching me. He made me touch him back. And then when I was fifteen..." She stopped a took a deep breath to give her the courage to continue. "When I was fifteen, he took my virginity."

"He forced himself on you?"

"There was no force involved. I was too scared to say no to him. All the fight had gone out of me long before. I lay there and suffered him night after night. Sometimes he even took the trouble to give me pleasure, to make me want his touch. Those nights were the worst of all. On those nights I truly felt that he had poisoned my soul."

"He raped you." The look of horror on his face mirrored the self-disgust she felt, she would always feel. His fists were clenched by his side as if he wanted to strike out again, she knew not at what.

"Until my belly swelled with child. My uncle's child."

"You are a mother?"

"I miscarried." The pain of losing her child was still with her. Though it was of her uncle's getting, she had mourned for it. "It was for the best. I would not want to bring such a child into the world."

"Your family never knew?"

"There was so much blood, blood everywhere, that there was no hiding my condition. I was in disgrace. Complete disgrace. My father has never spoken to me since then. He treats me as if I do not exist."

"Did your father not know who the father was? Did you not tell him you were not to blame?"

"I think my mother suspected the truth. But Uncle Ralph was her favorite brother, so she kept quiet about it. Certainly she never pressed me to tell her who was responsible. She did not want to cause a scandal."

"Your uncle raped you, and your mother was more worried about a possible scandal than about your welfare?"

Exposed

He did not understand the way it was in her family. It hardly mattered what evil deeds were performed, as long as they were kept quiet. Creating a scandal was the greatest sin of all. The only real sin. "She arranged for him to join a regiment off for a tour of duty in India. That was her way of protecting me."

"But then his regiment finished its tour of duty?"

A shrewd guess. As soon as the regiment was recalled, she'd known her days of peace were over. She'd known that as soon as her uncle was on English soil once more, he would come to find her, and she would be defenseless against him. Needing to escape, she'd run for the protection of a husband. Even marriage to a drunken miner who beat her would have been better than to be at the mercy of her uncle once more.

Instead she had found Gareth. Her precious Gareth, who had felled her uncle with a single blow. "I knew he would not leave me alone. He had promised as much before he left and repeated his threats in every letter he wrote to me. I was scared. Your proposal of marriage was a godsend. My mother encouraged me to accept you to keep me away from her brother, and I was frightened enough to agree. I was weak."

"You are not weak. You are the strongest woman I know to have survived so much." He stopped and took a visible breath before continuing. "And I love you."

What an ill-omened time for a declaration of love. He could not have understood what she had just told him. "I used you," she cried out. "I married you for my own ends, to escape my uncle. You cannot love me. I do not deserve your love."

"You have it, whether you deserve it or not. The real question is what you will do with it now you have it."

"You do not hate me?"

"Not at all."

"You do not despise me?"

"I despise your uncle. He was the one at fault, not you."

"You will not turn me out of your house, even though you know the ugly truth about me?"

"Of course I will not." He looked offended that she would even suggest such a thing. "You are my wife. I have sworn to love, honor, and cherish you."

Her knees buckled, and she sat down on the bed to stop herself from falling. "I have kept my secret for so long." She shook her head in wonderment. "I have held it to myself, protecting myself from hurt. I do not know how to behave anymore."

"Does no one else know?"

"I was engaged once before."

"What happened?"

"I told him the truth about what had happened with my uncle." She shuddered. "He joined the army the next day, one of the Scottish regiments, without even saying good-bye. I haven't seen him since."

"Were you in love with him?"

"I thought I was at the time. He was blond and aristocratic, even rather handsome in a desultory sort of way. Languid and rather bored with everything. I thought he was dreadfully sophisticated. He thought the same about me, I suppose, but he didn't like the reality of who I was inside. Appearances were terribly important to him."

"He was a coward to run from you."

"He was. I think I knew that even then. When he left, I did not mourn him for long."

"I will not leave you, Cora. I swear it. While I have breath in my body, I will be yours."

"You are stronger than he was. Stronger and more real." There were so many things she wanted to do with his love. Hold it to her heart, take it to bed with her every night, scatter it to the winds and watch it blow away, then painstakingly gather each piece up again. Before she could do any of those, she had a piece of herself to reclaim. "There is still one thing I must do. One last injustice I must do you." Though it would hurt him deeply, she needed to do it. Only then would she be able to face the world by his side. "It will cause a terrible scandal."

His whole body went still at her words. "You want a divorce?"

"No, not a divorce." The tension on his face eased. "But I have kept silent for long enough. I want to tell the world what sort of a man my uncle is. I want him publicly exposed as a manipulative schemer, as a rapist of young girls, of his own niece." She hesitated, aware of the enormity of what she was about to ask of him. "I want you to stand beside me when I do so."

"You are my wife. I will always stand beside you."

"He will deny my accusations."

"I will defend you."

"My family will disown me. I will be disgraced."

"The fault was never yours."

"The scandal will be mine."

"I do not care about scandal."

"You will lose the entrée into society that you married me for. Though I cost you many thousands of pounds, I will be utterly worthless. Less than worthless, indeed, I will be a liability on your good name. You will be known as the dupe, as the poor foolish miner who had a fallen woman foisted off on him as his wife."

"I did not marry for an entrée into society. I married you because I wanted to the moment I first met you. I fell so deeply in love with you that I would have paid any price to win you as my own."

"I need to do this." She carried on as if she hadn't heard him. "I need to do this for my own sake if I am ever to find peace."

"I understand."

"I am sorry to bring this trouble on you. I truly am."

Gareth gathered his wife into his arms. Now he understood why she had pushed him away from her, threatened to take a scoundrel as her lover, and tried to make him hate her. Her actions had been motivated by terror—terror that that he would find out her secrets, terror that he would turn against her and hate her first.

If only he could find the words to tell her how much he treasured her above everything else. He would stand beside her and be her rock and her anchor. He would devote his life to making her happy. "You have brought me great happiness, not great trouble. Before I met you, I was a shell of a man, devoid of human warmth. You were fire and passion, and I wanted only to warm myself at your fire. I married you for selfish reasons as well, because I did not want to live without you."

Her head lay quietly against his shoulder as she nestled into his embrace. For the first time since he had met her, she seemed to be truly at peace. The tension, the brittleness that had marked her was gone, replaced with a gentleness he would never have believed she possessed. "Now that I have come to know you, I would not want to live without you, either. You are strong and you are kind. I know you will protect me."

"Then we will stand together and tell the truth, and brave whatever scandal may ensue. Your uncle will have to flee farther than India this time to escape the censure of the world. And to escape the hangman's noose." Personally, he'd rather quietly slip a knife into the bastard's back in a dark alleyway and get rid of him that way, but now he was respectable, that was not an option. Mind you, he still had a few contacts in low places. He'd make sure the bastard knew that, and knew exactly what they were capable of doing if paid enough—it would be good leverage to keep him far far away from Cora.

"I do not care about him any longer. It is nothing to me if he hangs, or if he runs to Australia. So long as I never have to see him again."

"I think I can safely guarantee that. Between us, we will make England too hot for him. Hell would be cooler than England, once we have finished with his reputation." He would weather the storm and keep his Cora safe.

"Forget my uncle." She dismissed him with a wave of her hand. "Help me take off my costume and come to bed with me instead."

He pushed her skirts off her hips and pulled the strings of her tiny top so that it fell away. "Your wish is my command."

Naked and unashamed, she lay down on the bed and watched him as he took off his own clothes. "I owe you an apology."

Pausing in the middle of unbuttoning his shirt, he looked at her, his gray eyes guileless. "You do?"

"I have been a bad wife to you. I should not have come here with Felix Rutherford. He meant nothing to me but as a way of punishing myself for having married you."

"I had guessed as much, but I am glad to hear you say so, and to know he means nothing to you. That is all the apology I need."

"I will not always be an easy woman to live with." There was plenty of time left for him to regret marrying her. "I am too used to having my own way to take kindly to any attempt to control me."

His bare skin glinted golden in the gaslight as he pulled back the sheet and climbed into bed next to her. "Does this mean you will want to take another lover?"

"That is not what I meant at all, you silly fellow. You are more than enough for me. But I am no meek, retiring woman to sit in a corner all day and see to my embroidery. Such a life would kill me."

"I had gathered as much."

"Besides which," she added, raising her head and giving him a saucy smile, "you need have no fear of me straying. What would I want with another man that I do not already have from you? You make all my fantasies come true."

AVON

978-0-06-124085-0
$13.95

978-0-06-112864-6
$13.95 ($17.50 Can.)

978-0-06-089023-0
$13.95 ($17.50 Can.)

978-0-06-078555-0
$13.95 ($17.50 Can.)

978-0-06-085199-6
$13.95 ($17.50 Can.)

978-0-06-081705-3
$13.95 ($17.50 Can.)